Dangerous
Waters

Dangerous Waters

Bill Eidson

PIATKUS

Copyright © 1991 by Bill Eidson

This edition first published in
Great Britain in 1992 by
Judy Piatkus (Publishers) Ltd of
5 Windmill Street, London W1

**The moral right of the author
has been asserted**

*A catalogue record for this book is available
from the British Library*

ISBN 0-7499-0136-5

Printed and bound in Great Britain by
Biddles Ltd, Guildford and King's Lynn

FOR DONNA

Special thanks to Bill Eidson, Sr., Catherine Eidson, Frank Robinson, Richard Parks, Nancy Childs, and Shelah Feiss for their help with this book. And to my family and friends for the wonderful way they helped me celebrate the first.

1

We were standing at the Fort Adams dock in Newport, Rhode Island, waiting for the launch out to my boat. The lights of the Newport Bridge formed an arc like a cold white rainbow to my left and the sea breeze upon my face was soft and refreshing. All of it should have been very pleasant. *Would* have been pleasant if I was not about a half hour away from cheating on my wife, Ellen, for the first time in our ten years of marriage.

Ellen was not the kind of woman men would typically think of cheating on. She was the kind you see in a photograph, and think, My God, if only she were mine. Since she was a fashion model, this was an experience I had often enjoyed.

And perhaps I had been foolish enough to let that image be the basis for my love.

. . .

I had indulged in a bit too much scotch, and that was my excuse, I suppose, for being there on the dock with my arm around Rachel's waist. I did not love her. But I certainly liked her, and she was undoubtedly beautiful. She was an account executive at my advertising agency, and the impropriety of sleeping with an employee was also ringing alarm bells in my head. This is not right, was what I thought. What I said was, "We should have brought some wine."

She laughed. "Don't blame me. This isn't some client excursion. You're responsible for the liquor and entertainment on this cruise."

I was too keyed up to chatter, so I looked for the shape of my white sloop, the *Spindrift*, in the dark.

"What's with the oars, anyhow?"

"The dinghy," I said shortly. "Outboard was quirky last week."

Rachel took them from me and leaned them against the handrail for the ramp. She put her arms around my neck and touched her nose to mine. As I kissed her, I made comparisons . . . the taste of her mouth was different from my wife's, the shape of her lips. Her scent was of baby powder, Ellen's perfume. A bit of me watched from a distance; watched me make the comparisons and judged me none too favorably.

Rachel and Ellen were about the same age, early thirties, but were otherwise as different as possible. Rachel was blond, fair-skinned. A tall woman, well-proportioned, athletic. She knew how to laugh, and she could tell a joke well. I loved to watch her in presentations, and so did the clients, both male and female. She was one of those extremely competent people who seem to do everything with a certain grace, from outlining a multimillion-dollar media plan on the chalkboard to brushing a tendril of hair away from her eyes.

Ellen, on the other hand, was a dark beauty. Tall, with a great sense of style, her clothing loose and yet sophisticated. Her sense of humor was razor-sharp, with much more of an edge than

Rachel's. She had a quirky ability to pull random ideas together. If her underlying bitterness made her difficult, it made her interesting to me also. It gave her that much-vaunted air of mystery.

I heard footsteps on the ramp. A man's hand brushed down the rail and the oars started to fall. I let go of Rachel and caught one, but the other clattered on the deck.

The young man who had knocked the oar down bent quickly and handed it to me. "Sorry," he said, grinning. "Looks like I arrived at just the wrong moment."

I frowned back. His grin faltered, and I realized I was being churlish—he had no way of knowing Rachel and I were having an affair. He turned toward the parking lot and glanced at his watch, which appeared to be a Rolex. "The launch should be here any minute, right?"

"That's right," Rachel said.

He was blond, fresh-looking, and handsome. He had a duffel bag slung over his shoulder. I had the impression I should know him. With unpleasant clarity, I saw how I was setting myself up for a divorce. I could not place this young man, I probably didn't know him, but the mere fact he was seeing me with Rachel, this way, made it real that I was cheating on Ellen. The launch pilot would most likely recognize me, and if he was on tomorrow, he would see my wife joining me on the boat too. I was making myself beholden to all of these people, trusting them to keep my secrets.

I walked away from Rachel and the young man. She started to follow, then stopped and turned around. After a moment, I heard her starting up a conversation with him. I was grateful for her tact, and found myself thinking she deserved better than an affair with a married man—that when I asked her to join me, I was only thinking of myself.

Two hours ago, my partner, Nick, and Rachel and I were in the Ritz Carlton bar in Boston celebrating the kickoff of a new campaign with Carl Tattinger, the ad manager from Textrel. I had excused myself, saying I planned to call Ellen and have her meet me at the boat. Her answer was terse: "Not tonight. I'll be there by noon tomorrow, if at all." She sounded bored, sullen. The lump of anger between us had been festering for close to a year, for reasons that I had been frustratingly unable to nail down. When I hung up, I thought, Have I ever loved her?

When I returned to the bar, I found my year-long flirt with Rachel becoming real, or so it seemed. Nick asked me if I would be meeting Ellen, and I said, "Who knows?" in a tone made a bit too truthful by alcohol. There was an awkward silence. Nick made the mistake of filling it by telling me I should not drive all that way after the few drinks I'd had. With false cheeriness, I said, "Right, Granddad. I can still make the ten-o'clock launch."

Our eyes had locked. He let me know he was not too happy about being left in the politician role with Tattinger, and I let him know I was not too happy about his putting me on the spot in front of a client. Tattinger made a comment about how if Rachel and I were killed in a car crash, the deal was off. Nick's eyes still glinted, but he laughed along heartily enough. I knew I would hear about it come Monday. I offered Rachel a ride home and made a fast exit. Outside her condo on Beacon Street ten minutes later, Rachel agreed to sleep with me aboard the *Spindrift*.

She interrupted my thoughts by stepping in front of me and giving me a soft, quick kiss on the lips. I was conscious of the young man standing only a few steps away, of being watched. "I'm sorry about the shabby aspects of this. Hustling you off to the rental car agency in the morning, and all."

She put her hand on my chest and started to say something, then looked over my shoulder, her expression curious.

I turned toward the parking lot, and saw a man coming down the ramp. I glanced over at the young man with us on the dock. His face was white, and he crossed his arms over his chest.

I looked back at the other man. He was big, bigger than me. I'm six feet tall, and weigh just under one-eighty. A little of it is flab, but not much. From what I could see in the poor light he was a good twenty pounds heavier, and none of it was soft. He was wearing a green Lacoste shirt, and "wiry" would be the adjective I would have used for him if he had not been two inches taller than me. His close-cropped hair was kinky and dark. He looked to be in his mid-thirties. His teeth gleamed. "How's it going," he said genially to me and Rachel. He had the trace of a southern accent. "You'll excuse me and my friend for a moment." He jerked his head up toward the parking lot. "Come on up, Cory. We need to talk."

Cory shook his head. It seemed to me he was affecting nonchalance. "Can't. Waiting for the boat."

The man lowered his eyes and glanced away, mugging an expression of dismay, of embarrassment. "Now Cory, we don't want to discuss our business in public, do we?"

I looked out over the water. I could see the red and green of the bow lights of a small boat headed our way. Rachel followed my glance and met my eyes. "Getting tense over there?" she said.

"It looks like the launch to the rescue," I said quietly. "You think we could get a boat to the Jacobsen presentation next week?"

She laughed.

Green Shirt looked our way suddenly, and I automatically met his eyes. In the instant they locked, I felt sympathetic to the young man. Green Shirt was no lightweight, and he was ready to find insult where none was intended.

I glanced at the boy. He wasn't really a kid, he was at least in his mid-twenties, but he had an open appearance that made him look younger. He looked frightened, but was trying not to show it. "Leave us alone," he said to the man. "We're waiting for the launch. I'll call tomorrow and explain what's going on."

I stiffened at the "us."

The older man turned to look at me and Rachel and widened his eyes. "Are you three together? Am I bothering you?"

I wished for sobriety now. Something was starting, something I recognized back from my days as a street kid in San Francisco.

"Huh?" he said. "Am I *bothering* you?"

I met his eyes, but did not answer. "Oh shit," Rachel said under her breath.

"What's that?" He cupped his hand over his ear.

She turned her back to him and me and looked out at the approaching launch. I did not get the impression that he noticed the boat.

He stepped down from the ramp onto the dock. He looked at Rachel's back, and made a face at me, pursing his lips as if he had just sucked on a lemon. "Frosty."

"Go up to the car, Rachel."

"You stay right there, lady."

The young man moved toward the edge of the dock, slipped off the duffel bag, and reached inside. He said, "Come on, Cra—"

Green Shirt hit him with a backhand so fast I could barely see the blur. He swung a hook into the young man's stomach hard enough to lift him right off the dock. I hesitated a half-second, then moved quickly, feeling that my balance was good as I put my left foot behind my right, lining up for a kick to his thigh that I figured would knock him into the water. But he spun around outside me and buried his fist over my kidneys. It put me right down. I lost my dinner instantly. Soft, I thought. Drunk and soft.

"Disgusting," the man's voice said. I tried to stand, and he kicked me in the chest, knocking the breath out of me. I fell back against the ramp. "Stay there, hero. I'll be right back to find out why you're so brave."

Rachel came up behind him and tried to push him off the dock. He gave her a short vicious jab with his elbow, then locked his heel behind hers and shoved. She fell to the deck heavily, her blue eyes wide.

"Stay down," I croaked.

Green Shirt went over to the young man and hit him across the face with his forearm. It put the kid on the deck again. Green Shirt kicked him in the groin. "Now then, Cory, you pretty boy, your education is just about to start."

"Don't." The young man rolled quickly for the duffel bag, reached in, and came out with a small handgun, little more than a derringer. The older man did not hesitate for an instant; he kicked the boy's hand as if it were a football set up for a field goal. The gun splashed into the water.

"Cute," Green Shirt said. He grabbed the bag, rummaged through it disgustedly, then threw it into the water too. "Now about that education—did they teach you this kind of *stress* at Thorton? I bet they didn't." He bent down and grasped the young man's right hand.

"No!" The young man tried to scramble away on his back.

Green Shirt took the young man's forefinger and snapped it to the side. The young man shrieked and curled into a ball. Green Shirt grinned over at me. "Like that?" He turned his attention back to the young man, grabbed him by the hair, and slapped him across the face. "No, no. No fainting, you fuck-up, you pussy. You've got some explaining to do."

"Help him," Rachel said.

"Be quiet." I worked on getting in a full breath.

The launch was drawing closer. The pilot was standing up, looking at the scene. It was a woman, alone in the boat. "What's going on over there?" she yelled.

"Help us!" Rachel cried. "Call the police!"

"Shit!" Green Shirt turned toward the launch. "Get the hell out of here, lady, unless you want some of this!"

I rolled up onto my feet and grabbed one of the oars leaning against the rail and swung with all my might. Green Shirt apparently heard me, and twisted inside of it, so that the blow had less power when it landed against his heavy biceps. He snapped off a quick right punch toward my face, and I ducked. The blow rocked me, but hitting my forehead apparently did him more damage, because he swore and grasped his right hand. I shoved the oar in his face as if it were a rifle butt. I was vaguely aware that Rachel was yelling something as I hit him again, this time in the side. He staggered back and swept his arm down to make an effective block as I pivoted the oar to his groin. I feinted to his left shoulder, and when he rolled it forward, I snapped off a hard blow to his head, then shoved him into the water with the blade of the oar.

Rachel pushed me toward the eastern edge of the dock, and

that's when I realized the woman in the launch had brought the boat up. "Come on," Rachel urged. "Come on, Riley!" She and I grabbed the young man by the arms and dragged him into the launch.

The launch pilot apparently recognized him suddenly, and said, "Cory, is that you? Are you hurt?"

"Let's go, let's go," he said, cradling his hand. "Move this tub, Linda."

"Riley!" Rachel cried, turning. Green Shirt was pressing himself up onto the dock with apparent ease. His eyes met mine, and he grinned suddenly, with bloody teeth. I was chilled with my handiwork; all his attention was now focused upon me. He swung a leg over the side of the dock, and I leaned over the launch pilot and slammed the throttle down. She swore and twisted the wheel around. I grabbed the oar again and turned. Sure enough, he was already halfway to us, ready to jump into the boat. I shoved the blade at his face just as the stern of the launch banged against the dock. It worked to the extent that he was too off-balance to jump. But he parried the oar away with his arm, then yanked it out of my hands. In a quick fluid motion, he drew it back and threw it like a spear. I ducked. The oar splintered the cockpit coaming behind me.

"I'll remember your face, hero," he called, just loud enough for us to hear over the engine noise.

2

The pilot thought we were responsible for getting Cory hurt. "His hand—something's broken. Cory, are you all right?" She was young, dark-haired, and very angry. I'm sure the smell of alcohol on me didn't help. To me, she said, "What happened back there?"

Looking back at the dock, I saw Green Shirt was striding up the ramp. "You did the right thing to pick us up."

"Of course I'd pick up Cory. Who are you? What did you do— start some idiot brawl, and he had to pay for it?"

She cut the throttle and went to the stern to bend over him, saying, "Let me take a look at your hand." I took the wheel and shoved the power back on. I flicked off the running lights.

She stormed back. "Get your damn hands off the wheel." She tried to reach past my arm to the light switch.

I pushed her away gently enough with my forearm. "Look, I want to get out of sight of that guy on the dock. I don't want him watching the lights of this launch go right to my boat, understand?"

"I don't need you to crack up the launch. Now move it."

Rachel was sitting beside the young man. She was apparently feeling his hand gently for the break. I said, "Have you got anything to say about this, Cory?"

He snapped, "Leave him alone, Linda."

"Maybe we should call the police," Rachel said.

"No," he said quickly.

"I don't want to spend the evening with the police either." I reached into my coat, took two twenties from my wallet, and offered them to the launch driver. "Here, take the wheel if you want it and take the long route to my boat over there—see it?"

The pilot stared at my money.

"Please. I apologize for the rudeness."

"I don't like being bribed."

"You didn't have to come up to the dock, with all that was going on."

She shrugged and put the bills into her anorak. I went back to Cory. Rachel still had his hand in hers. His eyes were closed. His good looks and helpless expression irritated me.

"Let's talk, Cory," I said.

He opened his eyes. "Let's not."

"Who was that guy?"

He shrugged. "I don't know. Some pissed-off Georgia boy."

"Bullshit. He knew your name, you knew him. I want to know if I'm ever going to need to deal with him again."

"What's the problem?" He looked at me as if I were very stupid. "You paid your bucks to Linda. He's not going to be able to tell which boat you get on. And you could probably tell, he's not the yacht-club type. You won't be running into each other socially. Just forget it."

"What's his name? What 'business' did you have?"

"You're not listening."

"I'm listening, I just don't like what I'm hearing. We risk our butts for you, and you decide to be coy."

His lip curled back. "So what? I didn't ask for your help."

I felt the anger bubbling in me, pushing out from my chest into my arms. I grabbed the front of his shirt and pulled him half up. "Well, you got it. What's *your* full name, Cory?"

"Hey!" He pushed back ineffectually with his one good arm.

"Riley, let him go," Rachel said, her face chalk-white. "Come on, your adrenaline's pumping, let him go."

"Cut it out," the girl said, with a frightened edge to her tone. "I'll call the cops, so help me."

I suddenly saw it from her point of view: I was possibly drunk, and to her mind, violent. And she weighed about 110 pounds and thought she had to maintain order.

I let go. He fell back onto the seat.

"That's it, I want you off," she said. "We're going to your boat."

"Take the long route."

She threw the crumpled twenties back at me, and they flew over the stern. "No. I've had enough of you."

Cory went to stand beside her.

I spent the next few minutes straining my eyes toward the parking lot, but it was impossible to make out much detail. I thought Green Shirt was probably gone, but I really had no way of knowing.

Rachel pointed over my shoulder.

I turned, and the *Spindrift* was there, trim and perfect in her way. I reached for Rachel's hand. "Let's go."

Cory stood in front of me, looking at my boat. I pushed past, anxious to be free of him. He backed off quickly, eyes wide suddenly. He thinks I'm going to hit him, I thought. In spite of myself, I found myself feeling a little sorry for him. I said, "You'd better see a doctor. That's an ugly break."

He nodded. "Sure. Thanks." He gestured with his chin toward the stern of my boat. "That's yours?"

"Right."

"The *Spindrift*. She's a beauty."

Rachel and I climbed aboard, and the girl slapped the throttle down. I watched him watch us as the launch motored away.

Rachel said, "When did you learn to fight like that, using that oar like . . . what is it, a quarterstaff? Better yet, why did you mix into that one?" We were in the main cabin. I had just washed my face, and rinsed the taste of vomit from my mouth.

"First question, in the army."

She cocked her head slightly. "*That's* right. Nick said something about it . . . what was it? I know, you're the tough guy in the agency because you were in the Rangers, and he was in the National Guard. The Rangers are one of those special groups, right? Did you go to Vietnam?"

I nodded.

"How did I not know that about a man I'm about to go to bed with?"

"I didn't know it was a requirement. In any case, your second question, when I told you to go up to the car, he told you to 'stay right there, lady.' I figured if he was willing to throw around orders like that, and willing to start beating on this Cory, then he might do the same to us when he got around to it."

Rachel winced as she took off her blazer. "I thought maybe it was because you were drunk. Because my feeling was that he was a pro, and he would have mopped that Cory up, and then taken him up to the parking lot to continue their 'business' in private. That we would have been left alone."

"Could be. Could be that he would have killed Cory."

"Maybe you were showing off for me." She seemed to force a laugh.

I shrugged. "Maybe."

Her mouth twisted, but she said, lightly enough, "I would hope I have that much to hold against the bruise I'm going to have in the morning."

I failed to answer, thinking about Cory's reaction to my boat's name, and wondered if he was threatening us—pointing out that he knew how to find me and I didn't know how to find him. If so, it worked to the degree that I excused myself from Rachel to go on deck. I waited up there for about fifteen minutes, waiting for my night vision to return somewhat.

I saw the lights of a car leaving the Fort Adams parking lot. Of course, I had no idea if it was Green Shirt's or not. It was too far away and the angle was wrong for me to make even a guess at the make of the car. Another left a minute later, and then another. A few more came and went within the next five minutes. Proving only it was a fairly busy parking lot. I went below.

Rachel was sitting at the navigation station. An open bottle of scotch and an empty ginger ale bottle were sitting on the counter. She raised her drink. "No ice, but don't worry about me, boss. I've been thinking about our theories: drunk or not drunk; showing off, not showing off."

"And?"

"There may be some truth to each of them, but I don't think they carry as much weight as the real reason." Rachel's face was slightly flushed and her jaw was set. "You're pissed off. You're so angry at Ellen that getting in a fight is the best thing you could do. Even better than taking me to bed."

"That's ridiculous."

"Yes, it is. But it's true. I saw the anger on your face, the release you had in that fight, and afterward in the launch with that boy. This whole ride down, I've been chattering to keep up the pretense this was a romance, because I wanted it to be, but I could see you were hardly noticing me personally. I was just your escape, how you were getting back at Ellen."

I could have told her she was wrong, and almost did. Maybe she would have been happier had I made the effort. As it was, I slept in the bow that night, and she slept in the main cabin bunk. She took the first launch back in the morning, after an awkward breakfast of a shared apple and instant coffee. Luckily, another launch pilot was on duty.

I watched her motor off, as I had watched Cory the night before, and thought that perhaps I had made it through the night unscathed.

Stupid of me, really.

3

I was disappointed when noon came and went without Ellen arriving on the launch. Having told myself that the strange
incident on the dock had given my marriage a reprieve, that I
should think of the near-affair with Rachel as a real close call, I
was anxious to try to set things straight with Ellen.

I did quiet work on the boat, oiling the teak and polishing the
chrome, before motoring up to the Fort Adams dock to place a
call. My second oar was still there, miraculously, and I put it in
the cockpit. I walked slowly up to the phone, looking at the people who were scattered over the lawn, looking for someone with
kinky black hair and vengeful eyes. I didn't seriously expect to
see my assailant, but I realized it would probably be some time
before I would feel comfortable waiting for the launch at night.

I kept my back against the wall while I dialed the number. She picked up the phone without saying anything, a recent habit I found irritating.

I said, "Are you coming with me or not?"

"What did I say? I told you I'd be there by noon or not at all."

I paused, and then said, "Look, Ellen, pretty soon we're going to go too far, or one of us might."

"What does that mean? Have you already done that?"

"No. I haven't." The truth, but only technically.

She paused, then said in a conciliatory tone, "Go sailing yourself, and I'll meet you for dinner at the Rhumb Line at seven. How's that?"

"It's a start." I hung up.

Outside the harbor, I set sail, and began an easy series of tacks to the Texas tower about four miles away, just outside the mouth of Narragansett Bay. The modifications I had made to the *Spindrift*—self-tailing winches, an autopilot, roller reefing on the big genoa, plus a pedestal-mounted boom for a self-tending working jib—were indicative of my changing marriage. More and more, I was sailing alone.

I couldn't shake the feeling that I was losing everything I had fought to achieve since I was a teenager.

I had learned to sail while growing up in San Francisco. Jerry Caldwell, one of my mother's "friends," took an interest in me, telling her one day that some time on a sailboat in the bay might give me a different perspective from the Tenderloin district. I was recovering from a bad beating I had taken earlier that week from shoving one of her other friends.

I told Jerry to stuff his boat.

My mother had just poured her first glass of wine for the morning. She cracked me across the face and said she was going to be "busy" that afternoon, and she'd just as soon I was out of her hair.

I went.

He was a nice guy, Jerry, and he was remarkable in his willingness to take me out on his little sloop dozens of times over the next few summers, long after he had stopped coming around to see my mother. I did have a different viewpoint bounding along under sail. But clearly, *he* did not want to gain any more perspective himself about what it was like growing up without a father, with a mother who was a hooker. "I don't really want to hear about it, Riley. I figure it's bad enough, that's why I invite you out like this. Look, let's just enjoy the sail. Make your own decisions about what you want in life, then just go get it. Words are a waste of time."

Over time, I decided he was right. After all, other than his willingness to use prostitutes, this well-ordered man, with his sunburned face and hearty manner, seemed to have a clean, successful life.

So I made my decisions.

I hit the road when I was seventeen and thumbed around the country for a year, until, on my eighteenth birthday, I enlisted in the army. And my plans crystallized in Vietnam, over many nights lying belly down in the mud, the smell of the rotting jungle cloaking me like a blanket: I wanted a wife, children, my own business, with a partner I liked. Things in order. Clean. Money in the bank. No living with an alcoholic mother in a cheap residential hotel, no fighting with hard-eyed pimps who wanted to cut her for drinking her earnings. I would send her checks as long as she was alive, I told myself, but have no other contact. I began implementing that part of the plan late in my tour, and sent her a letter explaining that the checks would be coming automatically, and to expect no more from me.

She took too many pills on top of a jug of burgundy one night just weeks before my discharge. They sent me home for her funeral. I found the empty check envelopes in her top drawer, tied in a bow, as if they were letters.

I couldn't cry.

I wanted to so much, but I couldn't. I looked around the dingy little room, and found nothing I wanted to keep. Closed the door, and left for Boston University, vowing to forget her and Vietnam. To let go of the constant fear, the fear that made me expect to find explosives tied to everything, from a package of cigarettes on the ground to the bodies of my dead friends. And to let go of the cold anger that had helped me succeed in becoming a Ranger, that helped me when the reconnaissance patrols turned into search-and-destroy missions, when both the M-16 and I were set to automatic. I had learned not to talk of such times with my fellow students—of any times in Vietnam, really. I simply put my head down and worked. I had a lot of catching up to do.

Ellen and I first met in Newport, through Nick. He and I were both in our mid-twenties, and trying to make names for ourselves at Santachi & Bright. Nick was in the creative department, I was an account executive. One day he hauled me in to help tape a radio commercial, saying I had just the right authoritative growl. He was a muscular man with enormous energy and a quick sense of humor. His antics started me laughing, and he was pleased to find I had "natural talent" for radio mimicry. Pronouncing me a man who "has some uses after all" to the rest of the creative staff, he helped me bridge the usual distance between the "suits" and the "creatives."

I was pleased when he invited me to join him in Newport one Saturday for a sail, to take a look at his new boat and meet his latest love, Ellen. I was delighted with his Lightning—a beautifully kept wooden daysailer with blue-green decks and varnished trim.

However, it was Ellen Carson who held my attention. She had taken off her shorts and halter to reveal a surprisingly supple body within a white bikini. Beyond her obvious beauty, her sexuality was so undeniably strong that I felt cotton-mouthed. From my upbringing, I had no illusions that lust meant love, or so I told myself. But it was as if I contracted a fever from her. I tried to ignore my attraction. After all, she was with Nick. As the day went on, more and more of her attention focused upon me, and I could see the interest in her eyes. "I hope I see you again," I said at the end of the day.

"You will, I'm sure."

For the next week, I dreamed of her every night and thought about her all day long. Then she broke it off with Nick, and called me to say she had.

I stopped by his office and told him I intended to ask her out. His smile was rueful. "We weren't married, and you don't need my blessing." He put the tips of his thumbs together and framed me with his two vertical forefingers as if lining up a photo. "You two are a set of bookends. Both complex, moody, pains in the ass. You'll drive each other insane."

Ellen and I were married within the year, and Nick was my best man. And he was right, it wasn't easy. But in the balance, it was a good marriage for a long time. Sexually we remained almost obsessive about each other, until this year. In other ways we appeared well matched. She was a model and I was in advertising. We liked to do the same things, traveling, sailing, skiing, reading.

Nick and I became partners right about the time we both turned thirty, and shortly after, Ellen broke off from full-time modeling and took a job as an assistant manager at a small Newbury Street art gallery. I made the presentations, bringing the clients in, managing the accounts. Nick really delivered on the creative side, and we overstepped the profit line on my five-year plan by almost 10 percent. And it was an ambitious plan.

During that time, Nick and I first bought a boat together, a nice little J-24. But it was quickly apparent we needed more room, and more boat. So when Nick married a cheerful woman named Susan, we all agreed it was time to buy our own boats. I moved to a Soveral 30; Nick a Pearson and a dive boat. We spent many a weekend rafted together on the Elizabeth Islands, Martha's Vineyard, Block Island.

After two years, Susan walked away smiling with a substantial hunk of Nick's savings. He hunkered closer to us for a time after that, including the Virgin Islands vacation where we first saw the *Spindrift*, a custom-made forty-two-foot sloop with breathtaking lines that had seen hard service—very hard—as a bareboat charter. Belowdecks was a shambles, but the hull was hand-laid fiberglass and the decks teak. Nick and I flew back three weeks later and sailed her to Boston. We sold off the Soveral and Pearson and worked on the *Spindrift* evenings and weekends for a season before bringing it down to Newport. Ellen sometimes tried to get him to open up about Susan, but after a time I encouraged her to let it go, figuring his message was clear. As my friend Jerry had said, it's only what you do that matters, not what you say.

The agency continued to prosper, and he eventually asked me to buy him out of the *Spindrift* and bought himself another boat, a beautiful Hinckley. It was just as well, for right about then Ellen and I needed more time alone.

Things had started to crumble when Ellen turned thirty and still refused to consider having children. I had been pressing for some time, but she said that she had not achieved any of the things she wanted. Over the past two years, she had started a number of creative activities—acting lessons, pottery, dance. She gave nothing enough time, throwing herself furiously into one project and then into the next, working with joyless determination, and then moving on when she didn't achieve immediate results. She started taking more modeling assignments. Though never for my agency—that was a separation of church and state we thought best.

The past few months or so had been worse. There was an essential sadness about her that I did not know how to reach. I came home one day to find her crying in our bedroom. She shoved me away when I sat beside her, saying she didn't want to talk. This time I insisted, and finally she told me, pulling out a copy of *New England Monthly* to show me an ad she had done for a Providence-based jewelry manufacturer. In it, she was sitting across from a white-haired man, apparently her husband, and she was trying on a necklace as the young waiter poured champagne. The headline read: "Show her, shower her."

"And?"

She pointed to the husband. He had to be at least fifty. "The client said they wanted somebody 'who has seen what life has to offer.' That they weren't trying to suggest I was some cute little chickee for this man, but his long-term mate, that I deserved the necklace for sticking with him through the lean times."

I kept my tone light, but I felt more than mildly irritated. "That's advertising, Ellen. Besides, you're only thirty-two. That's not old by anybody's standard, except maybe a teenager's."

"I'm not crying because I'm vain . . . or maybe I am, I don't know. It's just that I look around, at you, this house, the money, the boat, we've got it all, but I feel so empty." She brushed her tears with the back of her hand. "I'm going to be *old*. I know I'm not yet, but damn it, time is just passing by . . . and when my looks go, I don't know what I'm going to have left."

She was twenty minutes late to the Rhumb Line. I was reaching for my second draft ale. Her entrance caused a discreet commotion, as the men looked her way and automatically smiled, as the women judged her cheekbones and clothing and could not find her wanting. I watched her with a long-absent flush of pleasure. She was wearing the sapphire earrings I had bought her the first year the company turned a profit, pleated pants, and a mannish striped shirt.

She put her hand on my shoulder and leaned down to kiss my cheek, then stopped. "Phew, beer. Well. You certainly got some color today. How was the sail?"

And so it went through most of dinner. Brittle conversation. As the evening passed, I tried to tag exactly where it had gone wrong, when we began playing old tapes from behind mechanical masks. Thinking how I had created circumstances where I couldn't even tell my wife that the night before I had fought with a man who was possibly a professional leg breaker. She was talking with forced gaiety about a customer at the gallery, and I had a false smile on my face—and then I just could not continue it any longer.

"Ellen, we've got to talk about what's going on."

She set her wineglass down and looked at the tablecloth. I continued quietly, "I want to reassure you that I love you, and I want you to reassure me."

"Keep it down." Two red spots had formed on her cheeks. In a furious whisper, she said, "Where's it written? I've said all I've got to say. There's nothing more."

"Our marriage isn't working. Maybe we should see somebody."

"Who? A shrink? I'm not crazy." She grabbed her handbag. "I'm sick of you analyzing me, trying to figure me out."

"I don't do that. I should do more, for God's sake."

Her tone turned self-mocking. "Don't you understand? What you see is what you get. Is that so bad?"

What *is* this? I thought. "Ellen, I know I haven't been the most communicative man, and you're no picnic in that department either—"

"Let's go."

I looked at my watch. "Calm down. We just missed the nine-o'clock launch."

"I reserved us a room at the Treadway Inn."

"Why? The plan was to be on the boat together."

"That's your plan maybe. Mine is to leave myself room to breathe."

4

The next morning, we took the launch out to the *Spindrift*. Our familiar routine took over as I checked the oil, opened the hatches, and flipped on the power to the depth gauge and wind indicator. Ellen packed the lunch into the icebox and put the cushions into the cockpit. "You oiled the teak," she said. "It looks good."

I figured I would go along with her attempt to return to at least a surface kind of balance, not just because I didn't want to argue any longer, but because I was feeling more and more hypocritical. I was not willing to tell her the truth about my near-affair with Rachel, so what right did I have to insist that Ellen be honest about whatever was bothering her lately? Maybe that's why she's so depressed, I reflected. So much compromise.

I kissed her on the cheek. "Let's go sailing. The breeze is up."

"Let's." She kissed me back on the lips. "And let's be friends again, okay?"

I pushed the starter button. Black smoke chugged from the stern, and I waited until the engine settled into a dull roar before giving her the word to drop the mooring. I slipped into reverse, and the engine pitch changed suddenly.

There was a thump under the waterline, and the gearshift shuddered under my hand. I slipped the engine into neutral. "Did we clear the mooring?"

"Sure did." She pointed over the starboard bow as the orange float bobbed into my view. Ellen slid the aluminum boat hook open like a telescope to its full twelve-foot length and leaned over the side to catch the marker. "Damn it!"

She had dropped the pole. It floated alongside the boat, out of easy reach. Her face reddened with sudden anger. "What's the matter with me? I can't do anything right anymore."

"Take it easy," I said, and used the dinghy oar to push the hook end of the pole deep into the water so that the handle stood in the air at right angles. When I slipped the oar blade off the hook, the buoyant pole shot into the air, and I caught it and leaned out as far as I could for the float.

"Joe Cool," she said wryly.

I missed it by about a foot and a half. "Looks like I can't do anything right, either. We caught something, but we're still drifting." I went back to the stern and leaned over. I couldn't see a mooring line, or lobster pot float. The wind was snapping the burgee overhead, and we were slipping past the stern of an unoccupied white ketch. Below us was a low gray racer with a thick mooring cable. I didn't want to drift on top of that with whatever was fouling my prop. I hurried back to the bow with the boat hook and snagged a stern cleat on the ketch. I pulled us close and Ellen attached a short bow line. The *Spindrift* swung into the wind, more slowly than usual, I noticed.

I lifted the hatch to the engine compartment to make sure the shaft wasn't showing any damage, and that there was no major leakage around the stuffbox. None. I slapped the hatch back down.

Ellen took the bag of snorkeling gear from the cockpit locker while I stepped below quickly and pulled on my bathing suit. Back on deck, I slipped on the fins, put on the mask, and took a few breaths out of the snorkel, while Ellen unsnapped the stanchion lines. She looped a line around the starboard winch and handed me the free end to take down in case I needed to haul off a stuck mooring buoy. She strapped my dive knife sheath onto my right calf, and leaned over to kiss me on the forehead. "My hero," she said, her smile genuine.

I swung over the side.

The harbor water was none too clean. I lay on the surface and peered under the *Spindrift*. Visibility was only about six feet, less in the shadow of the hull. There was a dark mass underneath the prop. It was bunched up against the prop. Seaweed? There was a faint patch of yellow. It was huge, whatever it was. I took a deep breath, jackknifed under the boat, and moved upside down along the hull. The thing began to take shape. It looked like a cloth, a bundle of cloth, until the *Spindrift* rolled slightly in the wake of a passing boat.

Then my body recognized it before my head could accept it, and I was scrambling up the hull back to the surface. I took some water down my throat on the way, and my mask was skewed half off before I hit the surface.

"What is it, Riley?" Ellen's voice was alarmed. "Riley, what's the matter? What is it?"

"Wait," I said, coughing water.

"Riley!"

"Wait." I had to think. It was the boy. It was Cory. And the rope around his chest was what was fouling my prop.

5

I needed to know more.

"Riley, answer me!"

I readjusted the mask and dove back under the boat.

It was him, all right. I hugged the rudder to keep from having to touch him, but nevertheless his knee brushed mine. I think it was the Rolex on his wrist and the blond hair that let me identify him in an instant. Because otherwise, this thing hardly looked like the handsome boy who had been on the dock the night before last. His skin was unnaturally white in the gloom under the boat. The fish had been at his eyes.

I went up for air to find Ellen above me. "What's wrong? What's under there?"

I dove back down. He was stuck against the rudder and keel on the starboard side, facing outward. His hair waved over his sightless eyes, each strand seemingly distinct. Something silvery glinted in his wide-open mouth. I kicked over to the port side and looked at the prop. Heavy line was tangled in the blades and around the shaft. Lines were tied to him in two places: one around his chest, the other to two cinder blocks around his ankles. There were only two possibilities I could think of. Somebody had dumped him in the water near our boat and it was just coincidental that we had picked him up while leaving the mooring.

Or, what I knew in my stomach to be true: the guy who had beat him that Friday night had finished the job, and stuck him under my boat as a message to me for interfering.

I swam back to the surface to explain it to Ellen.

I asked her to get me a towel.

She crossed her arms. She sounded more frightened than demanding when she said, "What's under there?"

"Please, honey, get me the towel."

Her lips compressed, but she hurried below and came back with a coarse blue towel and tossed it to me. I wiped my face and hair, and wished I could just keep my head in those blue folds and never tell her the truth. Finally, I put it across my lap and said, "It's a body, Ellen. There's a young man's body down there."

Her hand flew to her mouth, and she looked down at the cockpit sole reflexively. "Oh, how awful! We didn't—we couldn't have hit anyone—I was looking—"

I put my hand on her arm. "No, it wasn't a swimmer, nothing like that. I'd say he's been dead for a while. A day, last night maybe."

She took my hand in hers. "How can you be sure?"

"I can't. That'll be up to the police. But I've got to explain something to you first."

She sat down and seemed to shrink into herself. Her expression became wary.

I took a deep breath. *From here*, I thought, *she and I will never have a chance to get it back the way it was.* "Ellen, I know this man. I've seen him once before, this Friday night, in fact."

She drew back slightly. "You knew him? Who?"

"Nobody you know. But I helped him out of a bad spot, a fight, on Friday night."

She shook her head, half smiling, apparently deciding this was some bad joke on my part. She said, "Riley, come on. You weren't in a fight. You didn't say anything, not last night or this morning."

My mouth tasted coppery. "I know. That's because I had something to hide." I told her. About the guy with the green shirt. About him breaking the boy's finger. About Rachel.

She hugged her knees up to her chest. Goose bumps formed on her arms and legs in spite of the heat. When I was finished, she said, in a remote voice, "Was she a good fuck, Riley?"

"She's got nothing to do with this. We were just there."

"Tell it to the boy down there. Maybe if you had gone to the police he'd still be alive."

"He didn't want to go to them either. It was his fight. He was obviously mixed up in something. Gambling, drugs maybe."

"And now we are too."

"Yes."

She said with soft intensity, "I hope she was good, Riley."

"I told you we didn't make love."

She laughed, a short pained bark. "You poor bastard," she said quietly. "It wasn't even worth it."

The harbormaster was the first to arrive, and after hearing my quick explanation, he jumped over the side with mask and fins. He came up immediately and said, "No rescue there. He's been under there at least the night." Ellen paled and went below.

His radio squawked, and he climbed back into his boat and answered it. As the fire department rescue team arrived, he yelled to them, "He's dead, no doubt about it. Borenson's at the dock now. If I know him, he's going to want me to photograph the body just as it is. Stick it out here while I go get him."

We waited. The fire department boat was about thirty feet long, with swirling lights. It puttered fifty feet ahead and maintained its distance. Other boats began to mill near us, attracted like moths by the lights. By the time the harbormaster returned with the police, two windsurfers were tacking between the fire department boat and the bow of the white ketch.

The three policemen were in plain clothes. The oldest, a tall man of about forty-five with florid skin and reddish hair, said to me, "Lieutenant Borenson, Newport police. And you are?"

I gave my name. "Riley Burke."

"You're the one who called this in?"

"Yes."

"Well, hang on a minute." He said to the harbormaster, "Cahill, bring it up so I can get a look."

The harbormaster eased the big launch alongside the *Spindrift*, and I made their lines fast. Borenson put a swim ladder over the stern of his boat, climbed down, and put a glass-bottomed viewing box into the water. He grunted. "Jesus, this visibility sucks." The wake of a passing powerboat slapped up against the hull, splashing his pants leg. "Cahill, get that damn fireboat to move these gawkers away from me." He climbed back into the launch, and he and one of the others, a policeman in his mid-thirties with a mustache, stepped onto the *Spindrift*.

Borenson did not shake my hand. Instead, he turned to the two left on the boat. "Cahill, you've got your scuba gear and the Nikonos, right?"

The harbormaster held up a black underwater camera.

"Right. So you go on down. I want shots of the body head to toe, the prop, the whole hull. When you've done that, bring him up. Cut the rope only where you have to, and save whatever's weighting him down. Blair, you take the launch, but keep the radio open so you can come right back when Cahill's ready for you. I want to know who was on their boats in the immediate vicinity last night and this morning, if they heard anything, their phone numbers, addresses, the whole bit." He turned to the detective beside him. "DePetrie, photos. Every square inch topside. Get going."

He turned to me. "What's your name again?"

I told him, and said that I would like a chance to tell him what

I knew while Ellen stayed below, that she was upset enough already.

"It doesn't work that way. Just a moment." He stepped below and introduced himself to Ellen. He came up a few minutes later and said, "She's going to wait up in the bow, then I'll talk with her later. Let's get started."

And so I started, without leaving anything out. He listened quietly enough, making notes from time to time, keeping his face blank when I told him about Rachel.

But when I was finished, he shook his head as if I had just given a bad job interview. "I dunno, Mr. Burke. I still have a lot of questions. Why were you meeting this Cory? What was your and Miss Perry's relationship with him?"

"I told you, that was the first time I'd ever seen him."

"You're sure?"

"Yes, I'm sure."

"And Miss Perry? Was this the first time she had met him?"

"Yes."

"How do you know? Did she say so?"

"No."

"Then how do you know?"

"I just do. We weren't planning to go to Newport. I told you, we were waiting to go out to the boat, and he showed up. Then the other one."

"Yes. Tell me about him again."

I described him again, including his comment about remembering my face.

"You say you've never seen him before either."

"That's right."

"But you were willing to get into a fight with them. Why?"

"I didn't get into a fight with 'them,' I got into a fight with him. Because I thought he might kill this kid."

"Which you think he now did."

"Right."

"I see. So you just jumped right in. Now if I understand this right, you are a half owner of Burke and Daniels Advertising. That means this Miss Perry works for you, correct?"

"Correct."

"Do you have a background in the martial arts, Mr. Burke? A law enforcement background, perhaps, or military?"

"The Rangers."

He looked up from his notebook. "No shit? When?"

I gave him the dates.

"Vietnam?"

"Yes."

"Maybe you were reliving old times fighting this guy?"

I answered mildly, "I got in the fight because it seemed like the thing to do. I thought the big guy was going to kill this kid right in front of us, and when I told Rachel to go up to the car, he told her to 'stay right there.' I figured we were involved, like it or not. Plus, like I told you, I'd had a few drinks. As soon as I got into it, I saw I was out of my league. I was lucky that I had the oar."

"Did you draw blood?"

"Maybe. Yes, his mouth was bleeding."

"You say he threw an oar. Which one was it?"

Both of them were lashed alongside the dinghy. I pointed out a rough spot on the end of one of them. "That's probably where it hit the launch."

"Okay." He pointed the oar out to DePetrie. "Fingerprints," he said.

"Mr. Burke, have you had many instances since Vietnam where it's been the 'thing to do'?"

"None."

"You're sure?"

"Yes."

"Because we can check easily enough."

"Go ahead."

"You say the launch driver seemed to know him."

"Yes, she knew his name."

"And hers?"

"Linda, I believe. Yes, Linda. The launch *Dauntless*."

"Did you have the sense she was meeting him at the dock on purpose, that it was prearranged?"

"No, I didn't have that impression."

"Do you know what boat, if any, they went to next?"

"No. They may have just gone to shore."

"Which direction did they go?"

I pointed deeper into the harbor toward town, where the launch service kept its main docks. He stood at the binnacle and made a quick sketch of the harbor with arrows indicating our path from the Fort Adams dock to my boat, to their departure. He used the compass to indicate a rough course, then showed me the sketch. "Like this?"

"Right. The kid's finger was broken, though, so he might've gone to a hospital. I suggested he do that."

"Tell me about the break again."

I did.

"You say the assailant had a southern accent?"

"Yes."

"From where? Could you tell?"

"I couldn't. Cory called him a 'Georgia boy.' I don't know if he meant it literally or not."

"Yes, it's a common expression. Tell me, do you scuba dive?"

I blinked. "You do bounce around, don't you, Lieutenant?"

"You've got some problem with that?"

"No."

"Because if you do, I'll stop and read you your rights, and you can call a lawyer."

"It's not a problem. Yes, I dive. I don't have any gear on the boat, other than the snorkeling equipment. My tank and wet suit are back home in the garage."

"Have you had your gear on the boat recently?"

"Not recently, no. I dive occasionally off the boat, but more often as something to do on the north shore, Gloucester, Rockport, on the weekends when we don't go sailing."

"Now tell me about your day on Saturday. You say you went sailing by yourself?"

"That's right."

"It's a good-sized boat to take out alone."

"Are you a sailor, Lieutenant Borenson?"

"Power."

"Well, it's rigged for . . ."

Before I finished my sentence the diver broke the surface and said, "Take a look, Lieutenant?"

The body was apparently unweighted, and floating facedown on the surface. A small powerboat skirted around the fire department launch. A photographer stood in the bow, the fast click of his autowind camera just audible across the water.

"That's great, the press is here." Borenson spoke into the radio. "Blair, bring the launch back, and chase that photographer away. Cahill's got the body."

To the diver, he said, "How's it look?"

The diver flipped the body over, and my stomach clenched.

Behind us on the deck, I heard DePetrie say, "Holy shit."

The diver said, "It's not going to be a mystery for the medical examiner. Shotgun blast to the chest. Tight pattern—the shooter must've been close."

"Is a finger broken on the right hand?" Borenson asked.

"You've got it. Right hand, forefinger."

Cory's face looked even worse in the daylight, his skin colorless, the partially eaten eyes, his mouth jammed open obscenely by something I couldn't identify. Borenson asked the question for me: "What's in his mouth?"

"Baggie. Looks like somebody shoved a Baggie of coke down his throat."

"Cocaine?" Borenson turned to me, his watery blue eyes hard. "You didn't say a thing about coke, Mr. Burke."

"This is the first I've heard about it."

"Uh-huh. Well, I'm not taking any more chances with Miranda." He pulled a small plastic card from his back pocket and read the warning to me in an even tone.

When he was finished, I said, "First off, Lieutenant, am I under arrest?"

"No. I just wanted to make sure you understand your rights."

"Think about it, Lieutenant—would I have called the police if I had killed him?"

"You'd be amazed at the stupidity I see every day. Now do you want to call an attorney or not?"

Ellen came up behind him in the cockpit. She stared at the body, eyes wide, her hand over her mouth. Her face was bone-white. "His eyes," she moaned. "Look at his eyes. . . ."

Three boat lengths away, the photographer's telephoto lens was aimed at me like a gun. The detective in the harbormaster's launch was yelling for the press boat to back off.

Ellen sat down heavily. Her voice was almost a whisper. "What in God's name have you gotten us into?"

6

The police department was in a redbrick building across from a church. It was flanked by a Chinese restaurant and a tattoo parlor. Borenson gave me the phone to call the agency's attorney, Tom Windon. "The police?" Tom repeated. "You're kidding." Tom was not a criminal lawyer, but neither were the two attorneys I knew socially. He said he would be right down.

"Save us all some time here," I said to Borenson. "Check with the Treadway Inn. We were there all night, ground-floor room near the desk. I ordered cognacs for us around midnight, we couldn't sleep. We were up for breakfast at six-thirty."

"Lot you can do in six and a half hours," he said.

I extracted a photo of Ellen and me from my wallet and told

him again how we spent the evening, starting with dinner at the Rhumb Line.

He looked at me speculatively, then called out to Detective Blair. They talked briefly, and the detective left with the photo. Borenson turned back to me. "I'm cooperating with you, you cooperate with me. Tell me about the coke."

"I've told you all I know. We'll wait until my attorney and your detective come back."

"Suit yourself. In the meantime, we're bringing in Mr. Daniels, Miss Perry, and the launch driver."

"Is that really necessary?"

"Embarrassing, is it? That's too bad."

For two hours, Ellen and I sat at an empty desk in the detectives' area, watching them go about their business, answer phone calls, drink coffee. She refused to speak.

Tom Windon arrived, looking hassled and a bit uneasy. He requested a private room for us, and I explained what had happened while Ellen looked past me.

"I know this is rough," Tom said. "But, as you said, Riley, everything you'd want to hide is out in the open. First thing, Rachel and Nick will confirm what happened earlier in the weekend, the timing and all, and let's hope the police come back with something solid from the Treadway Inn. Mainly I think they're just trying to throw a scare into you, so that if you are involved you'll give." He looked uncomfortable. "Uh, you're not, are you?"

"No, Tom."

"All right. Well, good, you know, but I've got to ask."

Through all of this, Ellen sat with her arms crossed, staring across at the mirror above a little washbasin. "I suppose that's one-way glass."

"It may be," Tom said. "But I guarantee you no one is watching behind there now. That would violate attorney-client privilege, and that would throw their case right out."

"If you found out." Her eyes moved quickly to my face, and she looked back at Tom. There were goose bumps on her arms, though the room was warm. I put my hand on her shoulder, but she moved away like a cat. "Don't." To Tom, she said, "Can't you get us out of here?"

"Sure. You're not in custody."

"Let's get this over with," I said.

"Riley's right," Tom said. "I'm not going to argue with you that the police are being stupid. But there's so much pressure on the drug-trafficking thing around here that when they think they have a shot at tracking it down, they get very careful, and that means they don't take a chance on any testimony being thrown out because the suspect didn't hear his rights."

At that moment, a uniformed policeman escorted Rachel and Nick into the room. Ellen's lips tightened, and she squared her shoulders. She stared at Rachel.

"I don't know what to say," Rachel said to Ellen.

"I can imagine," Ellen said. "But don't worry . . . Rachel, is it? I didn't marry you, I married him. She's very pretty, Riley."

"Come on."

She yanked her arm away. "I'm being goddamn civil, under the circumstances."

"Ellen, let's sit back over here," Nick said.

Borenson stepped in at that moment with Linda, the launch driver. She looked very young, her eyes apparently red from crying. But she said, steadily enough, "Yes, that's him." She nodded toward Rachel. "And that's her."

Ellen rubbed her arm and stared defiantly at Borenson. He grinned at me. "Hey, the whole gang is here, huh? Time for you and your attorney to join me for a chat." We followed him back to his office. Borenson leaned his elbows on his desk and said, "Well?"

"Lieutenant. You don't have anything linking my client to a crime. He did what any good citizen should do, he called the police when he found a body. . . ."

And so on. They haggled a few minutes more about who was helping whom, and then I went through the story once again. Borenson tossed me a typewritten statement created from the earlier interview and asked me if it was accurate. Tom and I read it through carefully, and I said that it was. "Okay," Borenson said, standing. "You can sign it now, or after I talk with your friends and get the final report in on the search of your boat."

"Search?" Tom said.

I felt chilled.

"Hey, it's a crime scene." Borenson leaned close to me. "Look, we're sick of the money that's thrown around in this town on drugs, the attitude that if you're rich you can get away with anything. I see it all day long in the faces of the punks sailing those boats, kids driving Porsches to high school, frigging yachts complete with helipads. I'm up to my neck in the problems people like you bring into town, and if I find so much as a stick of pot on your boat, you're going to wish you never got that hard-on for Miss Perry."

"Hey, enough of that," Tom said, standing.

"Yeah, I've had enough of the two of you. Sign this or don't."

I signed the statement.

"Okay, time to talk with the rest of the happy crew." He waved us out of his office and began to close the door.

"Borenson," I said.

He turned back. "Lieutenant Borenson."

"How about giving me some mug books to look through? When you get finished playing your games, you'll find we're innocent, so how about we make use of some of this time?"

"Getting cooperative?"

"Always was. Just not putting myself in jail because it'd make your job easier."

"Sounds reasonable to me," Tom said.

Borenson grunted. "Sure, we've got pictures."

It passed the time, but I didn't see Green Shirt. A skinny police artist interviewed me to put together a passable likeness. He said he would talk individually with Rachel and Linda and refine it further.

Another few hours passed before the uniformed officer brought me into the big interrogation room with the others. Ellen looked straight at me. Nick shook his head wearily. Linda sat in the corner writing in a notebook. Rachel avoided my eyes altogether, staring at the tabletop. Tom simply looked uncomfortable.

Borenson entered, and held the final sketch in front of him. "Okay, you three claim this is the guy, right?"

I nodded, and so did Linda and Rachel.

"But no one like this fits the photos in the mug books, right? How did I know?"

Borenson stared right at me. "You'll be interested to know the final reports are in on the search of your boat. Guess what we found?"

I felt a sinking in my chest. If someone planted Cory's body under my boat, he surely could have planted a few ounces of coke in one of the lockers as well. I kept my face blank and said simply, "What, Lieutenant?"

He sighed and said, disgustedly, "It's clean. And the clerk at the Treadway does remember you and your wife, and says he left his post just once to go to the bathroom, and your door is within clear sight. We turned up a witness on the Albin three boats away from yours. He was there Saturday night, and couldn't sleep right about the same time you were calling for your cognacs. He went up on deck and saw a quahog boat, one of those skiffs with the little cabin on the stern, being rowed right beside yours. Thought that was funny. Those boats run about eighteen feet, and are usually wood. Kind of a heavy boat to row. He figured the guy was headed out to rake shellfish illegally, so he yelled out, and the quahogger started the outboard and took off. Too dark for any identification, he says. Plus the medical examiner puts Cory Dearborn's—that's his last name; sweet, isn't it?—anyhow, he figures Dearborn caught all that metal in his chest a little before midnight. Everything else checks out, timewise, and you'll be interested to know we followed up thoroughly. Oh, yeah, a Carl Tattinger said to let you and Mr. Daniels know how unhappy he was about the police calling him at home to verify your whereabouts Friday night. Made a point that I let you know, and he says to put everything on hold, he'll have *his* attorney contact yours first thing tomorrow morning."

Nick groaned.

Borenson grinned at me, then looked over to Tom and said, "Guess that would be you, wouldn't it?" He turned for the door.

"Burke, if you've got a minute more, stop by my office. It'd be in your best interest."

I almost didn't, but I decided to hear what he had to say. He was on the phone, but I walked into his office anyhow, and sat across from him while he dawdled over his call. Finally, he hung up. "Look, I think you're lying. I'm not sure where, but I think so. But whether you are or not, you're in shit way over your head." He pulled out several eight-by-ten photos from his left-hand drawer and splayed them across the desk. I winced. They were most likely taken at the morgue, of a young black man with a long deep gash along his throat up to his ear. There were cuts across his nose and right eye. Another set of prints showed the head of a white man, his hair shaved around a deep cut which had laid open skin and bone down to the gray matter of his brain.

"Penknife," Borenson said. "You'd think it would be impossible. The guy who did in these two weighed easily twenty, thirty pounds less than either of them. But they pissed him off. They were at his house, and he had just done a few lines and he figured they were trying to stiff him on a buy. He cut the black guy, then gut-shot the white one, and then went at his head with the knife. All this before they knew what was happening to them. *I* know this, because when we brought him in, he bragged about it. This shit doesn't make people crazy—he knew exactly what he was doing—but it gives them the attitude that they can do *anything*. That they're faster, smarter, and better than anyone else. And someone with an attitude like that, who is a head case to begin with, will do absolutely irrational and vicious shit, faster than you can believe. You're not set up to fight with them. If the head basher you told us about is real, and if he thinks you have something he owns, you've got yourself a serious problem. This is the time to tell me the truth."

"We've told you everything we know."

"Uh-huh." He eyed me silently, then shrugged. "Well, good luck, then. I'll call the Belmont police. Check in with them when you get home. Maybe they can pay your house some extra attention."

"Tell me, how about the fingerprints? Did you get anything off the oar?"

"Nothing we can use. It was too smudged."

"What do you know about Dearborn?"

"His wallet with twenty dollars in it was still in his back pocket, and the girl, Linda Noel, knew him. He was a local yacht sales-man, worked for Compton's Marina. My guess is he made more than a little money on the side with snow. He has a terrific apart-ment, stereo, Jacuzzi on the deck, the works."

"Was Linda planning to meet him at the dock?"

Borenson looked irritated that I was questioning him, but he answered, "No, she said she was surprised to see him there."

"Did he ever say which boat he was originally heading for?"

"No. But being a yacht broker, he could have access to a num-ber of boats moored in the harbor. You know, ones listed with his marina. We'll check those out as well."

"So she took him back to the main dock in Newport, not back to Fort Adams, right?"

"Right. She said she took him back to the dock, and he walked away, saying he was going to call a cab for the hospital, and that's the last she saw of him."

"Did she see him take the cab?"

"No. Though two other launch drivers confirm that he left without her."

"And you haven't found the cab driver yet?"

"Not yet."

"Dearborn didn't have a splint on his finger, either."

Borenson smiled grudgingly. "You're thinking like a cop. But there was a residue of athletic tape. That doesn't tell us much, though, since plenty of people have a roll in their medicine chest. We've checked with Newport Hospital, and they have no record of him or anyone who fits his description coming in. We're checking other hospitals and clinics."

Borenson leaned back in his chair. "Look, you want to show me you're on the level, how about you help us out, hey? Let us stake you out on your boat. You act like you've fought with your wife, hang out for a week or so, hit the bars, complain that you're lonely. See who approaches you."

"What makes you think I need to show you I'm on the level? Besides, why would anybody come to me? I told you, I don't have any coke. What's to say any has been stolen?"

"You think they stuffed his body under your boat just to make a point, huh? For interfering?"

"That's the only explanation I can see."

Borenson tugged on his lower lip, while staring at me. "Huh. Well, that's it, Burke. You got anything more to say, now's your chance. After this, you're on your own."

"Always was," I said.

Outside the station, Tom said, "I'm not sure how much I helped in there."

"You did," I said, but privately I agreed with his assessment.

"Uh, look. If this continues in some manner, I'm not the right guy for this job."

I shook his hand. "Thanks, Tom. Looks like we'll be needing you in tomorrow with Tattinger."

His face fell even further. "Probably not going to be complex, I'm afraid. He'll exercise his right to resign the account, and we'll cover him for thirty to ninety days, however long it takes him to get a new agency."

"Sounds accurate."

Nick drove me, Ellen, and Rachel back to the Fort Adams parking lot.

"Look, I know this sounds lame," I said. "But I'm sorry for all the trouble."

No one answered.

The tension was electric. We all kept our eyes straight ahead. When we reached our car, Ellen locked her door.

"Take your girlfriend," she said. "Nick will see me home."

7

Talker, our golden Labrador, looked as if he knew something was wrong by the time I arrived at home. Nick had already left, and Ellen greeted me with white-faced silence. Talker moved warily between us, apparently unsure if he was the cause of our increased tension, but certain that he should remain present.

I made a quiet fuss over him, scratching his muscled neck and behind his ears. Ellen went upstairs. I called the Belmont police and bounced around on the phone lines until I finally reached a Detective Swampscott, the officer who had talked with Borenson. Swampscott's tone was cool, but he said that they would indeed have the patrol cars drive by, and would I plan on stopping in to see him tomorrow?

Afterward, I made myself a cup of instant coffee and looked out the window, thinking of what I had to say to Ellen. Talker brought me out of my reverie by licking my hand and whining. I said, "All right, boy, let's go."

He ran up the stairs before me and pushed the bedroom door open with his shoulder. His tail started wagging, slowly, and he dropped his head. Ellen was sitting at her dressing table, her back to me. The lights were low, and she glanced at me in the mirror, but said nothing. Talker sniffed at her hip and pushed her with his nose. She ignored him. He growled softly and moved his lower jaw in the way that had earned him his name, and she looked down. "Sorry, boy," she said, petting his head. "I shouldn't have done that, huh?"

He slumped at her feet and heaved a big sigh.

She was wearing her bathrobe. She said to me, "You don't think we're going to sleep together, do you?"

"Ellen, I can't come up with an explanation that casts me in any positive light. But you've got some responsibility too. It's been no pleasure living with you for the past couple of years, you know that."

"We can change that pretty damn quickly!"

"Maybe it'll come down to that."

Her eyes dropped. "Is that what you want?"

"No. But I don't want to continue the way it's been." I pulled up a chair. "Let's talk about the next several days."

She turned from the mirror and faced me. Her normally fresh skin was putty-colored. She shook her head slowly and said, "Don't give me ultimatums or instructions, Riley. Giving you a little hell right now is just my idea of showing a bit of interest in our marriage. Because my true feelings aren't those of outrage, the way you'd expect. More like they're dead, or worse, nonexistent from the very beginning. I can think back to things you and I did, said, felt. But it's like watching some late-night movie, none of it's real, and it doesn't hurt so much not to have it now. The most I drum up is kind of a misty-eyed nostalgia. So think about that before you tell me what's so important."

I told her about Green Shirt's comment as we pulled away in

the launch, about Borenson's warning that we might still be in danger if we were suspected of holding on to a supply of cocaine. Some color came back to her face as she listened, and she sat up straight.

"So you don't think this monster's threat ended by putting that poor boy under the *Spindrift*. Does he know where we live?"

"I expect the Newport paper will carry our names, and that we live in the Boston area. We're in the phone book." I told her about my conversation with the Belmont police.

"They'll drive by," she repeated. "That's it?"

I shrugged. "Who knows?"

She grasped my sleeve and said, "Do you really know more about it? Did you steal something from that boy?"

I looked at her askance. "Of course not."

She dug her nails into my wrist. With her eyes locked on to mine she pleaded, "Tell me the truth. Are you involved?"

"No." She was shivering again, and I felt a heavy mantle of guilt for having frightened her. "Ellen, I do love you. I'm sorry about Rachel, and the police, all of that. But you're going to have to do what I say so you'll be safe until the police catch this maniac. He enjoys hurting people. He may think he has reason to get to me, and that could include getting to you."

Her face blanched. "Did he really hurt that boy?"

"With a grin on his face the whole time."

She hugged herself and said, "Stop. I don't want to hear. Just what is it you want me to do?"

"Leave town altogether. Maybe I'll put you on a plane to the Virgin Islands. You can't stay home alone like this anymore."

"Wouldn't that be sweet." Her face hardened again. "You can have Rachel come over and play house. You listen to me. I can't just take off from the gallery. I don't want to go out of town. I don't want to go lie on the beach and give you another opportunity to make a fool of me."

"That's not going to happen." I kept my voice even. "If this guy showed up at the gallery, what would you do? You wouldn't even recognize him. You've said Christopher has been doing a great job. You leave him in charge when we go on vacation. Do it now."

"No. You'd just better figure another way out, goddamn it."

"The only way I know to tackle that is to take Borenson's recommendation and go back to the boat, let them stake me out, and see if he approaches me. You can't come with me, and I can't leave you at home alone."

"Well, you'd better just find a way. Because I'm not going to change my life because you wanted to screw around on me. What am I, invisible or something? Besides, if this guy is as tough as you say, what are you going to do? You can't count on being able to fight him again. It's been almost fifteen years since you did that kind of thing." Her lips compressed. "You'll either never see him or he'll kill you and walk away while the cops are in the bathroom."

"Either way, there's no way you can stay here."

"Oh yes there is." She began to brush her hair. She said in a distant voice, "Leave me alone now, okay, Riley?"

I felt as if I was choking on a lump of mixed emotions: rage, soured love, self-fury. "Look, I don't care how angry you are at me. We've got to come to some sort of solution here."

She looked at me in the mirror and spoke in a tired and distant tone. "All right. Jocelyn has been sitting a house up in Manchester, and she invited me to visit. I'll call her tomorrow afternoon. The number's unlisted, and the owners are in Europe for a month."

"Good. But call her in the morning, and I'll drive you up before going into the office and try to make sure we're not followed."

"No! I'll go up tomorrow night. I can't see anyone right now, including Jocelyn. You go to work, and in the evening we'll go up, if that's okay with her. You said the police will be paying attention, and it'll just be for one day. Then you go down to Newport and put an end to this."

I was overwhelmed with a heavy weariness, and I was still far from certain we were in any real danger. "Fine," I said.

"Hey, Riley." She looked into the mirror, catching my eye. "Don't get yourself killed, all right? I want you to know what you've put me through, but I still want you around. I do know what I've put you through, too."

I squeezed her shoulder, and she held her hand over mine for a moment, then pushed me away. Talker got on his feet and followed me downstairs and watched as I made up the couch and switched off the lights. I tossed and turned for about a half hour, the events of the weekend playing in my head: Dearborn's ruined face, Ellen's sickened expression as I told her about Rachel, the bloody-toothed grin of the man as he pressed himself back up on the dock.

Talker's ears lifted curiously when I got up and loaded my .22 rifle in the dark. He gave it a thorough sniffing after I propped it up in the corner. I lay down on the sofa and pulled the blanket over me. He circled the living room, then jumped up to look out the window. His hackles were raised. He had caught my mood. He looked at me over his shoulder, questioning.

"Come here, boy." I petted him until he settled down on the floor by the sofa. He fell asleep hours before me.

8

Early the next morning, I drove to work, and started a list of next steps I should take. Most of our forty-odd employees were not in yet. Normally, I enjoyed this quiet time, the tick of the desk clock, the view of the river. Now it all seemed off-kilter, perhaps because topping my list of things to do was hiring a bodyguard for my wife.

She had insisted she would be fine that morning, and there in the kitchen, any danger did seem remote. But by the time I reached the office, I was convinced that for a while, anyhow, I should hire someone, and we should move her away from the house.

I was reaching for the phone to call Lenny Datano, one of our smaller clients, who included personal protection as part of his corporate security business, when Nick stepped into my office and said, "You look like shit." He sat across from me and put his feet up on my desk.

"So do you, as a matter of fact."

His face was drawn and haggard. He blew his nose. "Goddamn summer colds are the worst. And it's been a bang-up morning so far. It started with the Watertown cops pounding on the door at six A.M. Said they had a call from a Lieutenant Borenson from Newport, and that they would very much like to look at my dive boat. That they did not have a warrant, but would I show it to them anyhow. I said sure, and they went into the garage and took a few snapshots, and walked out saying that it didn't look like a quahog boat to them. I guess Borenson had a brainstorm last night. Then I called Tattinger just now. He was very pissy, acted like we had involved him in a drug scam because of those few drinks on Friday night. I gave him as sanitized a version as I could about what happened. Couldn't make it clean enough, though—he's pulling out. Says he has a responsibility to ensure that his vendors maintain the same level of integrity as Textrel, and he is no longer certain that Burke and Daniels is such a firm."

"Nicely put, Carl."

Nick smiled wryly. "Bet you waited up all night, right?"

"Good guess."

"No, I figured it would be just another night in the jungle for you, huh?"

"I'm probably being overcautious."

"That's not the kind of guy you are. Caution to the wind, that's you." As our creative director, Nick found clichés particularly amusing, and had jokingly sprinkled them in his conversation for so long that he actually ended up using them unintentionally sometimes. But his line about caution was not entirely facetious. He was somewhat defensive about his National Guard service, even though I had always maintained he showed more intelligence than me on that score. He said, "But truthfully, I think putting your marriage back together might be tougher. How's Ellen taking it?"

"How do you think?"

"I guess there's no way to treat this lightly, is there?"

"No." His tone was friendly, concerned. But I could feel an undercurrent of hostility. He was my partner, but Ellen was his friend, too. And losing the Textrel account would cost us a lot of money. "She barely said a word on the drive back," he said.

"Look, Nick, it was as unpleasant as you could imagine, but not a lot of screaming and yelling. She feels lost, I'm sick with myself, and I know you've got something to say too. So just say it."

"You got it, pal." Nick put his feet on the floor, leaned on my desk, and said softly, "I'd like to ask what the hell you were thinking of. Don't you know what you've got in Ellen? And how the hell did you expect to get away with making it with someone from the office? You can't screw around and keep good people. Christ, I'm divorced, and I leave the help alone."

"Just a reminder here, Nick—I may have messed my life up in a big, lurid way this weekend, but it's my life, not yours. And believe me, the problems with Ellen didn't just crop up between Friday and today."

"Yeah, well, just a reminder to you, Riley, I'm tied to you two, like it or not. We share a business, and I spend all my free time with you as it is. Losing Textrel is damn well my business. I had our team working overtime for a month and a half coming up with concepts to bring them on board, and now I've got to explain how you fucked it up. Literally." He rubbed his face in his hands, then said in a quieter tone, "Sorry. Look, you guys helped me out when I was going through my divorce, and now you're going through hard times yourself, and you didn't say word one to me."

I was at a loss. Normally Nick was so insular that it was hard to tell what he was feeling. I had never felt he accepted much emotional help from us after his divorce, but perhaps our just being there sufficed. Lamely, I said, "I guess we didn't just because you are that close."

He didn't meet my eyes, but he answered in a conciliatory tone, "Hey, I understand, I didn't talk much when Susan left. It feels like such a failure, it hurts just to look at it. You think it's going to come to that with you two?"

I shook my head. "Not if I can help it."

"Will firing Rachel help? Say it and she's gone."

"Two minutes ago you were reading me the riot act for screwing around with the help. How do you think everyone would feel about me firing Rachel because it didn't work out to be a pleasant weekend? Never mind how unfair it would be to her."

"We could weather that better than you continuing to have battles with Ellen because of her, then getting a divorce. Then having to dissolve the agency, or work with your hands tied financially, to pay some crazy settlement."

"Is that why you're really in here this morning?"

He laced his fingers across his stomach. "Like I said, I'm tied into you guys. What's best for the both of you is best for me."

My phone rang.

"Jesus, I told Lori we'd be in conference," he said.

I picked it up. My secretary said a little breathlessly, "I've got a call holding from the Newport police. He said it was very important and that I should break in. I hope it's all right."

"Yes." Inwardly, I sighed.

She put the call through.

"Guess who, hero?" There was no mistaking the southern accent. My chest tightened. "Aren't you cool. You and that blond chick, frosty. Gave me a real surprise when I figured out that you were stepping out on your lady."

My heart started to trip.

"Want to guess how I found out?"

I already knew.

"I've got somebody who'd like to talk to you."

I almost didn't recognize Ellen's voice at first. She was fighting to control her voice; it was too loud and shaky. "Riley, he's got a knife. He says he'll cut my face unless you do what he says—" She cried out in pain.

"Ellen!"

"Easy now, easy. I just gave her arm a little twist this time to get your attention. Next I'll use the blade on her face," the buttery-smooth voice said. "There's lots more pretty skin here. I might lose control and start having fun. You're crazy to leave this one at home—she's too tasty."

"I'll do whatever you want."

"That's good! Very good! First things first. I set the ground rules. Just like in big business, let's make sure we all have the same *expectations*."

Nick said, "What's going on? Who's that?" On a pad I wrote, IT'S HIM. ELLEN. Nick started to leave the room, I assumed to phone the police. I lunged across my desk, grabbed his arm, and pointed to the chair.

The voice said, "First off, buddy, if you call the cops your wife gets a new mouth. Right under her chin. I'll pull her tongue out of it, and leave her with what we call a necktie. Got that? You should know I've sliced up more than just a couple smartasses, and it doesn't bother me at all that some of them were women. If I went back to prison now on kidnapping, I would never get out. Never. So I might as well make it murder one. You got that?"

"I do."

"Good. I like a good listener. Now the next thing is, even though you deserve to have your teeth kicked in, I am a businessman first. So if I get what I want, your wife can walk away with nothing worse than a bad scare and a chance to find out what you were doing on that dock with the blondie. What was the blondie's name again? Huh, lady, what was her name?"

"Rachel . . . Rachel Perry," Ellen said.

"That's good, that's cooperation. See, Burke, she knows the meaning of a knife. Now, you give me what I want, and give it to me now."

"What is it you want?"

Ellen cried out, "Riley, he cut me, oh my God, he cut me!"

I stood up, knocking the chair over. "Leave her alone, damn it! Tell me what you want!"

"Jesus, Riley, what's happened?" Nick whispered. "I'm calling the police."

I held on to his arm and listened hard.

"Okay, calm down, everyone. Shush, honey. It was just a little slice along the back of her hand. I was nice enough to leave her face for the next time," the voice said.

I shook my head at Nick. My best chance was to get face to face with Green Shirt. I fully believed he would carry out his threat at the first hint of the police.

Green Shirt continued, "Nothing fatal, yet. But I've got this temper, and you're playing cute with me, hero. You hit me with that oar, then puttered off laughing with your girlfriend, and we both know what you've got that's mine. So you stop being cute or your wife's gonna do the bleeding for both of you."

I fought to keep my voice even. "Listen to me. You're talking about coke, right? That's what was stuffed down Cory's mouth, that's what the cops think this is about. But honest to God, the first time I saw Cory Dearborn's face was that night on the dock. I was lit, I'd had a few too many drinks, and I was down there with another woman. Are you listening? I did not know anything about you or him. I just got into the fight because I was drunk, showing off, whatever. That's all my involvement was."

"He's hung you out, sweetmeat," the voice crooned. "It looks like I made a mistake holding a knife on you. I should've gone for that long-legged Rachel."

"No," I said desperately. "I'll give you money, I'll go to the bank, but I'm telling you—"

A sudden roar filled the line. Ellen cried out, and the man's mocking tone turned enraged. "Get him off!"

I grabbed Nick on the way to the door. "Call the police. The dog's attacking him."

Nick was waiting outside of the parking garage as I came down the ramp. I hit the brakes, and he slid into the front seat. He said, "Take the pike to Storrow, that's the fastest way. I got through to the Belmont cops—they're probably there already. They've got good people. They'll mop this guy up. She'll be all right."

I stood on the gas pedal. "I've got to concentrate, Nick."

He nodded. "Sure." We hit 120 before slowing down to run through the toll gate and turn onto Storrow Drive. From there, it was like pushing through dough. I moved the Acura as fast as I could through the twisting, crowded roads, but nothing was fast enough. When we rounded the turn to my street, I saw the swirling police lights. "Oh, Jesus," I said.

"Steady," Nick said.

We ran to the house. A young uniformed policeman with a short mustache stepped forward from the doorway, his hand on the butt of his revolver. "Hold it!"

"It's my house."

"Yes sir. Your wife's okay." He turned to Nick. "Give me the weapon right now, sir."

I glanced back at Nick as I pushed past into the doorway. He was handing the policeman a long-bladed letter opener, saying, "We didn't know what we were going to find. We rushed right over."

"I understand, sir."

"Ellen!" I called.

Another policeman, an older man with a heavy belly, was sitting on one side of her on the couch, and Sara Pratt, our next-door neighbor, was on the other. "Here he is, ma'am," the officer said with soft heartiness. "Bet you're glad to see him."

Ellen was holding her left hand. Blood seeped between her fingers, and several buttons on her blouse were gone. She was wearing jeans and no shoes. She came to me, her eyes wide, dark skin paled. I put my arms around her and pulled her tight, feeling her fear in the rigid set of her body. "Oh, Riley," she said. "He was going to kill me. He was going to make you come home, and he would have killed you too."

"I saw him," Sara said, her mouth shaped by her disapproval. "A big brutish sort, running out of your house clutching his arm and limping, then making all sorts of smoke and noise spinning his tires as he left. I hurried right over. I knew something was wrong."

"You don't have him?" I said to the policeman. "He just vanished?"

"Who's him?" The cop took out a notebook. "What's his name?"

"I told you, he drove off!" Sara interjected.

"Damn it!"

"Talker was out," Ellen said in a rush. "I had let him out. I was making coffee, and that man kicked the kitchen door in. He just came right in, shoved me right off my feet, as if I was nothing, he was so awful, so cheerful. He had a gun in his belt, and wore gloves. He reached under my blouse and touched me . . . as if he wanted to show me he couldn't care less that he had no right. Then he pulled out this knife from behind his back, it was just suddenly there. And he talked about how sharp it was and what it sounded like when he pushed it into someone, and that if I didn't do exactly what he told me, he'd show me."

"Sir, when we arrived your wife was at the doorway, hysterical and with her hand bleeding," the officer said. "No man. Your wife gave us a quick description: dark hair, sunburned skin, yellow shirt, chinos, southern accent. Mrs. Pratt identified the car as a beige late-model Ford LTD, no plate identified."

"I couldn't see everything," she said. "Lucky I recognized the car. I used to have a Ford."

"We have other patrol cars out looking for him, so if he stays in the Ford, we'll get him. If he dumps it fast, it won't be so easy."

Ellen took my hand and said, "Talker is in the library."

I followed her in. He was on the floor, breathing shallowly. I knelt beside him. Blood seeped into the rug. He tried to whine. There were deep cuts across his face, one bad gash above his right eye. The worst wound appeared to be a deep puncture on his right side, where blood bubbled along his rib cage.

"You're a good boy," I said, rubbing him softly along his spine. I looked up. "It looks like a lung's been hit." My vision blurred.

"Oh, Talker," Ellen said. "He must have been roaming around. He came up through the cellar, as usual, and he must've heard the fear in my voice, because I've never seen him like that. He came charging into the room, his hair was standing all up, he looked huge. He was just roaring, ferocious. He actually scared that man, I saw the fright on his face. Talker went for his throat. I ran for my room, locked the door, and called the police. I could hear them fighting down here, you can see how the place is torn up. Talker just kept going after him again and again, and then I heard a yelp, and I knew that he had lost. I didn't dare come down until the police car pulled into the driveway."

Tears poured down Ellen's face now. I put my arm around her. "It'll be okay, honey, it'll be okay." Nick came through the doorway and said, "Oh Jesus, I'm so sorry." The cop looked out the window. We had bought Talker as a puppy.

I reached down to pet him again, and found he had already died.

9

Ellen withdrew into chilly silence immediately after I asked the police to pick Rachel up at my office. "I doubt he's headed right over there, but he did say on the phone that he should have gone after her."

Afterward at the Belmont police station, Detective Swampscott, a hard-looking man in his early thirties with a droopy mustache, said, "I just had a quick conversation with Borenson. If you do have a shipment of cocaine, you'd better tell me now. I'm not saying there won't be any pain resolving the drug issue, but better you clarify it early, because this guy is obviously violent, and we can't protect you if we don't know exactly what we're dealing with."

" 'Won't be any pain resolving the drug issue,' " Nick repeated wonderingly. "Damn, Riley, the detective is speaking our language, let's confess. Sure, we pulled off the ad-agency bit for years now, we admit it, we're the head of the Eastern Seaboard drug cartel. Congratulations, Detective, you'll make lieutenant on this."

"Nick . . ."

"That's enough of an admission for us to hold you for a few days, Daniels."

"It's not an admission, it's a joke. I'm sick of spending time being—"

"I couldn't care less what you're sick of."

"Hold it," I said. "Nick, shut up, please. Detective Swampscott, I do not have any coke and never did. I'm involved in this just as I told you, and Nick here is understandably upset. My wife has been attacked. Let's get on with resolving this, can we? Has there been any luck with the car?"

Swampscott stared at me silently for a moment, then gave a curt nod and said, "Found two beige Ford LTDs in the Alewife Parking Garage. One had the plates of an Audi 5000 and was listed as stolen from Dedham early this morning. When we showed it to your neighbor, she said it looked like the one. But it was wiped clean inside, not a good print to be found."

"So you figure he may have taken the subway into Boston?"

"Could be. Or found a car to steal there at Alewife. Lot of people leave their parking stubs right in the visor. The gate attendant didn't recognize the description we have, but then he says he never pays any attention to the drivers coming out—he's got a TV."

"So this guy could have been heading in to get Rachel."

"It's possible. But he would have to be totally soft to do that. If he has any sense, he would figure we would be looking out for her right now. Boston police just called a minute ago, said they picked her up at your office, and they're at her apartment now and will stay with her until they hear back from us."

"A regular harem waiting on you," Ellen murmured.

"Okay, where we left off," Swampscott said. "Tell me what happened down in Newport right up until this afternoon."

He had us run through the story twice before he left the room, presumably to call Borenson. After about fifteen minutes, he came back. "I've been talking over the jurisdiction and some of the forensics we've pulled together so far with Lieutenant Borenson. We'll touch base with some of the other law enforcement agencies, the state police, FBI, the Drug Enforcement Agency. But the investigation will primarily be split between our two departments. The perp wore gloves, so we're not likely to find any fingerprints, and the blood sample taken from your dog's teeth is in the lab now. The reason we took your blood sample, Mrs. Burke, is in case we have an opportunity to match the knife. He apparently came up on the sidewalk, so we weren't able to get a cast of his shoe, but there was a smudged footmark on the door where he kicked it in."

He had us go through a description again. Afterward, he showed Ellen a facsimile of the Identikit drawing, which Borenson had presumably sent him, and asked if there was any new detail.

She reiterated that his hair was kinky and he wore some cheap cologne. "I don't know what kind. And he chewed gum. That's right, the whole time he was doing this he was chewing on gum, Juicy Fruit, I think."

Swampscott wrote it down. "In any case, we should talk about the next steps. I'll put Borenson on the line now." He called the Newport police and switched on the desk speaker.

Borenson sounded remote, but his tone was heavy with bored disbelief. "Tell me your story."

Nick rolled his eyes.

I said, "Borenson, we do have a witness this time, our neighbor Sara Pratt. Do you think we've paid her off to lie to you too?"

"Get on with it."

"Shit," Nick said.

"Why don't you start, Mrs. Burke," Swampscott said.

She did. Then me, then Nick.

After he finished, I said, "So if you've got some ideas, let's hear them."

Borenson said, "Do what we were talking about all along, and come down here to see if we can draw him out."

"I don't think he would believe I would leave my wife at home for a sailing vacation right after his attack. And he'd be right."

Borenson was silent, then, "Yes, except it would also be very logical for Mrs. Burke to be upset with her husband right now, right?"

Ellen's laugh was brittle. "Very logical."

"I'm not talking about you going sailing, I'm talking about you living on the boat in the harbor like you and your wife have separated. You could spill it in a few bars how she dumped you and left the state. It wouldn't be that difficult for him to find out and believe. He'd be suspicious, but look how fast he moved last time. He'll jump, I think. I bet he's not working alone, particularly since we don't know him. I have to think that he's been sent from someplace else to take care of this problem."

"You'd do that for us, wouldn't you, Riley?" Ellen smiled bitterly. "Tell women in bars, 'My wife doesn't understand me.' "

"You've got the right, Ellen, but this isn't the time."

A flush spread up her neck. She said, "I'm not leaving the state, though. That creep can take a plane just as easily as anyone else, and I'm not going to be all alone waiting for him. I'll stay with Jocelyn. It's an unlisted phone, and nobody would have any reason to expect me up there."

"Where's this?" Swampscott said.

"In Manchester."

"I don't have any jurisdiction there."

"I'd expect some protection," she said. "But frankly, I'm a little sick of being surrounded by men. I want to be with her."

"I was thinking before about hiring Datano Security Service to provide a bodyguard," I said. "Obviously, I started too late. But we could put an around-the-clock guard up in Manchester, if Jocelyn is willing. We'd get one for Rachel too."

"And I'd stay with Ellen and Jocelyn up in Manchester nights, along with the guard," Nick said. "I've got a firearms permit to carry."

I saw the detective's lips curl almost imperceptibly. Nick picked it up as well, and his expression turned stony. He glanced at me. Swampscott said, "Who do you know at the security company?"

"Lenny Datano," I said.

Swampscott's features relaxed slightly. "Right to the top, huh? Yeah, he's good, he was on the Boston police for almost twenty years." He turned to Ellen. "If it's a go with your friend in Manchester, I'll take you up. We'll go back to your house so you can pack, and then the two of you'll drive to the airport. You'll say goodbye to your husband outside, and by then I'll be waiting for you inside. We'll take an elevator upstairs to the parking garage, switch cars, and I'm afraid from there, Mrs. Burke, you'll have to keep down on the backseat."

Over the squawk box, Borenson broke in to tell me to call him the next day after I had made the arrangements, and then he hung up. Ellen called Jocelyn while Nick and I discussed work briefly. I decided to stop by the office the first thing in the morning to pick up some work and my laptop computer.

"All set," Ellen said, putting the phone down.

"I'll go home and get a change of clothes, and my gun," Nick said. "We'll do what we have to do." Though he said it with a shrug, there was an eagerness in his voice that made me aware he was pumping up to the adventure.

I shuddered inwardly. Only the new guys were eager, and they were usually the first to be cut down.

After we met Nick at a rest stop off Route 128, Swampscott led us through a convoluted route to Manchester. Nick followed us in his big Suburban. Together we looked to see if anyone followed our little procession. We took an exit off the highway halfway up and headed south for a short time before looping back north. Then we used back roads both east and west of the highway. Once we waited around a corner in Wenham for twenty minutes as Swampscott jotted down the license plate numbers of the cars that passed. After we moved on, I kept an eye out for them as well, with no results. We drove all the way to Essex on Route 22, down to Gloucester on 133, then back to Manchester on 127.

The house was at the end of a long asphalt driveway, about a quarter of a mile from the nearest neighbor and surrounded by a thick wall of scrub pine. I did not think anyone had followed us, but I still felt uneasy. Ellen was rigidly silent as we all walked up to the front door.

"Lenny's going to be here any second—he just called me on the car phone," Nick said. "He's really good at what he does, Ellen. I figure I'll just be in the house, kind of a last line of defense, you know. We'll be ready for this bastard."

Ellen's lips twitched.

Nick looked at us sharply. "You think this is a joke?"

Ellen raised her bandaged hand. "Guess."

"I may not be an ex-Ranger," he snapped. "But I've learned a few things along the way, and we were all asleep at the switch, leaving you alone at the house so this guy could just walk in."

"Nick, I wasn't laughing at you—"

"Forget it." He turned on his heel as a blue Chevy with the security service logo pulled up.

Ellen shook her head. "He's done too many push-ups. Talk to him, will you?"

Jocelyn opened the door just then. She gave Ellen a quick kiss on the cheek and hugged her close. She said over Ellen's shoulder, "High drama out here, my God."

Jocelyn was a small woman with auburn hair, fair skin, lots of freckles. An artist with a multitude of friends, she managed to live from one house-sitting job to the next. She reached a hand out to mine and squeezed tight, her nails digging into my palm slightly. "You're causing big trouble these days."

"Can't argue with you there." I joined Nick and Swampscott as they met Datano. He was a heavyset man with thick shoulders and forearms, a small hard belly. We had won his account soon after he opened his doors, and though it would never amount to much money, we enjoyed dealing with him. His years as a cop apparently imbued him with a passion for controlling as many risks as possible. "I'm just a big pussy," he once told me. "So Lord help the scumbag who scares me or one of my customers."

Lenny's small eyes were generally friendly. Now they were concerned, yet appraising. I felt more secure about Ellen immediately. Swampscott and he exchanged quick pleasantries, and then Lenny turned to me and said, "Tell me what's happened."

I went through it quickly.

"I'm going to stop at the Manchester police on the way back and talk with Captain Ross," Swampscott said afterward. He lifted his chin in Nick's direction and said to Datano, "Mr. Daniels here is carrying a piece."

"Yes, I saw that."

"He's got a permit, but it's your choice."

When I thanked him for his help, the Belmont cop looked at me speculatively before saying finally, "It's all in the job." He drove away.

"It's also in the job for him to be suspicious," Lenny said. "He doesn't know you the way I do. Anyhow, Pete Barrow's sitting in Miss Perry's condo right now. I talked to him just as I was coming up the drive. She's none too happy."

He turned to Nick. "So you're carrying that .38 we were talking about last month? Let's see it."

Nick drew the revolver from the shoulder holster under his jacket and handed it to Datano butt first.

Datano broke it open, looked at the cartridges, and snapped it back. He said, "Nice." He walked around to the trunk of his car and locked the gun away.

"What the hell are you doing?"

"Sorry, Nick, I don't want to be an asshole about this. But we'll do the security work. I'm going to do some of the shifts myself, just to make sure everyone knows how seriously I'm taking this job. This guy isn't going to get past us. I don't want things getting hinky and my own guy shooting you, or vice versa. Plus with that load you got in there, those bullets wouldn't let a wall or two slow them down."

Nick started to argue, but Datano put his hand up. "I am dead serious, Nick. It's nothing personal. You just haven't been trained for this, and it's like anything else."

"We're paying Lenny for his experience," I said to Nick. "Let's do what he says."

"I suppose you're not carrying anything either?" Nick jerked his thumb at me and said to Datano, "Riley went out on long-range reconnaissance patrols. Meaning he set ambushes. You think maybe he has enough experience?"

Datano raised his eyebrows and said, "I think that was a long time ago. What do you think, Riley?"

"I agree. Anyhow, I'm going to be down in Newport, doing what the cops say."

"Good idea." He gave Nick a nightstick and a heavy black flashlight. "Here. With the muscles on you, anybody gets through to the house, they're going to be in serious trouble."

A vein throbbed in Nick's temple, but he smiled and faked a blow to Lenny's head with the club. "Don't bullshit a bullshitter, Datano."

"I'm not," Lenny said placatingly. "I wouldn't want to tangle with you." He grabbed Nick's biceps. "Jesus Christ, you still doing those triathlons?" He grabbed my arm also. "Too bad you guys weren't partners back in the army, huh? With the right training, Nick here could be a one-man ambush, wouldn't you say, Riley? Now come on, and introduce me to the ladies."

Before the sun went down, Jocelyn walked us around the grounds and out to the barn that she was using as a studio. The house was a weathered gray monstrosity that was probably called "modern" in 1962. The location was beautiful, however. It was perched on a cliff overlooking the Atlantic. A stone wall ran around the perimeter of the cliff, and below a short outcropping the sea crashed against the rocky wall.

"That'd make for a nice high dive," Nick said.

"Assuming you didn't break your neck," Jocelyn said. "The water's not that deep." She walked us into the house, saying, "I know, this place would make a great bonfire. But look at that view. And who am I to complain about a free house and privacy, anyhow?" The interior was decorated in oranges, yellows, and reds. Time had faded the colors, and the whole house had a hollow, shabby feel, as if it was on the verge of delaminating. I found it particularly depressing because it had the look of a home that might have been someone's dream at one time.

We sat on the sofa while Lenny outlined his plan. An armed

guard would be on duty around the clock, and he was going to take the first shift himself. Jocelyn and Ellen were not to invite anyone else over, and if they needed to go into town for groceries, or whatever, they should be accompanied by the guard. He talked with them for about a half hour, in his low-key, competent manner. I could see Ellen's shoulders relax and her face soften. She said, "I'll probably be stir-crazy in a day, Lenny, but right now your cocoon sounds pretty nice." She turned to Jocelyn. "There's no way I can thank you enough for this, Jocelyn. Putting yourself in jail with me so I can avoid this maniac. It was too much of me to ask, but I'm so thankful you said yes."

Jocelyn gave Ellen a hug and said, "Stick with me, kiddo, I'll take care of you."

I left early the next morning, feeling tired and grainy after a restless night. We had stayed in a big bedroom overlooking the ocean. Ellen remained aloof from me until she fell asleep, then she moved closer, touching me just with her forehead and knees.

I stopped off at the office, filled several manila folders with ad briefs, and picked up my laptop computer. Geena, our traffic and office manager, was having her morning coffee when I stepped into her office and explained that I would be working off the boat for a few days. I'm the boss, but I could see her eyes narrow as she brushed the crumbs from her muffin into a napkin and tried politely to suggest this wasn't the best time for me to be out.

I held up my hand. "It gets worse." I explained that Rachel would be staying at home with a plainclothes guard.

"What?"

I grew warm as I explained what was going on. It was worse than telling the police, telling someone who worked for me. But she had to know what was going on, because it was going to disrupt the office in a big way. "Well, what can I say," Geena said. "Except you're going to owe me after this."

"You'll have to stand in line."

A few minutes later, I left for Newport.

10

Along the way, I stopped at a phone booth and called Borenson. We agreed on the next few steps, and I continued on.

In Newport, I carried a light gym bag into the Treadway Inn and had a cup of coffee in the restaurant. At exactly eleven o'clock I went into the men's room. One of the detectives who had helped recover Cory's body was there. He was tall, sandy-haired, about thirty. He wore shorts, boat shoes, and an Adidas T-shirt. We shook hands.

"Jeff Blair," he said. "You brought the bag—good. Step into my office." We went into a large stall marked with a wheelchair symbol. After taping a wire onto me, he showed me how to turn the transmitter on and off and had me speak a few words. Next, a bulletproof vest. "This Kevlar is going to be as hot as a bastard, and you're going to have to keep your shirt on, but it beats letting a bullet tumble around inside your rib cage. That'll do while you pick up groceries and get ready for a long stay on your mooring." He eyed the way my shirt covered the vest critically and said, "Okay. You can take the wire off when you get onto the boat, but keep the vest on, even though I doubt we're dealing with a sniper here. Use this walkie-talkie for communication while you're on the boat. The frequency is supposedly private, but the idea is to keep conversation to a minimum." He put that and a roll of adhesive tape into my bag.

We stepped out of the stall, and he told me to talk about my sailboat if anyone walked in during our conversation. "We're all of three moorings away in a thirty-two-foot sportfisherman, the *Audacious*," he said. "Good name for it. We confiscated it earlier this year—the guy running it had filled every available inch below with bales of grass. This is nice duty for me and Neal, but we'll keep a close eye on you. Don't worry when you see us slugging down lots of beer—it's just ginger ale."

"What are you expecting to happen?"

"Hard to say. Chances don't seem really great that he'd approach you on the water. Even if that was him in the quahog boat. But we've got to be ready for it. What you need to do quickly is provide a plausible explanation for why you're down here away from your wife. You probably won't have an opportunity to do that until tonight. Meantime, if someone is watching your boat, we want you to be visible. Do you know anything about engines?"

"Sure."

"Good. If you've got work you need to do already, that's great. Otherwise, let's say the water pump goes. The engine hatch on your boat opens up right in the cockpit, right?"

"Right."

"Good. That'll keep you in sight. Take your time. Then maybe around four, you go in to pick up some parts. Say you'll need the impeller in the water pump—that's a cheap little part that goes frequently enough. That'll get you back on shore pretty early, and if he's looking for you, and he follows you when you go to get parts, that's going to be believable to him. You should come in on this side of the harbor, into town. We'll have people waiting to follow you. You don't need to know who, but they'll be there. And if you speak, they'll hear you. If our buddy doesn't show, then go back to the boat, kill a few hours. Appear to fix the water pump now that you've got the part. Then at eight o'clock go out to dinner. Use the Fort Adams launch, take your car into town, then walk around. Hit a bunch of places, have a few drinks, but don't get drunk on us. Say you hit the Ark, then One Pelham East, then Banisters Wharf. Maybe the Charthouse. You know, guy alone without his wife."

I looked for a smirk, but his expression was guileless. I said, "Yes, I know."

"You scared?"

I shrugged. "A bit."

"You should be. This guy doesn't sound like a cupcake. But you'll be watched the whole time. In any case, after tonight, the lieutenant says you have work to do on the boat, for your business, right? So then a couple of times a day, you can go to shore to use the phone, or fax the stuff in, maybe take a drink or two on the way back, come back later for dinner. You know how to act drunk? Talk very slowly, carefully. Focus your eyes on the lips of the person you're talking to. Walk slowly, and very straight. Don't weave around and slur your words. That looks fake.

"Now, I don't know you, but my impression is you're not a big talker. You're going to have to change that. Come across as a guy who's spilling his guts. Word gets back to this guy that you're hitting the bars, whining about your wife, he'll maybe figure you're no risk, and maybe that you're one of Dearborn's customers who just got greedy. What we figure, if this guy is connected, pretty soon somebody is going to want to talk with you, maybe somebody at a bar, maybe somebody tries to hustle you into a car, maybe our man shows himself. We'll be ready."

"What's to keep them from just opening up with a gun, or sticking a knife in my ribs?"

He shrugged. "Shit, they might. That's why the vest. But from the way he came after your wife, that's a risk you're under already, so you might as well be surrounded by all of us. And the thing we're all counting on is that if they do think you have his coke, he probably wouldn't try to kill you until he could find out where it was. Like you have it ransomed. Do you, by the way?"

"I don't, by the way," I said dryly.

"Better not." His tone was friendly enough, but his face hardened. "Because if we found out you were jerking us around, you'd find the Georgia boy with the knife wasn't such a bad guy after all."

It was hot working on the boat. The sun beat through a hazy cloud cover, and the harbor was flat calm. My eyes stung with sweat. I pulled out the water pump and left it on the deck. While I was at it, I changed the oil and cleaned off the corrosion forming around the battery terminals. From time to time, I glanced over at the *Audacious*. Jeff was casually polishing the chrome while Neal sat up on the fly bridge and drank beer after beer. I wondered if it truly was ginger ale.

By a little after three, I was ready to go into town. I rinsed off in the head, taped on the wire, and slipped on the vest. By the time I had the whole itchy package covered with a large Hawaiian shirt, the perspiration was rolling down my face again. I turned the transmitter on and said, "Are you with me, gentlemen?" The walkie-talkie crackled an affirmative. I called the launch on my marine radio.

Linda was not on duty, but the driver, a young man with a curly beard, looked at me appraisingly. I mentioned that I was going into town for a part for the water pump, and he simply nodded. When he dropped me off at the dock, I looked for the policemen tailing me, but no one appeared to be paying me any attention. I turned right on Thames Street and walked along with a closed expression on my face. Detective Blair said I should appear preoccupied; it fit the image of a man on the outs with his wife, and would make it easier for Green Shirt to tail me, and in turn be tailed. It wasn't a hard image to project.

The parts store had the impeller, and I chatted with the owner for a few minutes about how to break down the water pump. None of the half-dozen people in the store appeared to be listening. I left, and stopped off at the Ark for a drink. The bar was cool and dark in the late-afternoon heat. There were only a few customers at the bar, a young couple whispering and laughing together, and a construction worker who stared moodily into his draft beer. I took a stool and ordered one for myself.

It was odd, going through these motions. I could not visualize clearly what I would be saying and doing under normal circumstances. Every move I made felt theatrical.

After two beers the bartender picked up my mug and asked if I wanted another. I said, "Better not. I've got to call the wife soon. Things are bad enough as is—I can't sound drunk on the phone."

He shrugged and started to turn away, but I kept talking. I said in a self-pitying tone that I'd screwed up, but that she wasn't understanding a goddamn thing. . . . He listened, like a good bartender, and after a while I left for the boat.

It was harder to spill my marital disaster story than I thought it would be, perhaps because so much of it was true.

"Was there anyone out there last time?" I said into the walkie-talkie around seven-thirty.

Jeff's voice came back. "Two draft beers, right?"

"I'm impressed." Following his earlier instructions, I called for the launch to take me into Fort Adams. My heart sank when I saw Linda was at the wheel. She apparently had a similar reaction, because she dropped off her other passengers and came back for me.

"I wasn't going to pick you up, but I figured you'd try to get me fired if I didn't," she said.

"Think what you want. But I had about as much to do with Cory getting killed as you did."

Her mouth tightened.

"Maybe less." I looked at her indirectly. "Did you give him a place to stay that night?"

"Save it, mister. I already talked to the police." She pushed the throttle down all the way, and the launch sat back on its haunches, the diesel bellowing.

"What's bothering you? Did you care about him that much, or is it more than that? What else do you know?"

"None of your goddamn business. What are you doing here, anyhow? Where's your wife? Which one is she, the blonde or the one with the dark hair?"

My impulse was to tell her to shut up. But that missed the point of my being there. I said, "Ellen has dark hair."

"Where is she? She kicked you out, I bet."

"It's more complex than that."

"Sure it is." She banged against the dock hard, and I stepped off.

"You saw Cory again before he was killed, didn't you?" I put my hand on her arm. "Look, that guy tried to kill my wife later. He found our home."

She snatched her arm away. "Don't touch me."

"I'm serious."

"He attacked your wife?"

"He came after her with a knife. We were just lucky she wasn't killed. If you do know more about this, tell the police if you won't tell me."

She slipped the boat back into gear. "And you left your wife alone?"

"Well, obviously we're not getting on too well. As I said, it's complex."

"Uh-huh. Well, either you're a liar or the biggest bastard to walk the earth. Keep your advice to yourself." She pulled away from the dock.

Maybe both, I thought. Quietly toward the mike, "You should talk with her again, guys." I drove my car to the Charthouse for dinner, mostly because I knew there would be a crowd around the bar, even on a weeknight. I took a deep breath and worked my way into a conversation with Rick and Tina, an insurance adjuster and accountant, respectively. I told my sad story, and they glanced at each other and excused themselves.

I wondered again if the police were anywhere near, until I realized that a quiet man in his late twenties standing near the end of the bar looked familiar. He was clean-shaven, and wore a dark blue cotton shirt. I didn't know why he looked familiar until he looked my way. I thought his eyes flickered a little, but his face showed no other expression. With a slight shock, I realized it was the young construction worker from the Ark. Now he looked like a crew member from a twelve-meter yacht. Two draft beers, I thought. I followed his lead, and let my gaze fall away.

Next, I talked with a sullen young man who sat alone at the bar. He commiserated with me, knocking down draft beer after draft beer, saying, "You got that right, man, you just can't win with women. Either you don't do enough and you're a bastard, or you do too much and they think you're a fucking wimp. There's no winning."

I left him to have dinner, feeling slightly sick to my stomach, because his brand of self-pity was the type of image I was supposed to project. Afterward, I walked across to One Pelham East, and listened to a rock band for about an hour. I danced with two women, and asked a half-dozen more in a blunt, hungry way that assured they would say no. I stopped in at the Ark again and hailed the bartender as if he were a long-lost friend, telling him that I had made the call to my wife already, so I could indulge myself in a few drinks and have fun. He nodded politely. After intruding on conversations from one end of the bar to the other, I decided to go into the Wharf before driving back to Fort Adams.

The bar was crowded, and I couldn't see my construction worker–turned-sailor policeman, and I didn't care. The whole plan seemed foolish. I took the last seat at the bar and ordered a cognac, thinking if I had another few drinks, my escort might feel duty-bound to arrest me for drunk driving. The man beside me got up, and after a few moments, a young woman sat down. I took a better look at her and realized that she was gorgeous. Simply gorgeous. Probably in her early to middle twenties, lightly freckled skin, an imperious nose, high cheekbones. Chestnut hair and green eyes, flecked with gold. She was wearing a green cotton sweater and white pleated pants.

I said hello.

She smiled back politely. I considered calling it a night and not going into my spiel, which I quickly realized was just my pride not wanting me to look like a bitter, weak man in front of this woman. So I asked her if I could buy her a drink. She looked pointedly at my wedding band and said, "Thanks, but you're married."

I swung fully into my role, saying, "Just married. Meaning just *barely*, not just recently. . . ." And so on.

"Excuse me," she said, "but I didn't ask for your life story."

I felt the heat go up to my face.

She put her chin on her hand and gazed at me directly. "Funny, you don't look like a guy who normally sits around feeling sorry for himself. So I'm going to give you some free advice before I go someplace else for a quiet drink. If you don't like your marriage, either fix it or get out of it. Because this line of yours is none too appealing."

Couldn't argue with that.

She had started to slide out of her chair when I said, "Stay. I'll go." I gave the bartender a ten and said, "Please get the lady whatever she likes."

"You don't need to do that," she said.

I smiled. "You shouldn't give away your counseling services, especially when they're so good."

"I *meant* you don't have to go away. You do have to buy me the drink, for listening to all that whining." To the bartender, she said, "Chardonnay, please."

"And for you, sir?"

The woman patted my chair.

I nodded to the bartender and sat down. "Again."

When he walked away, she brushed her hair away from her high forehead, and put out her hand. "Alicia."

"Riley Burke."

"My, you are new again to the bar scene, aren't you? No one gives his full name at first." Though she was smiling, her brow wrinkled faintly. The newspapers had carried my name, so it wouldn't be surprising if she recognized it. She seemed to dismiss the thought, and said, "Are you a boater, Riley?"

I told her about the *Spindrift*, how we had brought it up from the Virgin Islands and restored it. Again, she showed some sign of recognition, but then talked easily about her own little sailboat, a Laser that she sailed frequently in the harbor. A few minutes later into the conversation, when I mentioned I owned an ad agency, her eyes widened. "Wait a minute. I read about you last week, didn't I? That awful thing—"

She drew away.

I was more than a little suspicious, but told myself it could be simply because I was expecting someone to approach me. She handled herself well, and I found her quickly likable. Yet it all seemed too pat. She asked me what had happened.

I told her what Borenson and I had agreed would be the best story—the truth. Or as Borenson had said it, "Keep to the same story you've been giving me." That I had intervened in a fight, and I believed Dearborn's body had been placed under my boat as a warning. I did not mention Green Shirt's attack on Ellen, instead saying only that she had left me.

Alicia took the whole thing in with little gasps of surprise, her attention focused upon me with growing admiration as she asked me to tell more about the fight, and murmured words of sympathy at Ellen's reaction.

With her throaty laugh and quick questions, she seemed genuine, and it would have been very pleasant to believe she was. She gave me the impression I was the most interesting man she had ever met. But I was certain she was pumping me. I figured I would make it easier for her, and swallowed the rest of my cognac and called loudly for another round. I remembered Blair's advice on acting drunk, and talked slowly and with great emphasis about how the essence of a man's character can be found in hand-to-hand combat, the lessons of battle, all of that.

Her eyes began to glaze over.

But she kept her face animated and attentive as I rambled on. After I finished that round, she began to make her move. "But was it worth it?" Her lips curved in a sad, sweet smile. "You get some charge out of it, I know. But you could have been hurt, fighting someone like that. All the things you have to live for. If you lost . . ." She shrugged. "What would you have to show?"

Under her lowered lashes, her eyes were now quite intent. "At least in the movies, someone who takes those kinds of risks, they win treasure, gold or jewels. Something." She laughed, throwing back her hair. "Money, sometimes. Big boxes of money. How about you?"

There, I thought.

But before I could answer, her attention faltered and she looked into the mirror behind the bar. Her lips compressed. I too looked in the mirror, and saw in the reflection a man staring at us from the corner. He was fat, with a couple of days' growth of beard on his heavy jowls. His face was deeply sunburned.

Alicia looked at me carefully, then seemed to make a fast decision. "Well. I have to get going."

I said, in a bewildered voice, "Already?"

She laughed merrily. "Already. We've been talking for over an hour now, and you *are* married. Which is a shame." She leaned over and kissed me quickly on the cheek. "Maybe I'll see you in the harbor sometime. The *Spindrift*, right?"

"That's right."

"Bye." A quick wave, flash of a fetching smile, and she was gone. I looked in the mirror as the door to the deck swung shut. He was gone too. I muttered in the microphone under my shirt, "Alicia. Somebody'd better see where she goes. There was a guy in the back left corner, with a balding head, gray sweatshirt, tough-looking. He scared her off."

11

The police followed Alicia back to her apartment on Old Beach Road, in Newport, but did not approach her. The name on the mailbox was Alicia Nadeau. Unfortunately, they lost the fat man. Detective Blair and I had another quick meeting at the Treadway Inn men's room. "Neal had already started following the girl when he heard your message about the other guy. I told him to stick with her. We had to scramble, get somebody else in place, but it was too late—there was no fat man hanging around the parking lot or deck. He must've taken off."

"Damn."

"Yeah, I know. Tell me what he looks like again."

"Didn't Neal see him?"

"Not really. He vaguely remembers a big guy in the corner, but nothing definite. It happens. But you didn't recognize Neal either, right? Not with those glasses and the longer hair. It's tough to peg everyone in a bar, and Neal had his attention on you and the chick. Anyhow, describe this guy again."

I did.

"That's it? Fat, balding, didn't shave? What else?"

He and I went over it for a few minutes, but I could not come up with much more detail. I had only that glance in the mirror to go by. "All right," he said dubiously. "We'll keep an eye out for anybody who fits this description coming near you. If you see him again, give us the word, and we'll follow him. But frankly, the lieutenant is not too impressed about any of it. The guy was just sitting in the bar. And we listened to the tape of what the girl said, and frankly, she could have just been trying to pick you up."

"I told you there was more to it than that," I said evenly. "She was working me."

Blair put his palms up. "The lieutenant is the boss. We'll do some very quiet investigating, but he doesn't want to bring her in yet. He'd rather see if she makes another appearance on her own." He grinned. "Just keep slinging that shit at the bar and let's see what happens."

I called Ellen the next four evenings. We never talked for more than a few minutes, and only when I was sure of relative privacy on the pay phone near some men's room or cigarette machine. My bar-crawling and role-playing were wearing on my patience, and the first few times I talked with Ellen, I found myself wound even tighter after putting down the phone.

Those times, she sounded bored with her confinement, and asked about the work I had done on the boat, which was kind of a shorthand for us: the *Spindrift* was shared ground, a good topic. I responded cheerfully, feeling more and more like a third-rate actor. On the fourth night, she asked, "When are you coming back?"

"I can't be sure. Although nothing much has happened, and the police aren't going to maintain this forever. Everything okay?" I did not feel comfortable talking about the girl at the bar with her, because after four days, I had begun to consider the idea that maybe she was just trying to pick me up. I was irritated with myself about this low-grade deception, and when Ellen repeated a question, I snapped the truth, on that score anyhow.

"I said, is Rachel down there with you?"

"No."

Her voice lowered. "Do you wish she were?"

"Truthfully, Ellen, sometimes yes."

I heard the sharp intake of her breath.

"Or someone like her. Someone I could feel easy around, like it was with you. It's been so hard to be with you for over a year now, particularly for the past few months."

"And that's my fault?"

"I don't care whose fault it is. But we've formed two armed camps."

"You tuned right out on me," she said. "It's as if I stopped being what you wanted to see. I always felt I fit part of this package of home, hearth—the business, the boats, the whole thing. And I was the pretty wife. You are very goal-oriented. And, I don't know, now that you have everything, you're bored. Bored with me too."

"And I see you feeling the same about me," I snapped. "Worrying about your looks. Poking and prodding everything we do to find the bad spots."

She was silent. I rubbed my forehead and took stock, before saying, "Look, my first reaction was to tell you I didn't miss Rachel, that all I hoped for was for you and me to be together again. You and I have made a science of half making up, of saying the words to avoid a fight, and that's going to finish us. We have to stop posing."

"Maybe that's all we've got. Maybe that's all we ever had."

"No. Not for me. I know without doubt I once loved you. That's why I'm saying what I am now—you're going to hear the truth, and I want the same from you."

"I wish I could see your face when you tell me you love me. I've been so lonely. Riley, I would do anything to have you back in my camp. Be careful."

Around eleven o'clock the next morning, I was down below reading the ad plan for one of our new accounts, a Boston-based retail bank, when I felt a bump against the hull of my boat, and the slight dip of someone climbing aboard. I didn't have the bulletproof vest or the wire on, and the detectives who were on duty now were on a town mooring, almost a quarter mile away. They must have been asleep, not to have warned me. I grabbed the walkie-talkie and said, "Pay attention, guys," and hid it under the cushion before stepping halfway up the cabin ladder. I held the butcher knife I had been keeping on the counter against my leg.

It was the girl, Alicia. The sail of her little Laser sailboat hung slack in the faint air. She said, "I figured I knew you well enough to stop by for a cold soda on a sweltering, dead-air day like today. I hope it wasn't too rude of me."

I slipped the knife into the cabinet and said, "Not at all."

She was wearing white shorts, boat shoes, and a Kelly-green cotton shirt. Her sunglasses hung from a loop against her fine breasts, even though the sunlight was painfully bright. The better for me to see her eyes, I thought. She shaded them now, and said, "And you struck me as a man who wanted to talk."

"I had a bit too much to drink that night. But I enjoyed our conversation." I gestured for her to have a seat in the cockpit and then reached down into the icebox for a soda. Her legs were just a few feet away as I dug through the ice, her calves well defined.

"You've been through a rough time," she said sympathetically. "I'm sure you can handle it—God, that fight you told me about sounded awful. And it must've been tough finding that boy's body, then telling your wife, and going to the police."

Poor baby, I thought sarcastically, the image of my mother talking about her johns arising unbidden. "Prop them up as men, then let them be babies," she would say, lying on the couch with a wet towel draped over her forehead. "That's what I do for a living, honey." She would laugh. "Think of your mom as a shrink—that make you feel any better?"

As I handed Alicia the soda, I wondered if she was a pro. She was not hard the way my mother had been, but certainly she was after something beyond my good looks. The question was whether she worked for Green Shirt or was coming in from some other angle. "What do you do for a living, Alicia?"

She wrinkled her nose prettily. "I'm between jobs right now."

"And when you have a job?"

She shrugged. "I've done some consulting."

"Consulting about what?"

"This and that. Boring stuff. Maybe we should go for a sail. The wind just picked up."

I looked up at the burgee, and indeed it was snapping. "Maybe."

"Mind if I use your head?"

I gestured for her to go below. As she went down into the cabin, I saw her look around carefully. When she saw me watching, she said, "Let's leave my boat on the mooring."

I got onto her sailboat, unstepped the mast, and handed myself along the *Spindrift* to tie the bow line to the mooring line. As I swung myself back aboard holding on to the stays, I was able to see her in the main cabin through one of the Plexiglas hatches. She was back in the main cabin, rummaging through the side compartments, my suitcase, and two of the bunks. I tensed. If she looked much further, she would find the walkie-talkie and other police gear. I walked quickly back over the cabin roof, and when I stepped back into the cockpit and looked forward, she was coming out of the head, as if she had been there all along. She had pulled her long hair over her shoulder so it covered her left breast.

"Come on down," she said playfully. "Take most of your clothes off, and let's act like we're sailing in the Caribbean."

Perhaps she was looking for a listening device, I thought. Or maybe coke, or perhaps she was simply looking to snatch whatever she could find. Either way, I saw no choice but to follow along with her. Narragansett Bay was crowded with enough boats for the police in the sportfisherman to follow at a discreet distance. Their boat could do over thirty knots, so there was no way the *Spindrift* would outdistance her. I wondered if Alicia was setting me up to get shot, or if perhaps Green Shirt was waiting with a fast boat out in the bay to pick me up. My butcher knife was not the weapon of choice if he brought a gun.

No matter what, the only thing to do was to move forward.

She watched as I took my shirt off, then went up above. If she was worried about it, she now knew I was not wearing a wire. A few minutes later, we cast off. As I put the boat in gear, I felt a strong sense of *déjà vu*, my body half expecting to feel the jar of Cory's body under my hull.

After taking off the sail cover, she said, "Where do you keep your winch handles?" I pointed to the small locker near the galley, and she took out two handles, dropped one into the plastic sleeve in the cockpit, then took the other to the bank of winches I had mounted on the cabin roof. As we motored past the red nun at the tip of Fort Adams, she glanced back at me. I turned the *Spindrift* into the wind and tailed the halyard as she cranked up the main. We fell off the wind toward the bridge, and she pulled out the jenny. She trimmed it nicely, keeping a critical eye on the sail and the wind indicator. The *Spindrift* bounded along under a close reach, hitting just under seven knots.

"Perfect," she said. She stood just behind me, holding on to the backstay, and if there was a false note in her voice, I couldn't hear it. We went along that way for about a half hour, sailing under the expanse of the Newport Bridge, deeper into the bay. She chatted along pleasantly, and no motive other than her appearing to enjoy my company seemed apparent. She did not suggest a direction for us to head, and the police maintained ample distance.

"Your boat's quick," Alicia said, taking off her sunglasses, her green eyes alive, excited. She put her hand on the back of my neck, a gesture so simple, yet evocative, that I was angered by my own response.

I said, "Particularly now that we cleaned Cory off the rudder."

Her head jerked slightly, as if I had slapped her. She began to slip her glasses back over her eyes, and I grasped her hand and pulled them away. "Who are you?"

"What? Why—"

"You knew Cory, didn't you?"

"Who?"

"Bullshit. Who sent you? Was it him, the guy with the knife? Kinky black hair, drug smuggler—he sent you, didn't he?"

"What are you talking about?"

"Cory's chest was blown open with a shotgun."

I knew I was hurting her wrist, but I had grown too impatient with her game. I pulled her down beside me and leaned close. "Look, your story, your flirting, it's a crock, we both know it. My wife's life is on the line, so you'd better tell me what your game is. I'm fresh out of patience."

"Let go of me," she said, shoving her forearm against me. She wrenched her arm back abruptly. I held on until she stopped struggling, then I let go.

"All right, so talk."

"Tough guy," she spat.

"Who sent you?"

"Nobody." She rubbed her arm. "Turn the boat around."

"Were you following me in the bar?"

"*You* talked to *me* first. Remember?"

"You knew Cory, didn't you?"

"Who?"

"Now tell me what you want."

"I *wanted* to help you."

"How?"

"By listening. Just being there. You were so depressed at the bar, and I thought, here's a guy—"

I said quietly, "Alicia."

She stopped.

"Tell me what you want. Who knows? Maybe I have it."

Recognition there. Her chin came up. Her eyes met mine with cool calculation. "You might have what?"

I said, "First off, tell me your full name, and how you knew Cory."

She shrugged. "My name's Alicia Nadeau, and okay, I knew Cory."

I had a hard time believing she was in mourning. I said, "Were you lovers?"

"*What* do you have?"

"First things first."

Big sigh. "We lived together for a while. Until about a year ago."

"And why have you been trying to get to know me?"

"Why do you think?"

"You invited yourself onto my boat. You tell me what your interest is."

She made a face. "I think this is a mistake. You're a lot different than you came across in the bar, you know that? Let's go back."

"Tell me what you expected."

"Not until you tack around."

I put the boat over, and we headed toward port. She shrugged. "Forget the whole thing, anyhow."

"Let's not." I repeated, "What were you expecting?"

"Oh, somebody less defensive," she said. "Somebody looking for some fun, I guess. Maybe you were drunk."

"Maybe. But what were you looking for?"

She looked to the sky and rolled her eyes. "Oh, I'm sick of dancing around this. I was trying to get to know you because I thought we might be friends. And if we became *good* friends, maybe those consulting services I mentioned might be useful for you."

"Which are?"

"No. Good friends only."

"What makes you think I have anything that I need consulting about?"

She stroked my jawline mockingly before I pushed her hand away. "I might be wrong. But getting to know you really wouldn't be so bad anyhow. So I don't have much to lose."

"Cory lost, in a big way. Can I assume he was a coke dealer? Is that accurate?"

She hesitated, apparently trying to decide if she was implicating herself. Then she said, "Yes. That's accurate. After I moved out, he started. But I had nothing to do with it."

"So if you're just looking for money, Cory must've been rich. Didn't he leave you anything in his will?"

"He was not rich, and he didn't have a will as far as I know. He should have been stinking rich, but lately he was doing the worst thing you can do in his business—putting the product up his own nose. Making bad decisions. Around here, he kept a low enough profile—a nice apartment and car, but nothing fancy. But he actually owns one of those high-speed racing boats down in Florida. And a ski house in Aspen. Add to that gambling—bets on jai alai, football, basketball, horses, dogs, you name it, he would bet on it. He pumped cash out like through a firehose." Her bitterness was unmistakable. "He was generous enough with presents, but no real money came my way. He should have had enough set aside to cover a loss."

She was quiet for a few minutes.

"What do you know about the man who attacked me on the dock?" I said.

"Nothing," she said emphatically.

"How about the fat man in the bar? You got scared when you saw him."

She shrugged. "He looked familiar, and he was looking right at me. I thought for a minute I had seen him talking to Cory once, but it was from a long ways away then and maybe it wasn't the same guy."

"Where?"

She shrugged. "Just a guy in one of those quahog boats, tied up to the dock. Talking to Cory last summer. Cory was scared when he walked away, his face was all white." She looked tired all of a sudden. "Cory could be a real prick, but he didn't deserve what happened to him. He was usually careful with the way he made the money, if not the way he spent it. He focused on upscale customers, businessmen, lawyers, engineers, restaurant owners, people who have cash. No one too dangerous. And he said more than once that his suppliers asked no questions about who he sold to as long as he delivered his cash on time. That's a very important 'as long,' understand. Cory was very scared of these people. But he figured there's a lot of dope coming into this town, and he might as well be the one to make the money."

"His customers were around here?"

She shook her head. "Most were up in Boston. He could've sold it here just as easily, but he figured it would be safer to sell it away from his home port."

"And is that where your consulting services come in? Helping me reach those people?"

She raised her eyebrows, but said nothing.

"There's one big problem, Alicia. I don't have any coke. I never did."

"Somebody sure thinks you do," she said, looking me right in the eye. "Why else leave Cory under your boat with a Baggie of it stuffed down his throat?"

I had her take the wheel as I furled the sails. She smiled up at me as the wind whipped her hair. My mouth tasted dry; she might have given me a solid link to Green Shirt. She had said the man in the bar was a quahogger and that Cory was afraid of him. A quahogging skiff had been seen beside the *Spindrift* the night Cory's body was planted. At the very least, the police needed to pull that man in for questioning. What I couldn't be sure of was how much further Alicia was involved. I thought it likely she was lying about not being involved in the coke trafficking; she seemed to know a fair amount. Whether she knew Green Shirt or was in fact working directly for him was still an open question. I figured it would be best to remain on good terms with her, and tell the police I would try to get her to be more forthcoming while I was wearing the wire.

There was still something I found likable about her, too, as much as I mistrusted her. On one level, I wanted to shake her and tell her what a fool she was to play in Green Shirt's territory, to tell her about the attack on Ellen.

But again, she might already know all about that. So when we reached my mooring, I simply offered to tow her sailboat from the mooring to the dock rather than have her restep the mast.

"I thought we were going to stay on the mooring together." She looked hurt. "Riley, I've been straight with you ... *pretty* straight, anyhow. It's just that we don't know each other that well yet—but there's a nice way to do that."

"Thanks, but I'm married."

She looked at me as if I had said something rather cute.

As I spun the boat upwind to land the *Spindrift*, the breeze brought Alicia's faint scent of clean hair and perfume. She stepped beside the binnacle, casually offering her body. "You sure you want to drop me off? I might see you again, I might not. This could be our only chance."

I threw the *Spindrift* into reverse as we approached the dock. "Let's meet for dinner later, discuss your consulting services."

She stepped in front of me and said softly, "First things first. I want to get to know you better." She leaned in to kiss me. In the millisecond before our lips touched, I saw her eyes flicker open, and I had the sense that she was looking over my left shoulder. I jerked my head around immediately, expecting to find Green Shirt standing above us at the railing.

But it was Ellen, her face stark white. "Oh, Riley," she said. Tears glistened on her cheeks.

"Oh boy," I heard Alicia say.

"You bastard." Ellen turned and ran.

I jumped onto the dock and took a few seconds to get the boat tied down to the pilings, cursing the lack of cleats on the short-term dock. By the time I ran up the ramp into the parking lot, she was in a car I didn't recognize, a blue Ford. She pulled out, tires smoking. "Liar!" she screamed, alone in the car. I touched glass and then she was past me and gone.

12

I squelched my first reaction to run back to the boat, grab my car keys, and chase after her through Newport. If I was to work my way back to Green Shirt, my first priority had to be maintaining a link with Alicia. Better the police follow Ellen, I reasoned. Borenson could have her pulled over with a phony speeding-ticket routine in case anyone was following her.

The tide was low enough that if Alicia remained on the boat, she wouldn't be able to see me over the top of the ramp using the phone. I called the station and asked for Borenson. I waited on hold for a full minute before a harried-sounding detective named Rengles told me Borenson was out. DePetrie was out too.

When I started to explain to Rengles that I was part of the stake-out in Newport Harbor, he said, "Just a minute," and put me back on hold. He came back on a moment later and said, "Now who did you say you were?"

"Damn it!" I slammed down the phone. I couldn't exactly use the walkie-talkie in front of Alicia to call the two on the sport-fishing boat. There was no choice but to try to get rid of her quickly and catch up to Ellen.

I jabbed in the number for Manchester. Lenny answered.

"What happened?" I said, and told him how she had just taken off before I had a chance to explain.

"You tell me. She wanted me to drive her down to see you yesterday, and I said no chance, we might blow the whole operation. I guess she decided to do it on her own." He quickly sketched out how she had gone to the market with one of the guards, Castiano, and had apparently slipped out the side door. Castiano assumed she had been abducted. He notified the local cops and called Lenny, and they spent an hour searching for her, circulating copies of Green Shirt's Identikit drawing. But the police found she had rented a car from a local gas station, and that she was clearly alone. "We looked like assholes," Lenny said. "I've got to tell you, Riley, this isn't what we were hired for, not to look after someone who's going to make the job harder. That's bullshit."

"Look, I've got to catch up to her. You keep trying to get through to Borenson or somebody on the Newport police who will pay attention, and give them the plate number for her car. If they don't get moving on it in the next few minutes, she'll be out of their jurisdiction, and I don't think we'll have any luck per-suading the state cops to stop her. Also, call Nick at the agency, tell him what happened, and ask him to go to my house in case she heads there first. If she doesn't, he should meet us in Man-chester, because this changes everything. We'll have to figure where else she can stay."

"You've got that right," Lenny said. "Unless she's awfully damn careful about not being followed back, we can't count on this place being safe anymore."

. . .

Alicia looked contrite when I got back to the boat. "That was your wife?"

"I've got to go," I said, stepping on board and grabbing my keys.

"I'm sorry I put you in a bad spot." As I stepped back on the dock she said, "You're leaving your boat here?"

"I'll call the harbormaster," I said over my shoulder as I started up the ramp.

She reached out for my arm and said, "I can see why I was having such a hard time turning your head. She's beautiful."

It was all I could do to control the trembling in my arms. I wondered if she could feel it. I was certain she knew more, but I didn't have the time or patience to work it out of her, short of holding her underwater until she confessed. And I didn't have the stomach for that. "So are you." I ran my fingers through Alicia's hair, and she smiled, a bit nervously.

I clenched my fingers and she winced. "Easy, that hurts."

"I don't want my wife to get hurt," I said. "You explain that to him."

"I don't—"

"Explain that. Make it clear. I'll do whatever I can to accommodate him." I recognized in the half second how I was slipping into the agency jargon. "What he wants is what he gets. But if he touches Ellen again . . ." I tightened my grip.

"Hey!"

"If he touches her, he will simply not believe what happens to him next."

"Why tell me? I—"

"Be quiet."

"Christ, Riley, I don't have any connection with that guy, honest. I just wanted to sell the coke. Make a one-time connection, and then take off someplace they'll never find me. Look, you can come with me, it'll be good between us."

I shook my head. "I've got to get him off my back. You find a way to help me get the stuff back to him, so I can end this. I'll make it worth your while. I've got the money to do that."

"So you do have the coke?"

"Sure," I said. "You never doubted it, did you?"

I let her go.

I kept the car at a steady eighty-five, slowing only when the radar detector beeped. I didn't have time to waste on explanations to a traffic cop, particularly the way I was already seething about police communications.

There were several blue Fords that I passed along the way, none with Ellen at the wheel. There was no way to be certain she was heading back to Manchester, or even Massachusetts. For that matter, she might have called Jocelyn by now, but I didn't want to take the time to find a phone. I cursed myself for having pulled the car phone out a few months ago—why had I rated my privacy so highly all of a sudden, damn it?

Going to Manchester seemed to be my only option, since I figured that would be Ellen's as well. I didn't bother with the creative routes Nick had been reportedly taking each night to the house, I just went straight there. She was typically a fast driver, I told myself, and in all likelihood she would arrive just before I would. We would definitely need a new hideout.

It took me two and a half hours to get there. About a quarter mile from the driveway, I noticed a red Corvette headed my way. I saw it jerk slightly, apparently rocking with full power shifts, then it roared past. I looked over as the driver's mirrored sunglasses turned my way.

I floored the Acura.

The driver was the fat man from the bar. And even in the time it took the Corvette to flash by, I could recognize the passenger by his sunburned skin and kinky black hair.

I flew down the driveway and skidded to a stop in front of Lenny Datano's car. He was slumped outside the open door, his face covered with bright blood. I tripped climbing out of the car and scrambled over on my hands and knees. There was a red hole in the center of his forehead, ringed with white. His eyes were wide open, bulging.

Nick's car was in the driveway.

So was a blue Ford that looked like Ellen's rental car.

"Oh God, no," I heard myself say. Even though I had seen the two leaving, I took the gun from Lenny's hand and ran to the house, automatically keeping my head down until I was directly underneath the windows. I cocked the revolver, hesitated beside the open doorway, and listened.

Nothing. Not a sound.

In my heart, I expected the worst.

I swung into the room with the gun clasped between two hands and found Jocelyn's body. She was sitting in the right corner of the foyer, her eyes open, surprised. Her legs were splayed wide. Behind her, the wall was streaked red.

"Ellen! It's Riley! Where are you?"

She wasn't in the living room. Or the kitchen. I ran up the stairs, bargaining, *she's gone for a walk, she's gone for a walk, and I'll go outside and explain what's happened.* . . .

The door to our bedroom was ajar, the wood around the lock splintered.

"Ellen!" I called.

Silence.

The room was empty. I wrenched open the closet. Nothing. "Ellen!"

A patch of red outside caught my eye. Something on the flag-stones. The balcony door was open, and a cool ocean breeze blew in, barely cooling the sudden tears which cut into my cheeks like acid. The patch of red was my wife's blouse, the one she had been wearing in Newport hours before, the one she was wearing now. It was just hours ago that her heart had been broken by what she saw, and Christ, I was only minutes away from reaching her in time, minutes away from having another chance for us to make it work.

But from the angle of her head, the way her body was twisted on the flagstones beneath the balcony, I knew that chance was gone forever. My wife was dead.

13

I found myself beside her a moment later. No pulse in her neck, her wrist. No heartbeat, not the faintest touch of breath against my palm when I cupped her cheek. No bullet wounds, either.

He must have thrown her from the balcony.

Death had left her shocked, her eyes open, lips pulled back from her teeth. A numbing sense of distance began to slip over me. *This isn't Ellen, this isn't my wife,* I thought. *This is a broken doll.* I hugged her.

The ghastly way her head rolled, loose on her shoulders, broke my self-deluding reverie. As in the cliché, her life swept before me: the photos I had seen of her as a child, a little girl on a tricycle; the love her parents lavished upon their pretty daughter; our brief courtship; the day we moved into our old Victorian and she flung all the windows open and cheerfully started to work. And then the bitterness of the past few years, our boredom and unwillingness to pull together.

It was all over. No more chances to make it right.

I had been harsh with her the last time we spoke. I'd told her I loved her, yes, but I'd been harsh too. She must have had a second or two of consciousness before dying to wonder why things had turned out the way they had. Did she wonder why I wasn't there? Did she think I just didn't care? Her body's warmth was slipping away. I said into her hair for the last time, "I'm so sorry, babe."

The heavy black nightstick Lenny had given Nick was beside her. Had she attacked her killer with it? I thought, and then remembered Nick's car was in the driveway. I called his name.

No answer.

There was a scuff mark on one of the flagstones going in the direction of the stone wall which ran along the edge of the cliff. Brushing the salt from my eyes, I followed the marks in the grass up to the wall and looked down.

Nick.

The waves lifted his body like a piece of driftwood and slammed him against the rocks. I called out for him, but there was no answer. His body was left high on a barnacle-crusted boulder.

Sickened, I almost turned away and missed it.

As he slid down the rock, he cried out, and tried to hold on. The razor-sharp barnacles must have cut through his unconsciousness.

"Nick!" I yelled.

He looked up, just as the water closed over his head.

I kicked off my shoes and stood on the stone wall. Below, the sea just beyond the rocks turned from deep blue to green as the water receded before the next wave. As the swell lifted, then surged back against the shore, I jumped.

I leaped out as far as I could, and clasped my arms about my head as I crashed through the surface. The bottom came up hard, and then the waves tumbled me over immediately. I caught sight of Nick clinging to the side of the huge seaweed-covered rock, and then the next swell lifted me and flung me beside him. I cried out as the barnacles tore at my hands and knees.

Nick said, "Can't get up." He tried to pull himself up, and then slid back.

"Stop it." I grabbed him by the collar and shoved both of us away as the wave receded. We went back with the swell, and I yelled into his ear to swim along to the right.

We made only a few strokes along the shore for every time we were pushed back into the rocks. But it was enough. I was able to keep Nick conscious enough so that when we hit the rocks, he too would put his feet first, and not waste his energy trying to climb out until we reached the spot I had noticed from above, where the water rushed into a narrow cut that provided solid footholds. Even then, Nick barely made it out. There was a bad gash along the back of his head, from which blood streamed, only to be repeatedly swept clean by the seawater. He was groggy, but he worked himself up the rock face until we were free of the crashing waves.

Blood immediately covered the right side of his head. He vomited. I held his shoulders until he was finished, and rolled him onto his side for a closer look.

The cut ran from behind his right ear along his temple. The top of his ear was gone, and the blood ran freely down his neck. His face was squeezed tight in pain. "They're all dead, aren't they?" he said.

"Yes."

He opened his eyes. "Ellen too?"

I nodded.

"Oh, God. Oh, God." He started to sit up, but I pushed him back down. "I'm sorry, Riley. I'm so sorry. I fucked up. I really fucked up. He was just so . . . fast, methodical, he just walked in shooting. . . . Lenny had locked my gun away, I didn't have anything but that goddamn nightstick. . . ."

I looked up the cliff. It would be a relatively easy climb, but there was no way he was going to make it in his condition. "Look,

I saw them pulling out. I've got to call the cops and get an ambulance for you."

"You saw them?"

"A couple of streets away. Red Corvette."

"Was it the guy on the dock? Can you identify him?"

"He was in the passenger seat."

"I only saw one. He was wearing a ski mask."

I started up. "I'll get that ambulance."

He closed his eyes, but said vehemently, "Fuck that. Call the police. They'll be able to pick these guys up. You might not get another chance."

Sure I will, I thought, climbing up to where my wife's body lay. Sure I will.

More police, more forensics, more talk. I called Detective Swampscott at the Belmont station initially, figuring he could break through the clutter more quickly with the Manchester police, perhaps get the state police involved in the search for the Corvette. As I expected, it was found on a side street in Manchester within the hour, wiped clean of prints. It was listed as a stolen car from Newport. The plate had been switched with that of a Ford Escort. Much later that day, the night manager of a convenience store called in to say he had awoken to find his Buick LeSabre had disappeared from the driveway.

People talked at me, expressed concern. Angry members of Datano Security Service, including a white-faced Castiano, offered advice to the police. In general, they were ignored. Borenson and Swampscott drove up to meet with the local police, headed by Captain Ross. They talked among themselves of jurisdiction, and the other agencies they needed to involve. They asked their questions, their professional mixture of sympathy and suspicion a language in which I had become fluent. At the hospital, they grilled Nick as much as the doctors would let them: You say the shooter was wearing a ski mask—describe it. What else was he wearing? Do you know what kind of gun it was? Describe it. Did you see anyone else? Did he say anything? Did you notice his shoes? Where were you? Describe the sequence of events. Did the assailant demand any cocaine? Did he give any reason for the killing?

I listened to all of this with an apparent lack of emotion that worried the police. I heard them whisper around me about shock, and they brought a doctor by who offered me a sedative and recommended counseling. They asked me if I wanted a priest or minister. I politely said no, and asked them to stop talking while I was listening to Nick. He talked slowly, his face almost as pale as the white bandages around his head. Though he answered their questions, he looked at me the entire time, telling me what had happened.

"It started about ten minutes after I got there. I talked with Lenny outside for a minute—he said that Ellen had just arrived. I told him I wanted my gun, and he gave me the same stupid argument. So I hurried inside, and Jocelyn told me that Ellen was upset, and she didn't know why."

Nick went upstairs and knocked on Ellen's door. It was locked, and she called out that she didn't want to talk. He insisted, but she refused. It sounded like she was crying. He left, went downstairs to the room that he used as a bedroom to change clothes.

That's when he heard a popping noise outside. "All the time I've spent on the range, I still didn't recognize it. I don't know if it was the distance or because I was inside the house or what. I guess I never really believed it would come to this."

Jocelyn apparently opened the front door. Nick heard her scream and the noise again, much louder, and he recognized it as a gunshot. He grabbed the nightstick and ran out into the foyer, and saw her bloodstained body. "I knew she was dead. I looked up the stairway. A man was pushing the bedroom doors open. He had a big revolver, a .38, I think. It was cocked." The man was wearing a ski mask, gloves, and a long-sleeved plaid shirt, and carried a green backpack.

The man came to the locked guest bedroom door, Ellen's. He stepped back, Nick figured to kick it open. "I lost it then," Nick said. "I could hear her scrambling inside—even from downstairs

I could hear her trying to get out. I ran up the stairs. I couldn't just stand there."

"Against the gun?" Captain Ross said. His tone was faintly skeptical.

Nick's eyes left mine. "I didn't think it through, all right? And I wasn't a hero. When he turned around and put that gun on me, I hugged the stairs. He missed. It went over my head. He pulled off another one, and it splintered the banister."

Ross wanted more details on those shots. When he was finished answering the captain's questions, Nick continued. "I fell back down the stairs, and he kicked in the bedroom door. She must've been out on the balcony, because I heard her struggling, fighting him, and I started up the stairs again, and then she screamed."

Nick paused here, and everyone waited silently until he could continue.

Seconds later, the killer stepped out of the bedroom and went after Nick. It took a few minutes for Nick to outline to Ross's satisfaction his path through the house. The killer fired another shot as Nick ran through the back door. "I was frantic. I figured my only chance was to jump off the cliff and take my chances. But I saw Ellen."

"Yes?" Ross said.

To me, Nick said, "I loved her too, you know. Different from you, of course, but I loved her."

"I know you did, Nick." My voice sounded rusty.

"I froze. I saw her there, this woman who's been my friend for how many years? I just got enraged. . . . He came out the door, and I turned and threw the stick, and I still can't believe I didn't get him. You know when you do something physical, and you _know_ it's going to connect? It was like that. Maybe it wouldn't kill him, but that stick was heavy, and it was flipping end over end, and it was going to punch him right in the chest. But he was so goddamn fast, he just twisted and it slid past his shoulder and hit the doorjamb. I stood there gaping. He stepped forward, the gun out as if he was going to place it against my forehead. I could see his mouth moving, through the slit in the mask, and I thought he was going to say something, and I couldn't understand it, and even then I got a whiff of his breath and realized it was chewing gum, the guy was chewing gum while blowing us away. I snapped out of it just in time to run. I don't know if he was playing with me or what. He was close enough to have shot me there."

"He was low on bullets, what he was," Swampscott said. "That's five so far. The gum fits with the description Mrs. Burke gave us after the previous attack. Juicy Fruit?"

Nick frowned. "I guess. Anyhow, that bit about him being low on bullets makes sense. He was running along beside me, and just behind, you know, and I kept anticipating that the bullet was going to hit between my shoulder blades, then I made it to the wall. Then he touched my head, and I must've twisted my head just right when he pulled the trigger so that I only have this bad graze. It was like my head was on fire. That's what I thought as I jumped—I actually had time to think on the way down that it was good I was going to be landing in water, since my head was on fire. That's all I remember. When I came to, I was getting scraped against those rocks, and Riley was there."

Ross gave a summary that night. We were sitting in his office, along with Swampscott and Borenson, and an officer from the Drug Enforcement Agency. Borenson and Ross were not working well together, I noticed. Throughout the day, I had watched them go about their jobs, making small jokes when they thought I wasn't listening, working hard, yes, but working at jobs nonetheless. "We could trace most of what your partner had to say through footprints through the grass, and one real clean print of a work boot on a piece of paper that the shooter apparently stepped on chasing him through the house. Your partner's gun was in the trunk of Datano's car as described. It hasn't been fired recently."

"Big surprise."

He shrugged. "Got to check. Anyhow, there are skid marks adjacent to Datano's car that match the Corvette's tires. We figure they blew straight in and shot Datano. Which of the two was the shooter we don't know. It looks like one stayed in the car, while the other went through the house."

Borenson said impatiently, "Tell me, did the girl, this Nadeau woman, did she say she knew Dearborn?"

"No," I lied. "It didn't come up."

Borenson looked a bit perplexed, but Ross interrupted before he could question me further. "Excuse me, Lieutenant. This happened in my bailiwick, I'll ask the questions. Now Mr. Burke, I got hold of the owners of the house, the Hodges, in Paris. They're coming right back. They had no idea their house was being used this way."

"It was inconsiderate of us," I said.

They all looked at me oddly.

Ross looked uncomfortable. "That's not exactly what I meant."

"Help me with something," the DEA officer said. He was a small man with a trim sandy mustache and wire-rimmed glasses. His name was Wameling. "I've talked to the other officers here, but satisfy me you are not connected with the drug trafficking."

I shook my head. "No. Satisfy yourself. I've said all the words I can say, done what you experts have recommended. My wife is dead."

"We want the guy who did it too," Borenson said. "You know we do."

I stood up.

"You're still the key here," he continued. "So just have a seat and let's go over it again. If your wife did what she agreed—"

"Lieutenant," Swampscott said warningly.

Borenson raised his hands. "Okay, Burke. I know you're upset."

"Yes, Captain, I am upset. But I've still got nothing more to say."

"Sit down," Ross said.

"Not unless I'm under arrest. Am I?"

"No."

"When can I have her body? I have to bury her."

"Sit down."

"Her body, Captain."

"We have to do an autopsy in a homicide."

"I know that. I've been listening the past week. How long?"

He shrugged. "Three days."

"Fine. I'll talk with you then." I turned for the door.

"You're letting him walk?" Borenson said to Ross.

"Just what the fuck do you suggest?" Ross answered.

"Where are you going?" Borenson asked me.

"To my house."

"I don't like this, gentlemen," Wameling said.

Swampscott stood up and put on his coat. "Hold up. I'll follow you down. Look, let us set up something for you, some other place to stay tonight. We can't guarantee he won't show up for you there. You don't want to be alone if he does."

I could read genuine sympathy in Swampscott's expression, but that was a meaningless emotion for me just then. I said, "You're wrong there, Detective."

14

Swampscott followed me to Wellesley to Ellen's parents' house, and waited out front. Their car was in the driveway and lights were on upstairs. They had been on the West Coast for the past two weeks, and had probably been home for only a few hours. Ellen had told me she had said nothing to them about the events in Newport. And the police had assured me no names had been released to the media regarding the killings in Manchester, "pending notification of next of kin." They had already talked with Datano's family, and were trying to get in touch with Jocelyn's.

Geoff and Sylvia met me at the door. Geoff's eyes narrowed sharply once I stepped into the light of their foyer. "What's wrong?"

"Where's Ellen?" Sylvia asked.

"Geoff, Sylvia, I've got some terrible news." I told them Ellen was dead. I told them the whole thing, leaving nothing out. Sylvia sat down heavily, stunned. Geoff attempted to remain calm, and I sensed he was not letting himself believe what I was saying. He asked questions without waiting for answers. What was she doing in Manchester? What did they want? Why didn't you give them whatever they wanted, for God's sake? Where were you? "Ellen didn't use drugs," he said. "I'm certain of it."

Sylvia said, "We were supposed to have lunch the week before last, and I canceled." She burst into tears. "Why are you telling us this?"

"Ellen said nothing about this craziness down in Newport," Geoff said angrily. "Nothing! She would've called us—we're her parents!"

"I know she didn't. She didn't want to say anything to you until we figured out what we were going to do ourselves."

"Who's the policeman in charge?" His voice had turned hoarse, and I could see in the sag of his shoulders that he was accepting the truth that his daughter was gone.

I gave him Ross's name.

"You'd better go now."

"I'll call you tomorrow."

"Don't. Just get out." His hand shook as he pointed toward the door. I looked back as I stepped onto the porch to see him sit down beside his wife and pull her head to his chest.

I sat in the armchair in the living room until just after midnight, listening to the new silence of my home. An unmarked police car waited out front as well. I resented their presence actively, because I knew with them there, Green Shirt would not come. It seemed unreal that he had emptied my life and I knew him only by his face, his voice, the color of his shirt, the fact that he carried a knife, that he chewed Juicy Fruit gum.

For a time sitting there, I drifted in my mind's eye, looking into every corner, every closet of our home, seeing our accumulated possessions, Ellen's clothes, her books, her photos.

It was the faint scent of her perfume that roused me. She liked to read in the chair I was using, the coffee table had a number of her magazines, and a novel was opened facedown. For a second, I thought my eyes would fill again. I was cut by the thought that she would never finish that book, that she had taken it from the library to read, and someone had snuffed out this minor plan of hers, and all the others that make up a life.

But the tears didn't come. Sylvia and Geoff could cry for their daughter, and for themselves, but I couldn't. I inhaled deeply, but Ellen's scent was elusive. A sudden fear coursed through me: how long would it take before her smell would drift away entirely, before there would be no living trace of her in the house?

Up in our bedroom, I found her perfume bottle. With it, memories flooded back, memories of good times overshadowing the bad, like the day we had brought Talker home as a puppy, and he first treated us to his conversational ways. She had tussled with him on the floor and growled back that we loved him, and would he like a baby brother someday? The two of them made me laugh then, touched me in a way that I rarely allowed.

I lay back on our bed and stared at the ceiling. In my head, the scenes of the day snapped into clear color focus: Ellen screaming at me from the dock, the bullet hole in Datano's head, Jocelyn's body in the foyer, the bright red of Ellen's blouse on the flagstones.

I squeezed my head between my hands and bargained with God for different scenes. *Let me have another chance, and I'll make it all work. I just didn't understand the stakes.* I saw myself catching up to Ellen in time, holding her in my arms. She said she understood, and we laughed at the foolish mistakes we had both made. Colored in sepia tones, I saw us grow old together, time dissipating the anger between us into nothing more than a faint memory.

But the real pictures only grew brighter and clearer. As real as if I were holding her in my arms right there in our bedroom, I felt the looseness of Ellen's head on her shoulders, felt with grinding certainty that I would be growing old alone.

I let the truth settle into my heart and harden my sweeping anger into a solid knot of resolve—the responsibility for Ellen's death was mine. For starting the affair with Rachel, for trusting the police to wrap it up, for leaving Lenny and Nick to guard Ellen. But most of all, for not finding and killing Green Shirt and his companion before it was too late.

At least I could still kill them, I told myself. That was something I could still accomplish.

A reporter from the *Boston Herald* called me at six the next morning. I had been exercising since four-thirty, doing push-ups and pull-ups, and working out on the long-unused heavy punching bag down in the basement. My breathing was ragged when I picked up the phone. "What're you feeling?" he asked. I put the phone back down, took a shower, and made myself eat breakfast.

On the way out to my car, the cop waiting in the unmarked car said, "Where are you going? Swampscott figured you'd be here all day, and I'm about to be relieved."

"He figured without talking to me."

The cop got on the radio, and by the time I had pulled out, he had an answer. He leaned out the window and said, "Swampscott says if you don't cooperate, we can't help you. We don't have any jurisdiction out of town. You want to run around like this, you'd better hire somebody."

He followed me to the town line, and from then on, I kept an eye out for other cars behind me. If anyone was tailing me, I couldn't see him. I stopped at a newsstand on the way to the hospital to visit Nick. The *Globe* and the *Herald* ran articles about the murders, the latter referring to them as the "Manchester Massacre." In both articles, cocaine trafficking was suggested as a possible cause, and though the police were quoted as saying that "Riley Burke is not a suspect," they were candid in outlining the earlier events, starting with the fight on the Fort Adams dock. There was a picture of Cory's body being pulled from the water, courtesy of the *Newport News*. Rachel was mentioned, and the *Herald* openly questioned our relationship. The *Globe* ran a sidebar interview with Wameling from the DEA about white-collar cocaine abuse. "People are learning the hard way," he said. "Cocaine isn't just a harmless party drug, and the people who traffic in it are notoriously violent. Unfortunately, some people have to learn through tragedy."

Nick had the same papers on the table beside his bed when I walked in. His color was bad, and he looked exhausted. I asked him how he was doing.

He grimaced. "Too much time to think. But the doctor says I'll be okay."

"I know you're tired," I said. "But I need you to go over it again." I pulled a chair up to his bed. "Give me everything."

"None of it's going to do a thing for Ellen." His voice was dull. "The chance to do that is gone."

"Tell me anyhow."

He looked at his hands, big powerful hands that could do many clever things, from splicing a line to drawing clear, fine illustrations. Now a faint tremor shook them as he rubbed them together as if he were washing. "Easy enough to do. It's been running around and around in my head like a looped roll of film. They were totally out of our league. Christ, we're a couple of guys who own an ad agency—who were we fooling?"

"Did this guy say anything? He just kept shooting, didn't say anything about Cory Dearborn, or coke, or money?"

Nick shook his head. "Not a thing. Strictly revenge, I guess. Like with the Colombian gangs you read about in New York, they figure you messed with their business, your whole family gets it." He went through it again slowly. When he got to the point where he found Ellen on the flagstones, he began to cry. "I did what I could."

His breath shuddered in.

I patted him on the shoulder, feeling awkward not because he was crying, but because I was the freak for not knowing how to respond to him. It was as if my heart had been cauterized during the night. Part of me felt his pain as my own. Greater, though, was the feeling of impatience. I had a lot to do.

"I'll let you rest, but hang on with one more. You say he was wearing a plaid shirt, right?" I asked.

"That's right." He rubbed the tears with the back of his hand.

"He wasn't when I saw him in the car. I remember a dark blue shirt, maybe black. You said he was wearing a backpack, right? He probably just stuffed the gun and gloves in there. Had a clean shirt, and a towel to clean off with. You recognize the make of the backpack? EMS? Jansport?"

He shook his head. "Green."

"Kelty? EMI?"

"Green! Damn it, what would you have done?" He stared at me, wanting an answer.

"I don't—"

"Would you have run up those stairs? If you had, you'd be one dead hero, because there were *no options!* Understand? You and Lenny settled it for me, you left me unarmed. I did all I could do."

He clutched at the bandage on his head, and when I reached out he shoved my hand away, and then sank back onto the pillow.

"I'm not blaming you, Nick."

"Yeah, well, I'm blaming you," he said between gritted teeth. "If you couldn't protect her, you shouldn't have hobbled me. Maybe you think that's not fair, that I should say the right things, try to help you. But that's the way it is right now."

On the way home, I stopped at a convenience store and picked up a copy of the *Want Advertiser*, a classified-listings publication. My hands were shaking too as I flipped to the firearms section. Nick was in pain, I told myself, feeling envious of his tears. Unless I kept moving, I felt as if I would stop breathing.

There were two pages full of guns. I called several listings before I found someone at home who had what I wanted: a collector selling off several handguns and an assortment of shotguns. His name was Larry Keiller; I told him my name was Carl Jorgensen. I expected a fair amount of dancing around over the phone; I knew from handling Lenny Datano's business that many gun owners were security-minded and might screen people carefully before inviting them over to buy a gun.

But there was the other kind of gun owner too, the type who

seemed to feel possessing a firearm ensured their superiority in the roughest of situations, and I quickly judged Keiller as the latter. "Cash," he said. "Get that straight up front. These are sweet pieces I've got here, plenty of people are ready to snap them up, so I'm not going to dick around on price."

"Cash is not a problem."

"Yeah, see that it's not. I had somebody come out last week, put a few bills down on a Walther, then started after me on a Beretta, wanted me to take a check for that. You know, I've got a selection, he sees, he wants, but I said come back with the cash and I'll set you up. Checks I haven't got time for. He gives me some shit, guy was acting tough, I show him the Police Special I keep in my shoulder holster and tell him that this is the only one in the fucking house that's loaded. Get my drift? I've got the paperwork, and a selection. I'm a guy who can set you up with what you need, but there's only room for one hardball in my house at a time, and that's me."

"Got it. When can we meet? You're in Watertown?"

"Yeah. I dunno, probably tomorrow morning, late, like eleven. I've got to go to work now, so take these directions down. I'll see you then, right?"

"Right."

"And remember . . ."

"Cash," I said.

I drove home, shaved, and put on some old painting clothes. I took a small daypack from the closet and threw in a clipboard, a pair of gloves, a baseball cap, a screwdriver, a hammer, a ski mask, a roll of duct tape, and two thousand dollars from the safe in my office. The irony of using the little backpack wasn't lost on me—I could see why the killer used one; it carried everything I needed and left my arms free.

I threw it in the front seat of Ellen's Jeep and started out around one o'clock. I put in about forty-five minutes on and off Route 2 and the back roads of Lincoln and Concord before heading back, confident that no one—police or otherwise—was following. In

Watertown, I pulled into a parking lot behind a movie theater and unscrewed a license plate from a Volkswagen Jetta. I adopted a nothing-to-hide manner, to the point of giving a cheerful hello to a couple who looked at me curiously on the way to their car.

I figured the same attitude would work at Keiller's house. I parked the car with its new plate about a block away just after two o'clock and walked up the sagging steps to his front door and rang the doorbell. Gun owners are often prime customers for security systems, so I looked for an alarm keyhole. None. When no one answered, I walked around the house with the clipboard, jotting down comments regarding the gutters, chipped paint, and rough dimensions to fit my cover story of being a painting contractor. There would have been plenty of work for me had I been legitimate—gray wood showed through the peeling paint, and the banister of the small porch in the back was rotting. A rusted Ford Bronco was up on blocks outside the garage. Through the basement window, I could see a finished room, which looked to be some sort of den.

No one approached me. The immediate neighboring houses looked closed, and there were no cars in the driveways. Everyone was at work, I assumed.

The back door provided the best possibility. It was locked, of course, but a tall hedge provided me with enough screening in case anyone *was* home next door. I pulled on my gloves, then quickly taped the pane of glass beside the doorknob. Even though no alarm system was apparent, I decided to leave myself only a minute and a half to find the guns and get out. That would beat the typical police response time with plenty to spare. Taking a deep breath, I set the timer on my digital watch for ninety seconds, activated it, then cracked the glass with the hammer. A bit tinkled onto the floor as I reached in. My eyes strayed up and I noticed a small metal hook over the door. I wondered briefly if Keiller had an awning, and then I withdrew my hand.

The hook was stainless-steel. And the shaft going into the wood looked as if it had been oiled.

And Keiller considered himself a hardass.

Stepping back, I took a closer look at the doorway and the

window beside it. The window lock on the inside did not look like anything special, but razor blades had been embedded on each side of the casement and carefully painted white. Someone raising the window by the brass lifting tabs could easily lose a finger or two.

Keiller had his house booby-trapped. Which meant he probably did not have the police tied into a security system—he was a guy who preferred to take care of things himself.

Walking away was the best idea. No way I could rush in and out in ninety seconds under these circumstances.

Then again, there was no way I could restrain myself from moving forward. I stood to the side of the door and turned the hook. It twisted smoothly, and a short length of line dropped inside the door window into my view. I reached back through the broken pane carefully and unlocked the door, then opened it—again, standing to the side.

Nothing happened.

I stepped inside to find a short-barreled shotgun mounted on a tripod, facing the door. A trip line ran from the trigger to a pulley screwed into the wall behind it, then back over my head to the door. Had I opened the door without twisting the hook outside—and thereby releasing the line from the jamb on the inside—the pressure of the opening door would have been my exit out of this life.

Nice guy, Keiller. A very illegal defense mechanism; he could be up on a murder charge if he killed a burglar that way. Particularly if it was a teenager looking for a stereo or TV. But it made me feel a little better about stealing from him, especially since I was going to leave more cash than I would have if I had been willing to register the guns and let him see my face.

"Hello!" I called loudly, walking carefully through the ground-floor rooms. Living room, dining room, small office. There was another gun trained on the front door. The house was a curious mixture: the walls and floors were poorly kept, there was a layer of dust over everything, yet most of the furniture seemed quite new and of high quality—though completely mismatched. Like a glass-topped table surrounded by Shaker-style chairs.

Downstairs there was a lonely male playroom, dominated by a glassed-in gun cabinet. There was a big-screen television, a VCR, and a stereo system. Stacked in the corner were several televisions in cartons, several microwave ovens, a refrigerator, and stereo components. The room smelled of dampness, stale beer, and old sweat. My take on it all was that Keiller's house was full of stolen goods. He probably would not have let me downstairs had I come by normally.

Interesting. I turned my attention to the gun cabinet. Inside were a Beretta and a big Smith & Wesson revolver, in addition to a hunting rifle and an Ithaca shotgun. And centered in the cabinet was a Colt automatic with a silencer attachment. What luck, I thought. Not only was Keiller willing to kill the random burglar, he had read too many spy novels as well.

After searching carefully for more tricks, I broke past the lock with the screwdriver. The Colt, the Smith & Wesson, and several boxes of ammunition went into the backpack. I wrapped the shotgun in a small throw rug. I left the money in the cabinet, thinking this part anyhow had turned out to be relatively easy.

But as I hurried up the basement stairs, I heard a faint snicking sound from upstairs, and stopped dead. Sweat popped out on my forehead. Keiller? Or was some unlucky son of a bitch about to take the shotgun blast in the face?

The front door slammed loudly.

Keiller. I had left the basement door open just a crack, and I heard someone walk by quickly, his tread heavy. "Jesus *Christ!*" I heard him mutter in an irritated tone, and I figured he had forgotten something.

If I was lucky, he might head right back out.

Unless he went into the kitchen and saw the broken glass and open door. His office was just down the hall from the kitchen. If he did see the broken window, I had no doubt his first step would be to draw the gun he said he kept at his side.

It was bad enough that I had broken into his house. I didn't want to hurt him too. But I didn't want to get shot either. I quietly loaded the shotgun, without pumping a shell into the chamber because of the noise. I could hear Keiller slamming through the desk drawer in his office as I loaded the clip for the Colt and pulled on the ski mask.

"Goddamn it," he said. There was a gurgling noise, and then he said again, but with an entirely different emphasis, "*Goddamn,* but that cures it."

Keiller was a drunk, home for lunch.

He was probably at his bravest right about now, if not his most steady. Bad time to be pulling a gun on him. Go out the way you came, I urged him silently.

I put my eye to the crack and saw him in the hallway, walking toward the kitchen. Damn.

He was a big man of about fifty, with sloping, muscular shoulders, a hefty beer belly, and a beak nose. Under his rumpled sport jacket I could see the outline of his shoulder holster.

His face went slack.

I kicked the basement door open, pumped the gun fast, and yelled at the top of my lungs, "Police! Freeze!"

He did.

Good thing, too. His hand was already around the revolver. His small eyes took in the ski mask, the gun. "That's my shotgun," he said. "You're not a cop."

"That's right, Larry. I made it past your little surprises, and I'll kill you right now if you don't take your hand away from that Police Special."

"You know my name. That was you on the phone—" He shut up abruptly.

"That's right. Now, with your left hand, use your thumb and forefinger to take that gun out and put it on the floor."

He hesitated, and I raised the barrel up to his eye level. "Do it."

He laid the gun down on the floor.

"Shove it into the corner with your foot, then turn around, grab that chair, and sit down on your hands."

He complied, his face drained white. I pressed the gun just behind his ear. "Do you have any security on this place, or you counting on just the guns? Because I promise you, Keiller, if you lie to me, I'll cut loose the first siren I hear."

"Just the firearms." He shook his head dully. "That's it." I felt that he was probably telling me the truth, but even if he was not, there was no choice but to spend a few minutes tying him up. I slipped the backpack off and used the roll of duct tape to bind his hands behind the chair. Keiller's wrists were slick with perspiration. As quickly as I could, I put a folded paper towel over his eyes, then wrapped a length of tape around it and his head.

"All right, Keiller," I said in his ear. "I've got some good news and some bad news. The bad news is, you're not going to report this to the police. If they come around and ask how guns registered to you turned up at a crime scene, you say you sold the stuff to a guy about fifty, gray hair, horn-rim glasses, and no, you did not ask for his permit, he offered top dollar, and you took it. You might take some shit, but if they track me down through you, the cops are going to hear about your shotguns trained on the windows, about the silencer you owned—but more important, all the stolen goods downstairs."

On that last one, I was bluffing. But I felt him stiffen under my hand. Good.

"But all of that's the icing. What you really need to worry about is me or one of my friends coming back. And all the shotguns and razor blades in the world aren't going to save you if I take my time and use a rifle and a scope. Got that? You could be walking down the street, going to work, going to the goddamn liquor store, and your head would just explode. Now who did you sell it to?"

"Gray hair, horn-rim glasses, about fifty. His name's Carl Jorgensen."

"That's fine, Larry. Now the good news comes in two parts. First, I'm going to leave you one of your kitchen knives here on the kitchen table. It'll be awkward, but you're not tied to the chair too tightly—you'll be able to back over there and find it fairly soon. My guess is you'll be able to free yourself within twenty minutes to a half hour." I slapped the knife down so he could hear it. "Second, you'll find money for the guns downstairs. In cash."

"How much?"

I had to smile. "Two thousand."

"For that, you could've just talked to me. You didn't have to do this."

"I'm shy, Larry. Just remember what I bought. I'd hate to have to come back." I taped his mouth, and after making sure he could breathe all right, I took off the mask and drove home.

I went to work that afternoon, and Lori, my secretary, guiltily began to move aside the two newspapers on her desk. I asked her to have Geena join me in my office. Work had piled up, and there were over fifty messages stacked neatly to the right of my desk.

I didn't care about any of it.

But it seemed only fair that Nick have a business to come back to, and for my employees to have their jobs. Advertising is all based upon service and creativity, and if I could not provide the former myself, I wanted to set it up so that they could.

"Oh my God," Geena said a few minutes later. "I am so sorry," she began and went on to express her condolences.

I listened as long as I could, then got to the point. "Tell me where we stand businesswise right now."

She looked taken aback, but she outlined the major issues: two large presentations coming up; several of Rachel's larger accounts had complained that she hadn't been out to see them; Bendon-away Clothing was unhappy with the program strategy statement she had sent along, and their ad manager wanted to know why he hadn't heard from me in the past week.

"That answer he'll read in the paper," I said. "I'll call him this morning, too." I told Geena that I would be out again for an indefinite period, and it would be at least several days before Nick was back in. I gave her a signatory authority release.

We were interrupted by Rachel and a tall older man I took to be a plainclothes policeman. I was surprised to see her at the office, and Geena used the opportunity to excuse herself. I could tell Rachel had been crying. "I'm so sorry, Riley. I couldn't believe it when I saw the paper. . . . I called you this morning. I sure didn't expect to see you in today."

The man with her spoke up before I answered her. "So this is the happy couple, huh?"

His suit hung off him, and I could see the outline of a shoulder holster and gun. Everything about him was pale, but his eyes were bright and alive, and at that moment, they were scrutinizing me with open hostility.

He showed me yellow teeth, and a badge. "Boston police. Detective Sheenan."

I recognized the name. "You were Datano's partner when he was on the force."

"That's right."

"I didn't know that," Rachel said, looking at him. "You didn't say that when you relieved the other policeman."

He shrugged. "Now you do. I've got some bad news. We're not going to be able to protect Ms. Perry, officially, much longer. Not stake out her place, anyhow. Other than what happened in Newport, no action has been taken against her, no face-to-face threat. And we *do* have people who're being beaten, raped, and shot at all day long we have to follow up on. We're not set up to guard people against what *might* happen."

"You are set up to pick up the bodies, is that it?" I said.

"All too often. And arrest the creeps who made the bodies bodies. Don't forget that."

"So what are you doing here?"

"I figured we could commiserate."

"Commiserate?"

"Yeah. I went to the funeral home yesterday, I saw the hole in Lenny's head. He was all floured up with makeup and a silly grin stuck on his face. I've seen a lot of bodies, but this made me sick, the kind of a sick feeling that makes you want to hurt people, break things. I expect you know what I mean."

I nodded.

"See, we're commiserating. Now, I'm supposed to keep away from this case, first off because it's not a Boston police problem, and second because I've got a personal interest. The lieutenant says I won't be objective. Says maybe I should take a vacation, that a cop all churned up about his ex-partner's murder isn't a

cop who's giving his all to the job. My lieutenant talks that way."
He looked at Rachel. "How'd you like me over to your place for
my vacation? Invite me, I'll accept."

"You want to use me like a tethered goat—just hoping this
guy will show up so you can kill him."

"So what?" His bright eyes flickered between the two of us.
"Think about it. We all want him dead."

"One man can't do the job alone," I said.

"I'm not by myself." He tapped the gun under his coat.

"No. This guy is fast, and he's a streetfighter too. I'm sorry,
but we need someone young, and fast."

The gun appeared in his hand, and he placed the barrel against
my chest.

"Sheenan!" Rachel said.

I might've been able to beat his hand away in time, but it
wasn't worth the chance. He said, "You don't need young muscle. A bullet'll rip that up just as easy as the old stringy stuff on
my arms. You need to be awake, sharp, and able to pull about
four pounds of trigger pressure. The load in here is cross-
hatched—one slug'll rip this guy's fucking arm off, if I miss his
chest. And I won't." He slipped the gun back into his holster.
"Let me tell you, having a cop nail this guy is about the cleanest
way this could happen. Because if we managed to track him
down—and with all the different police forces stepping on top of
each other, it isn't going to be so easy—the DA is going to have
a hell of a time getting a conviction. Maybe assault charges for
the fight down at the dock. But from what I hear, all you've got
on him up in Manchester is a glimpse as he drove by in the car.
Unless their physical evidence is very strong, you're going to
have problems with that."

I backed away and sat on the edge of my desk. I looked over
at Rachel. She nodded slightly. I said, "The first job is to protect
Rachel. And show me your quick draw all you want, but if we're
to agree, you'll need to hire somebody else, someone good in a
hand-to-hand fight."

Sheenan stared back at me hard, then jerked his head abruptly.
"I'll get a cowboy for her that'll jump in front of a bullet. If and

when this guy shows up, there'll be one of us to look out for her and the other to shoot him. And I'll let you guess who gets that job."

I looked over at Rachel. She nodded.

"Okay," I said. "I'll pay for that."

15

Borenson called me at home early the next morning. "You said you saw the driver of the Corvette, right? How about you come down here this morning and look at a lineup, see if you can ID him for us."

"How did you pick him up?"

"I'd rather not say just yet."

I pushed the point, but he remained adamant. We agreed to meet at ten.

"The other thing I was calling you on is the girl, Nadeau," he said. "We're keeping an eye on her, but I figured we don't have enough to pick her up, not unless you've forgotten to tell me something about her. If she knows you're working with us she'll just clam up. I'd like you to call her while you're down today, set up a meeting. No luck getting a court order on tapping her phone; we just don't have enough. Articles ran in the *Providence Journal* and the *Newport News* about your wife's death because of the link down here. So she must know by now what happened whether or not she's tied in with these guys. I assume you've got no problem calling her while we're listening in this morning."

"Anything I can do," I said.

In truth, I did not want to have the police listening in while I talked with Alicia. Therefore, I called the funeral home and woke up the director. He changed his tone of sleepy irritation immediately when he found out who I was and agreed to meet me early in the afternoon, leaving me a reason the police could follow up with as to why I could spend so little time with them.

I filled the backpack again, and headed down to Rhode Island. In Providence, I stopped and rented a beige midsized Chevy, and continued on to the Newport police station.

Borenson met me at the front desk and said, "There's an attorney upstairs representing the guy we have in the lineup, name of Mort Gillespie. I'll deal with him."

We went upstairs to a small dark room outfitted with a one-way mirror. It reminded me of a tiny theater. Borenson introduced me to the lawyer, a stout man of about sixty with pale, blotchy skin. He was wearing a dark blue pinstriped suit with highly polished shoes. He gave me the briefest of nods and said to Borenson, "Can we get on with the charade?"

I felt a sense of unreality as I waited for them to bring the suspects onto the little stage. This was so like countless television shows and movies I had seen, where the police wait breathlessly for the witness to finger the murderer. And I could sense that type of excitement from Borenson. From Gillespie, I felt a heavy boredom that was hard to peg, either genuine or simply his attempt to show me that my viewing his client was simply a waste of everyone's time.

A uniformed officer led six men out on the stage. I recognized the man from the bar who had scared Alicia and driven the Corvette. His face was sunburned and dirty-looking with several days' growth of beard. Freckles were scattered over his bald dome. He was enormously fat, and carried his weight with the sullen defensiveness of an angry teenager. His mouth had a sour, fat-baby cast. He was probably used to scaring people with his bulk, I thought. He would be hard to fight. Punches would be absorbed by that softness, and if he ever brought that bulk to bear in a tight space, it would be like battling with so much rancid dough.

I spent equal time looking at the other people in the lineup. They were all of essentially the same heavyset build: a blond man in his forties with a sullen expression; a biker type; a flabby man with even features; a Hispanic man who coughed nervously; and another man who also looked as if he spent quite a bit of time in the sun.

"Recognize anybody?" Borenson said.

"No," I said slowly, rescanning the faces. "No, I wish I did, but I don't."

His face sagged. "You're sure?"

"Who am I supposed to point out?"

"If you don't see him, it doesn't matter." Gillespie stood abruptly.

Borenson stared at me hard. "Nobody even looks familiar? Forget the guy in the Corvette—have you seen anybody up there ever before?"

"Lieutenant! His answer was no. Stop wasting our time."

I looked at them again and shook my head. "Afraid not."

Borenson looked disgusted as he said into a microphone, "Okay, Mario, file them out."

"That's it?" I said. "We just forget whoever you had up there? Why'd you put them up?"

"Just following a hunch. A patrolman made a note that one of these men was parked in the Fort Adams lot a little before your wife came in and saw you with the Nadeau woman. And he has a quahog boat. We were keeping a list of the plate numbers, or boat registration numbers, of any guys who came anywhere near you who were close to your description of the guy in the bar. So far we have about five pages of fatsos. But this is the first who owned a quahog boat."

"Hardly a crime to be fat," Gillespie said. "Hell, why don't you arrest me?"

"So just because I can't identify him," I said, "you're going to let him go?"

"The idea is, you arrest him if he's the right person," Gillespie said. "Not that you identify him after the police tell you he's the one they would like to put away. The other witness, the one who saw the quahog boat the night Dearborn was put under your boat, he couldn't ID my client either—reason being, my client had nothing to do with your problems. Now, again, Lieutenant, let him out of here."

"Yeah, yeah," Borenson said. "It'll take just a few minutes. Wait for him downstairs, will you, Mort?"

We went back to Borenson's office. He picked up the phone and said, "Kick our fat friend. Yeah, that one. I know, I know." Borenson looked disgusted with me. "I didn't have big expectations for the witness from the Albin. He said it was too dark, he never did get a good look. You I expected to come through."

"Look, Borenson, I'm going to be arranging funeral plans for my wife in about an hour and a half." I leaned across his desk and watched his face darken with blood. "I want the right guy. Not just the first guy you don't like."

"Come on to me like that again, Burke, you're going to be spitting teeth. Now, sit down." He made a pushing gesture with his hands. "All right, let's calm it down."

"Has he got any sort of record?"

Borenson made a face of disdain. "He does, and it's mean shit. School in his town complained that he was hanging around too much. The file says that he tried to talk some of the girls into his truck, but they ran away. Said he smelled bad, and scared them. Cops say he's been around for a long time, in and out of this kind of stuff, and some breaking and entering, and there's every chance he does quite a bit of illegal digging, and gives not one shit about who eats poisoned shellfish. . . . But he's caught just one short stint at the Adult Correctional Institution for the B&E. Funny thing, the cops who picked him up said he had crucifixes tacked up around the house. Another thing that smells wrong—Gillespie's a damn good lawyer and not cheap. Our boy's got a regular job, and there's the quahog digging on the side, but nothing that would make big bucks or need a topflight attorney on retainer. . . . But we've got nothing on him, so he's off."

"Any sort of drug connection?"

"Nothing on record."

"What's his name?"

"You don't need to know that," Borenson said flatly. "You didn't recognize him, so he's gone. Let's talk about the next step with the girl."

I looked at my watch. "Five minutes, all right? I've got to get back to the funeral home."

He made no attempt to hide his impatience. "You say she didn't know Dearborn—so what do *you* think her reason was for picking you up?"

"She acted like she was just coming on to me, period," I said carefully. "But I don't buy it. I think she's after the coke, but whether she's on her own or connected to the guy who killed Ellen, I don't know. I think we should go slowly with her."

"All right. *When* you have time, I think the only shot here is if you act like things were so bad with your wife that you're more concerned with your own hide than any grief about her." Borenson took a tape recorder from his bottom drawer and said, "Do it from home then, and tape it." He looked at me carefully as he showed me how to use the suction-cup attachment. "It's legal to tape her if you give your consent. I assume you do?"

"Sure."

"Tell Nadeau that you're scared for your own life, and you want out of the whole thing, and you figure the best thing you can do is sell the coke—and leave town. Ask her if she would know how to set it up for you. If she's smart, she won't discuss it over the phone too much, so set up a meeting, and we'll send you in with a wire and listen to what she has to say. My thought is she'll lead us either to the guys who did the murders or to Dearborn's customers. If we get to his customers, we might at least shake out who got this whole thing rolling. Because one thing we can probably take to the bank—somebody stole that coke and got this whole thing stirred up."

I drove around the block and parked so I had a view of the police station. Quickly, I took off my shirt and tie, pulled on a dark blue T-shirt, and put on my baseball hat and sunglasses. I sat in the passenger-side seat, rolled the window down, and turned on the music softly, hoping that I would appear to be simply waiting for the driver to return from a quick errand.

The fat man and Gillespie came out within the hour. I slid behind the wheel and followed them around the block, my attention focused upon the digger. They got into Gillespie's big Lincoln and pulled away.

I followed them over the Newport Bridge, through Jamestown, and onto Route 1 North. We both eventually picked up 95 North, and I faded back as far as possible, letting several cars keep between us. They took an exit for Warwick. The traffic became more congested, and the houses along the road had the added-on look of summer homes that had been converted to year-round use. When they turned down into one of the subdivisions, I gave him ample distance, then followed. I almost missed them as they took a left turn up ahead, and I stepped on the gas to catch up. Sunlight reflected off the little inlet to my left. Dust still lingered in the air when I reached where they had turned. It was a private dirt driveway. I could see the glint of water through the scrubby brush closing out the view, and the green roof of a small house. "Beware of Doberman" said a sign planted by the driveway. From the sound of a slamming door and the welcoming woof of a dog, I assumed my man had reached his home. The mailbox had a hastily painted name: D. Lowe.

I turned the car around and drove a block up to the vacant lot I had passed along the way that ran down to the waterfront. I could see a small nun buoy in the little inlet, and I made a note of the number. I was lucky that I had not brought the guns down. I might not have been able to do the smart thing, to wait until dark, wait until the attorney was gone, wait until I had no appointment to keep.

No, D. Lowe was safe from me for this afternoon. But his house was just two lots away from the red nun, and easily accessible from the water. Good enough for now.

The mortician was about my age, and he wore a somber appearance like a suit of clothes: hunched shoulders, sorrowful eyes, a concerned frown. From his tan and the laugh lines around those sad eyes, I could envision him on the golf course, telling his friends about the stable nature of his business.

"So particularly sad when it's someone so young," he said. "I can only imagine what you're going through."

"Let's get this done."

He glanced at his watch. "I received a call from your wife's father," he said. "He would like to join us, so I gave him the time of the appointment. I hope that was all right?"

I told him that was fine, but inwardly I felt myself retreat another notch. Geoff and Sylvia had not returned my calls. Had they, I would not have really known what to say. We had never been close. They had always been friendly enough, but there was an essential reserve toward me because of my background. When they first asked about my mother and father, I told them the truth. During the early years of our marriage, they looked at me as Ellen's form of rebellion. This changed somewhat after I started the business and we prospered, but I always had the impression they were watching me, waiting for my blood to tell.

I barely recognized Geoff when he came through the door now. His normally ruddy skin was shockingly pale, and loose. He must have lost a half-dozen pounds since I had seen him last. His lips were purplish, and he was using a heavy cane, something I had never seen him need before. It was a heavy oak stick with a silver head.

I stood up, and the mortician hurried around the desk to grab a chair. "Mr. Carson, let me express my condolences," he said. "Words can't touch what you're feeling, but all I can say is that we'll do our best to make your daughter's final rest easy and peaceful."

"That's not what I want," Geoff said, looking at me.

The mortician blinked. "Sir?"

Geoff drew back the cane like a club. I stepped into him and wrapped my arms around him, pinning his arms to his side. "Let go!" he raged.

"Mr. Carson!" the mortician said.

I ran my hand along his arm and twisted the cane away. I stepped back.

He punched me in the mouth. He rocked me with a blow to my chest.

"That's enough, Mr. Carson!" the mortician said, a ring of authority escaping past his professional mien.

Geoff's breathing was ragged, his face flushed. I put my hands on his shoulders and said, "Sit down, Geoff."

He knocked them away, and took out a handkerchief and scrubbed tears from his cheeks. "Goddamn you, Riley. Goddamn you."

"Look, you knew things weren't going well with us. We might've even reached the point of a divorce soon. But I loved her. And I'm going to do the right thing now."

He glared at me. "What does that mean?"

I gestured to the chair. "Sit down."

The mortician interjected, "Please, yes, let's do that."

Geoff stared at me hard, then sat down. He wiped his forehead again. He folded the handkerchief. "What does that mean?" he repeated.

"Her death won't be peaceful."

"I don't understand," the mortician said.

"You're really going to do the right thing?" Geoff asked.

"Yes."

He handed me the handkerchief to wipe the blood from my mouth. "All right," he said. "First, we bury her."

At home that night, I placed the little suction-cup attachment from the tape recorder on the phone as Borenson had showed me, and dialed Alicia's number. I had toyed with the idea of replacing the batteries with dead ones to give me an excuse for keeping my communications private. I decided against it, since I could always erase the tape if she said something useful. If what she said was innocuous, I could give the tape to the police to show that I was being cooperative.

She answered after the fourth ring. Her voice was subdued until I identified myself. I heard the sharp intake of her breath. "I haven't been able to think about anything else," she said. "I'm so sorry, Riley. I read about it in the newspaper. Did . . . did they follow her down right after she saw us?"

"It looks that way."

"I was afraid that was true, you know, just from the timing. Riley, you've got to know that I didn't have anything to do with that."

I hesitated, striving for the right tone. "You're right, Alicia, it is hard for me to believe you're not tied up in it somehow, seeing the way you showed up and all. But my gut tells me you're not. And right now, that's all I can go on."

"I can see why you'd feel that way." She waited.

I plunged into it. "Look, I've got to get out of here. Leave the state, maybe the country. It's only a matter of time until those two come after me, and the cops only half believe I'm not involved. Anyhow, I need cash, so I've got to sell something."

"Whoa. Let's talk about our date instead. I want to know you a little better. Bring me flowers, or maybe some chocolates. That's it, that would be a good start, I have a sweet tooth . . . but just a taste. I mean it, don't you dare bring any more than that. I don't want to get fat."

I considered refusing, since I didn't actually have even a "taste." But it was reasonable for her to expect to sample the product. I said, "Sure."

"So where are you taking me to dinner tomorrow night?"

"I can't do it tomorrow. Ellen's family, you know. The funeral is Thursday morning."

"Mmmm . . . I'm surprised they're speaking to you. Call me right after the funeral. And don't wait too long. It wouldn't look right if I showed up at yours."

. . .

I made a cup of coffee and listened through the tape twice. The way I saw it, there were three ways to go about getting to Green Shirt, in addition to setting a trap for him at Rachel's apartment. One, go after the quahog digger, D. Lowe. He was the most direct link. Two, try to find out who had stolen the coke in the first place, and Alicia might be able to help there if she knew Cory's customers. Three, find out why Dearborn was on the dock that night, and exactly why Green Shirt was chasing him.

Not the least of the difficulties was making the police think I was being cooperative while doing all this.

I erased the tape of Alicia and slipped old batteries into the recorder. Afterward, I put a call into Borenson to castigate him for the sloppy upkeep of his equipment. He was out, but the detective taking the message said with unfeigned skepticism, "You're right. That is hard to believe."

16

Alicia was, of course, correct that Ellen's family would not want me to join them the night before her funeral. It was just as well: I needed to figure out a way to supply her with a taste of coke.

I spent much of that morning in the office thinking about it, drawing a total blank. Other than a rare hit off a joint at a party, I had never used drugs myself.

It wasn't until Geena came into my office with layouts for the Bendall account that I had an idea. She was wary of me, as they all were in the office, still unable to reconcile my presence in the agency so soon after Ellen's death. "Rachel called in and asked you to take a look at these for her, and to let her know if they're okay."

I looked at photos of a computer CAD screen, thinking to myself that I should stop by to see who Sheenan had hired to help protect Rachel. And that's when I thought of Derby Tucker.

He was the free-lance photographer who had done the Bendall shoot. Ours had been one of his mainstay agencies, but just earlier this year he had bought a new studio in Roxbury and was now aggressively pursuing new business. Nick and I liked him and had offered to make referrals to help him along.

He had joined Rachel, Nick, and me for the briefing meeting held by Curt Donner, the Bendall ad manager. Curt favored hand-tailored shirts and elegant seven-hundred-dollar suits. His briefings were little performances in themselves—he apparently felt it was his job to be the dynamic visionary; we creative types from the agency were mere elves. On the way out of the meeting, Derby nudged me and tapped his nose. "What do you think— that boy's been tooting his horn a tad too much, huh?"

Pretty thin for a lead to buy coke, but it was all I had. Derby and I were good business friends: I certainly respected his talent, and found him good company. He had invited Ellen, me, and Nick to an opening party at his loft earlier in the year. I couldn't make it, but Ellen and Nick had gone and had said later they'd had a great time. And she had modeled for him a few times. Still, trying to buy coke from him was pushing beyond our relationship. But I saw no other choice.

I flipped through my Rolodex and found his card. His answering machine picked up. I put the receiver down without leaving a message. Not leaving traces was becoming a habit with me these days.

I drummed my fingers, frustrated. I decided to stop by his place later.

In the meantime, maybe I could find out some more about Cory Dearborn. Green Shirt had said something on the dock about Thorton, which I assumed was the small private college just about an hour and a half west of Boston. I called information and asked for the number of the alumni office. A few minutes later, using a hurried tone, I explained to the woman who answered that I was a reporter from the *Boston Globe*, writing Dearborn's obituary, and could she tell me his graduating year and degree? She made some official sounds about privacy, but when I snapped that I preferred not to bother the family with such small details at a time like this, she agreed and came back with the news that Cory Dearborn had left in his junior year, and had not finished his degree in business administration. I asked her the name of the dean of that school, and she gave it to me: Evan McArthur.

I figured the chances of the dean knowing much about an individual student several years back were slim, but then again, Thorton was a small school, with an excellent student-to-professor ratio. One of my clients, Chick Bannard, was on the board of Thorton, and a major contributor. I called him to ask for some help getting in to see McArthur. After he expressed his condolences, I told him what I wanted, saying, honestly enough, that while the police were not terribly concerned with Dearborn, since he was already dead, I was curious about him and thought maybe I could talk to one of his former professors. I asked if he could get me an appointment with Dean McArthur, without going into details. "Sure, sure," he said, wheezing slightly. "All the money I give them, I should have some influence, hey?"

So in a few hours I found myself walking through Thorton's small, gemlike campus. Rock music pounded from speakers that had been set up in dorm windows; the smell of popcorn wafted down. Impossibly young looking students eyed me with friendly wariness as I walked through the quad in my business suit.

Dean McArthur welcomed me in his high-ceilinged office and offered me coffee. A well-built man in his mid-forties, he had sharp blue eyes and a professional manner. He got to the point, saying that Chick Bannard was a well-respected member of the board, and if he could help in some way he would be happy to.

"It's about one of your former students. He was killed two weeks ago, and this Sunday my wife was killed. And the same person is the murderer."

"Your wife?" He looked shocked. "Who was the student?"

When I told him, his expression turned guarded, but not as much as I might have expected. "I didn't recognize your name from the papers. Perhaps you could excuse me for a minute."

He left the room, and I waited for a few minutes. He seemed tense when he came back. He tapped a pencil against the desk lightly. "I have a bit of a problem," he said. "A board member who is a substantial contributor would like me to help you. And, personally, given your recent tragedy, I too would like to help you wherever I can. But I don't want to reopen this thing. You see, we just heard about Cory last week ourselves."

"So you knew him?"

"Oh yes. Although I wasn't involved in the incident—I became dean two years ago, and Jack Reynolds was head of the department during the scandal. He's retired, lives in Arizona now."

"Scandal?"

He looked perplexed momentarily, then said, "I assumed you knew—forgive me. You see, we had quite a scandal about five, six years back. It seemed as if all the media on the East Coast were focused upon our little campus."

"And Cory was in the middle of it?"

"Yes, although that was not made public. I had him for several classes myself, and you are talking about a very charming but extremely manipulative young man. He had a talent for knowing how to say just what you wanted to hear. There were always girls crowding around him, alternately happy and heartbroken over his attentions." McArthur smiled wryly. "As a professor, you try to ignore the love interests of your students, but several of us commented to each other that Dearborn was indeed having the time of his life. And Judd Streeter was in line to be dean of the English Department, and he also was one of those professors who made comments. I guess in retrospect, he was a little more envious than he should've been."

"And that's where the scandal comes in?"

"That's right. Understand, he was a very proud man, about forty-five, good family, Rhodes scholar. He had money, took his role as a professor very seriously. But he was a lonely man—his wife had left him not long before. Not to defend what he did. . . . Anyway, a photo appeared in the *Thorton Crier*, the school newspaper. A photo taken of Judd through what was apparently his bedroom window with a young, naked girl. The caption was 'After-Hours Pointers,' or something to that effect. How the photo got into the paper was a big question. The faculty adviser who approved the mechanical swore the photo in its place was of a new exhibit at the student union."

"And Dearborn placed it?"

"That was never proved, but he was on the newspaper staff. It turned out the girl was not a student, and even younger than was first assumed. She was sixteen years old. The police said she was a runaway, and suspected she was a prostitute, although she had no record. Judd wrote a confession within an hour after the paper came out, admitted he slept with her, but claimed she approached him in the student union one day, and that he thought she was older, and a student, though not one of his. That in spite of his better judgment, he had fallen in love with her and didn't find out about her until it was too late. It was pathetic."

"*Wrote* a confession?"

"Before he jumped out the window," McArthur said flatly. "Seven floors, stone steps underneath."

"And where does Dearborn come in?"

"He was prominently mentioned in Judd's suicide note. At the tender age of twenty, Dearborn had been blackmailing him for one hundred thousand dollars. Judd refused to pay, but was unwilling to live with the scandal."

"Why wasn't Dearborn arrested?"

"He denied any involvement. So did the girl. The police could prove nothing. Can't convict somebody on a suicide note. We managed to keep his name from the newspapers. All we could do was find a way to kick him out, which took a month or two, but we succeeded. He had a girl, someone else, up in his room after hours. Normally not the type of thing we look at twice, truthfully, but it was sufficient."

"And the prostitute—what was her name?"

McArthur's brow wrinkled, and he said, "I forget. Because she was underage, the papers didn't carry her name—and the *Thorton Crier* issue with her photo was pulled. Otherwise we could call it up on microfilm for you. Does it matter?"

I wondered if Alicia could have been that girl. She was about the right age. "Maybe. If you could find out, I'd appreciate it."

He steepled his fingers and said, "As long as there's no need to bring the police into this. . . . None of what I read in the Boston papers about your situation seems to have anything to do with Thorton, true?"

I nodded. I certainly didn't want him calling the police on my behalf either.

He brightened, pulled his phone closer, and took a number from his Rolodex and dialed. "Jack Reynolds," he said, his hand over the mouthpiece. Someone answered, and apparently Reynolds was out. McArthur left a message for him to call, then took my home and work numbers.

"I'll get back to you as soon as I can," he said, walking me to the door. "Again, my condolences about your wife. And none of this need come back against the school, correct? I see no correlation, yes?"

I agreed, and he seemed satisfied. "This must all be a nightmare for you. I know it's wrong to say this, but I'm not surprised or sorry Dearborn is dead. He just loved to play with people, as if we were all trick dogs in his private circus. Looks like he tweaked the tail of a dragon this time."

Back in Boston, I stopped at the bank and cashed a check for fifteen hundred dollars. It took me a half hour to find Derby's building, which was apparently a former warehouse.

Beside the doorbell was a grim-looking photo sealed in Lucite of him holding a growling Doberman back by the collar. A caption underneath read "And he bites, too."

I pushed the button. The sound of barking started upstairs, faintly, and a moment later Derby's voice came on the intercom, asking who was there. I told him and he said, "Who?"

"Riley Burke."

"You're shitting me."

"No, Derby. You going to let me in or what?"

The little speaker over the door was silent except for the barking of the dog. When I looked up, I saw Derby leaning out the window three floors up. "Hey," he called. "It is you. Hold on."

He opened the door a moment later, and we shook hands. "Man, what the hell are you doing here? Come on in."

"I didn't know you had a dog."

"Yeah, he's a beast. I'm the only one here nights, and I like the protection." Derby led me to a small elevator and took me up to his loft. Once inside, he pushed the rewind button on a tape recorder underneath the intercom and said, "This is how I feed the dog." He looked over his shoulder at me, and I had the sense that I made him nervous. Well, what does one say to a man whose wife has just been murdered? He said, "No dog food, no hair, no taking the pooch for a walk, no waiting for him to crap when you're freezing your ass off, no *dog*."

Derby was just over thirty. His skin was coffee-colored, and he moved with a quick, sure energy. He had earned the name by the hat he wore on his bald head; a graphic of the same hat appeared on his business cards and letterheads, like a trademark. He grasped me by the upper arm and said, "What'll it be? Beer, coffee?"

"Coffee."

He strode back to his kitchen area off in the corner, and I looked around the large studio. The wide-planked floors were painted white, the walls too. Large blackout curtains were drawn off to the side to let the light pour in. I was sure he could reduce the room to pitch dark in minutes.

"Here you go. Drink it black like a man," he said, putting two mugs on the kitchen table. "Because I'm out of cream."

I sat down across from him and took a sip.

"How do you like it?"

"It's awful."

"Yeah, isn't it though. I drink it for the brain power, not the taste."

An uncomfortable silence stretched between us, and he spoke a half second before I did. "Why the fuck're we sitting here talking about coffee, man? I am so sorry about Ellen. I only worked with her a couple of times, but I sure did like her. I'm sorry as hell."

I nodded, and said thanks. Derby's expression was sympathetic, but I could sense his wariness. The silence lengthened, and he said, "What do you want, Riley?"

"I'd like to buy some coke, and I'm hoping you might have some, or know someone who can help me."

His head jerked back a half inch. "From what I read in the paper, that's the last thing you need. What're you telling me, man, you were actually in on that? And why're you coming to me?"

"I wasn't in on it."

"Then why are you coming to me?"

"I just want a small amount."

"That doesn't answer my question."

"I've got fifteen hundred on me. And Derby, I've always sent a lot of business your way, and if you help me with this, I'll do more. But this is important to me."

He drew back farther and crossed his arms. His tone had turned remote. "Man, I'd like to help you, things are looking pretty bleak right now for you, but I can't. Just because I'm black doesn't mean I'm some kind of Superfly, you know."

"Can't or won't?"

"What's the difference?"

"None really. Are you going to help me?"

"No."

I sighed inwardly. "Look, Derby, I'm going to have to hurt you if you don't help me out."

"What?" His voice rose slightly, and he placed his hands on the table. "What sort of bullshit are you trying to sling, you're going to *hurt* me?"

"I don't want to do this, but I need to make this purchase, Derby. And if you don't have access to coke, you know some-body who does."

"Says who?"

"Says me. This is Roxbury, you grew up here, you'll know somebody. I'm not saying it's fair, because it's not, but if you don't help me on this, then you're off the Bendall account, and we will not send another dime your way. Further, I'll do worse than not recommend you in the business, I'll put out the word that you're unreliable."

"You fucker." He stood up and walked over to the sink and dumped his coffee out. "You agency fuckers," he repeated, shaking his head. "You go put your dick in Rachel there, and I've got to pay? You try to blackmail me into doing shit I fought my way out of when I was fifteen. And you make the *assumption* I can get it for you because I'm black. Maybe I should just beat the shit out of you and dump you down the stairs. How about that, Riley?"

"I made the assumption because you made a joke about it after the meeting with Curt Donner. The rest is true. As I said, it isn't fair. But do this, and you're done, and I can get out of here. You've got a good business going, but you're poised on the edge right now, and any talk the wrong way could hurt you."

"You'd do this just to feel good? You'd threaten me to get high? You're pathetic."

"Maybe so. Don't go down with me."

He stared hard at me, and I felt he was restraining himself from swinging. Then his features softened, and he shook his head. "No. I don't buy it. I don't know you that well, but I know you well enough. You're running something."

I shook my head.

He put his palm out like a traffic cop. "You got that right—I don't want to know."

He took a key from his pocket and unlocked a massive padlock that secured the door of a walk-in closet. He went inside and came back a moment later with a small Baggie of white powder. "Here. I keep some around for those ten-hour shoots when I need to keep sharp."

I took out the bank envelope. "Fifteen hundred okay?"

He waved it away. "I'm not in that business anymore. And the only reason I didn't kick you down the stairs is I figure you're going to need your strength, man. If you're playing the games I think you are. If you're not, if you just got the urge for some snow and came to your friendly neighborhood black man to get it, I hope you eat shit and die. Now get out."

In Newport three hours later, I used the pay phone at Fort Adams to call Desmin Lowe. That was his full name, the name that fit the address in the phone book. Someone picked up the phone without answering, and I said loudly, "Lizzie? That you?"

He hung up. I caught the launch just before seven, and carried on my scuba gear. The driver was a blond girl in her late teens who smiled and said have a nice evening.

The Colt and the shotgun were in the equipment bag. After I left Derby, I had cut the stock and barrel off the shotgun. Given the sour taste left in me from bullying him and Keiller, I was looking forward to putting a gun up against someone who deserved it. And I figured from the way Cory's chest looked, a sawed-off shotgun was the type of weapon Desmin Lowe respected.

I went below and lay down in the bunk and waited.

I tried to sleep, but couldn't. My eyes were itchy, and I was keyed up. Instead, I thought about how I had helped build my separation from my wife with this damn sailboat. I thought of how I should have spent more time with her instead of running down to Newport and cajoling her to join me. We should've traveled more. We should've spent more time together. We should've had children. We should've talked more honestly. We should've, should've, should've . . . I should've left Rachel alone.

The hours passed slowly. After cleaning both guns, I fixed myself a sandwich and drank some juice. I plotted a simple course and punched the numbers into the loran, then inflated the dinghy and put on the outboard. And waited.

Just before eleven, I dropped the mooring and motored up the bay toward Warwick Neck. The water was calm, and the *Spindrift* made good speed, just under seven knots. After about two hours, the loran beeped for the third time, and I killed the engine and dropped anchor.

I quickly pulled on my wet suit and set out in the dinghy for the mouth of the shallow inlet leading to Desmin Lowe's house. A sense of unreality swept over me as the moon slipped from behind clouds to reveal me alone in the little boat, the minor chop slapping at the sides. The shotgun and the automatic were in the backpack up in the bow. The inlet narrowed, and I checked off the buoys as I passed by, until I reached the one that was two lots from his house. I cut the outboard and began to row. A quahog boat was tied to a small floating dock. The house was nondescript, closed off from the neighbors by a high wooden fence. A pickup truck dominated the driveway, alongside the dark shape of a car, a Trans Am perhaps. A big motorcycle gleamed in the moonlight near the back porch. Desmin had some new toys, all right. The dog was nowhere in sight; I assumed he was inside.

I continued past the house and let the dinghy drift up to the neighbor's beach. The time was just after one in the morning. My teeth were chattering slightly, although it was hot and sticky in the wet suit. Nerves. Up to this point, I had moved along through the logistics, preparing the dinghy, cleaning the guns, doing the navigation. Now was different: my plan was really no more complex than to force Desmin Lowe to tell me about his partner. Take him at gunpoint back to the *Spindrift*. Lash his hands behind his back, put a scuba tank on his back and the regulator in his mouth, and drop him overboard with a rope around his ankles and then wait. He would have no mask, no wet suit, no control. If being cold, blind, and underwater at the whim of the man whose wife he had helped murder didn't loosen his mouth, then perhaps I would simply kill him and dispose of the body.

But you don't know that he did it, I thought. Maybe he didn't kill her himself—maybe Green Shirt was the one.

I took several deep breaths and tried to relax my shoulders.

Either way, Desmin Lowe was on the scene when she was killed. I saw him. And that was reason enough for me to make him talk.

That he was going to do.

I waded around the edge of the fence and into the yard, the automatic with the silencer extended in two hands. The sawed-off shotgun was within easy reach over my shoulder in the partly open backpack.

The Doberman hit instantly. I had expected to deal with him, but inside the house—and I sure as hell hadn't expected him that fast and quiet. He launched himself for my throat, and on pure reflex, I jabbed my elbow into his face. His paws hit me square on the chest, and he knocked me down. I saw the white of his jaws as he angled his head to rip my neck. I cracked him over the head with the gun butt. He yelped and went for my right hand. Even as I yanked it away, I felt a sharp tug, and then I hit him with my left. He whirled, his teeth clicked in the night air, the age-old game of teasing a puppy between two hands saving me. Before he wised up, I jammed the gun under his jaw and pulled the trigger.

The silenced gun made a sharp puffing sound, and the dog dropped to his side, his legs scrambling madly in the sand. I put another bullet in his head. I looked over to the house. The lights remained off. There was a deep gash in the wet suit along my right forearm, and my heart was beating wildly, but I had come through otherwise unscathed.

The dog had clearly been at least partly trained, given the silence of his attack. After scooping up the spent cartridges, I dragged his body against the fence, then hunkered down and waited.

Five slow minutes passed.

Ten.

I waited for Lowe to come out. Come out looking for his dog, and I would take him on then. A lot easier than breaking into his house.

Thirty minutes.

Finally, I edged along the fence toward the house, my muscles tight from kneeling so long. There were three windows in a row along the first floor, all partly open. The window farthest from me showed the faintest glow of light, giving me an image of Desmin Lowe reading in bed. That, along with the memory of Borenson's saying crucifixes were tacked up around his house, jarred me for a second: did I have the right man?

He confirmed it for me himself.

"Right there, asshole." He extended a rifle out of the window beside me and aimed it in my face. "I'll take your head clean off, fucker. You stole my shit, you killed my dog. Only reason I haven't pulled the trigger yet is I want to know just who the fuck you think you are. Now drop it."

.　　.　　.

I dropped the gun and faced him squarely, hoping that he hadn't noticed the grip of the sawed-off shotgun sticking out of the backpack. He pointed the gun below my waist and said, "Okay, cowboy, I'm gonna climb out of this window nice and slow. I got this pointed at your balls—I figure all the pussy you chase around, you consider them pretty important. If you've got to sneeze, you'd better hold it until I'm on the ground."

He slid the window up with one hand and then wedged through, the gun cradled in his lap. He landed heavily and stepped over to me and jammed the gun under my chin. "Killed my dog this way, why shouldn't I do the same right now? Huh?" He shoved the barrel up so I had to stand on my toes, my head angled back. "I could make a fucking Roman candle with your head. But you took something of mine and my partner's, and I want it back."

"I'll give it to you."

He arched his eyebrows. "Oh! Hey, you'll *give* it to me! What a good guy, and all this time we thought you were holding out." His voice was oddly high-pitched, and even in that circumstance, the smell off him was overpowering: rotten fish, and under that, a heavy sweat stink.

"You told Cracker that you didn't have it, even when he had a knife to your wife's throat. Shit, when Cracker told me that, I'm a chump, I said maybe you were just some dumb fuck, didn't know what was going on, maybe you really *didn't* have anything to do with it."

He bared his teeth suddenly. Even in the poor light I could see his top front teeth were missing. "See that? Cracker put a two-by-four across my face because someone picked up our pot, stole from us. Then I find you creeping around in my yard, killing my frigging pet, and find out you lied to him when he was all set to slice up your wife, and you do have our coke."

"That his name? Cracker?"

He stepped back and clubbed me in the face with the rifle stock. It put me down. He put the gun barrel against my throat. "*I* ask the questions," he hissed. "All you've got to do is answer them. Then you're gonna die."

17

Acting dazed was easy. Trying to force clear thought into my head was the hard part. I figured he might kill me, but not with the rifle. Too much noise with the neighbors around.

My sawed-off was digging into my back.

He pressed the rifle barrel against my throat.

Slowly, so as not to startle him, I put my hand around it and lifted.

"Let it go, fucker," he whispered.

"Kill me and the coke's gone."

He knelt on my chest, holding the gun out by his side, and said, "Did I tell you to talk?" His weight was incredible; I felt my ribs giving way. "In a second, I'm gonna get up, and then I'll let you tell me where it is. And if you don't, I'm gonna start using your body as sweat equity. You know what that means, don't you? Sweat equity. I'll do the sweating, working some pay-back out of your body." He stood up. "You want to make me work?" He jabbed me with the barrel.

Even in the poor light, I could tell he was trembling. His being scared too made it even worse. I felt he could pull the trigger any second.

"*Say it*, man."

"No."

"Now stand up."

I sat up and got to my feet, careful to face him directly, so he couldn't see my gun sticking out of the backpack. My breath whistled in and out; I couldn't get enough air. I raised my hands.

He shook his head, wheezing angrily. "You've caused me some trouble, fucker, you really have." Abruptly, he jabbed me in the groin with the gun, and I was on my knees instantly, barely containing a scream. "Now, right now, where is it?"

He thumped me on the back with the gun butt, and I heard metal on wood. "What's in the backpack, cowboy?"

I tasted dirt, then was up and reaching back for the sawed-off with one hand and grabbing for his gun with the other.

"Jesus!" He pinned the fully drawn sawed-off against my shoulder with his heavy boot before I could bring it to bear, and yanked his own gun away. I rolled onto my back, he kicked me once in the face, and I almost had him lined up when he connected with my hand and the sawed-off flew off into the darkness. Another kick to the head, and this time I felt loose, and still he kicked, and used the gun butt, to my head, my ribs, and as I faded out, I thought to myself, Good job, Riley. You've pissed him off.

I awoke coughing out a mouthful of seawater. When I opened my eyes, the open jaws of the dead dog were only inches from my face. I jerked back and lifted myself up, and then sank down slowly. I was lying in the bottom of Desmin Lowe's quahog boat, and as the bow lifted, the foul-smelling bilgewater rushed underneath me. I kept still, taking stock of my injuries. Breathing caused pain; it felt as if I had a cracked or bruised rib. An upper back tooth felt loose. My legs seemed intact.

"Cowboy, I know you're awake," he said behind me. "Puke in my boat and I might lose my temper again. And you know what that feels like."

I sat up and found my ankle tied to a couple of cinder blocks by a thick piece of hemp. We were heading out of the little inlet, and the moon was just clear enough for me to see the outline of my sloop.

Lowe was standing in front of the little wooden cabin, holding the steering arm of the outboard by an extension. My dinghy was trailing behind. He had a battery-powered lamp in the cabin, muffled by white cloth. It gave off enough dim light for us to see each other. "Those cinder blocks are just to keep you steady in my boat. I don't want to take a chance on you jumping overboard, or maybe pulling some karate shit, you're such a big fucking surprise."

"What're you going to do with me?"

He kicked me in the stomach. "No questions. Answers. I can either take this automatic with the silencer you gave me, and put one right behind your ear so it's over nice and easy. Or I can take my time, maybe blow your dick off for starters. It doesn't make any difference to me. Either way, I'm gonna get my coke, and get Cracker off my back. Next run he's up, I've got to deliver my end, or it's me he's coming after. He's gotta deal with the Colombians already. This kind of low-level shit is giving him a slow burn, man, and I am not gonna be on the fucking receiving end when he goes off. So where's my shit?"

"Cracker's got you scared, doesn't he?"

He aimed at my groin. "Right now, asshole. Where's my coke?"

My insides shrank, and I said, "All right. Hold it. The stuff's on the boat."

"Liar," he said distinctly. "Why would you be carrying it there?"

I hesitated.

He straightened his arm.

"Because I planned on killing you," I said quickly. He hesitated.

"I was going to tow your boat into the bay, with you in it. I'd leave some of the coke with you, enough so the cops would think you'd had some sort of falling-out with your partner, but you still had the coke. That would get them off me."

He licked his lips. "Cracker was right about you, man, he should have killed you that first night." He raised the gun to my head. "Where is it in the boat? Then I'll put you down easy."

"I'll show you."

He fired the gun. It made a chuffing noise, and beside me several quahogs in a basket shattered. Splinters of shell and bits of foul-smelling fish hit me in the cheek.

"Stuff's rotted, hasn't it?" he said. "Now where the fuck's the coke?"

"Hidden on the boat. You could find it, but it'd take you hours."

"Nice of you to worry about my time like that, cowboy. Now why do you want to get on that boat?"

"I get to live until then." I rubbed my face. "I've got to explain that?"

He studied me for a few seconds in the faint light, then snorted. "You're looking for another chance to get cute. Well, first try, I blow your balls clean off. See how that wife of yours welcomes you to heaven like that."

He had me tie up to the *Spindrift* and cut me free of the cinder blocks. "Okay, you first. Climb up there and stretch out belly down on top of the cabin." I did as I was told, while he stepped up.

"Tell me something," I said. "How come you stuck Cory's body under my boat?"

"Shut up." He grabbed my arm and hauled me to my feet. His strength was appalling. "None of your chatty bullshit. Just give me the stuff."

"It's down below."

"Well then, let's go." He shoved me into the cockpit, and stood on the seats as I pulled out the washboards.

"I want some light on down there," he said. "No more than one, and keep it faint."

I reached in and flicked the power switch on, and set just the port-side interior light over the galley area. He nudged me with the gun, and I stepped below. He followed, and pressed me down against the counter as he pushed by, so he could stand behind me. "Where is it?"

I pointed to the open storage bin just behind the icebox, underneath the electronics panel. The food cabinets were at right angles to the bin, and I could see in the faint light the gleam of the butcher knife, right where I had tossed it when Alicia had come on board in Newport. He leaned forward, trying to peer down into the bin, but it was too deep. All he would have found had he reached in were a few six-packs of soda and beer. But it was large enough for a suitcase-size packet of cocaine.

"Get it," he said. "Cracker's gonna be one happy trucker come Saturday, and when that bastard's happy, I'm happy."

"Who are you guys?" I asked, letting my voice shake.

"Who I am is richer than you'll ever be." He sounded more triumphant now, almost friendly. Cracker clearly had him more scared than my showing up with a gun. "And I'm sure as shit going to live longer." He shoved me toward the bin. "Hurry up, slick. I'm gonna watch your hand real close, and if anything comes out of there other than my snow, I'm going to spread your brains all over this boat." He put the gun to my head and stood just behind my left shoulder.

I reached down with my left hand and grabbed hold of the plastic loop of a six-pack and started to pull it up slowly. I yawned nervously, my mouth dry. With my right, I braced against the edge of the cabinet, and when I sensed Desmin was leaning forward over my left shoulder to look down into the bin, I grasped the knife handle. "Did you kill her?" I said, facing the cabinet.

"Cracker," he said impatiently. "What's it matter, cowboy? I'm gonna do *you*."

I spun around to the outside, knocking the gun off my head

with my right elbow. The gun chuffed. I grasped the sleeve of his right arm and pinned his gun hand between my upper arm and chest. The knife was right in his face, and he roared, shoving me back against the galley counter, his strength lifting me right off the cabin sole. He dropped his chin down, and I couldn't get at his throat. He spun me around and ran me at the forward bulwark.

Sticking my foot out, I tripped him, and swung his shoulder against the bulwark. He tugged at the gun, and I kept my elbow and left hand tight against it, hugging it close. When he reared back, he pulled me on top of his belly, and I lost my footing. He punched me with his left, a blow that knocked the breath out of me. His own breath was rushing in frantic gasps. I couldn't get much leverage with the knife, cramped up like that, but I twisted my wrist up and did what I could.

I sliced off most of his upper lip.

His voice rose into a high-pitched scream, his mouth black with blood in the poor light, and when he reflexively put his head back, I cut his throat. Blood spumed against my face and shoulders, and he screamed again through the tug of steel through flesh, his eyes wide and amazed, and then he slumped against the bulwark.

I pulled him back against the stairway, then climbed out and hauled him with desperate strength up into the cockpit. I shoved him over the side into his boat. The whole time, his warm coppery-smelling blood was raining down on me and the deck. The thump he made as he landed in the work boat did it for me. I hurried to the opposite side and vomited again and again, until I was empty.

After I was finished, I sat in the cockpit, trying to consider my position. I had murdered a man—by any legal standards—and his blood covered my boat, and it was smeared in my face, hands, and hair. And I was anchored a few hundred yards offshore in one of the most popular bays on the East Coast. And behind the physical nausea, and the heart-pumping exhilaration created by adrenaline, I sought some response, some recognition that killing him had provided some vindication for Ellen.

There was no blessing, there was no real appeasement. Simply a recognition of something necessary done, a checkmark.

One down, another to go.

I set the boat on autopilot for Hope Island, and found a bucket and a bar of soap. I washed my hands in the sink, then put a line around the handle of the bucket, threw it overboard, hauled it up, and doused myself a dozen times in the cockpit before I began to feel clean again. I quickly mopped up the blood in the cabin, and used the lights as much as I dared to see how well I was doing. I used plenty of fresh water and soap, but knew that none of my cleaning would make much difference if a police forensic team went over the *Spindrift*. Luckily the bullet he got off had lodged itself in the radio, so I did not have to deal with a sinking boat.

Now that I had killed Desmin, I did know something that I hadn't known before—I didn't want to get caught. That was important to me, not only because if I was in jail I couldn't get to Cracker, but because I did want to have a life after this.

I scrubbed harder.

My every desire was to cut the quahog boat free and sink it right there. But the water was only about twenty-five feet deep in much of Narragansett Bay, and so heavily fished that I could envision some quahogger dropping his rake right on Desmin Lowe. So I doused the light in his boat and turned on the *Spindrift*'s running lights, figuring that under the bright moon I ran more risk in the bay of the Coast Guard approaching me for not having them on.

Once at Hope Island, I set a course for the Jamestown Bridge, and from there, out of the bay into Rhode Island Sound. The *Spindrift* plowed along, barely making over four knots with the heavy wooden motorboat and the dinghy in tow. The ocean swells started soon after the bridge, and I went forward, occasionally using a high-powered flashlight to look out for lobster pot buoys. At some points, they formed a veritable minefield, and more than once I hurried back to the wheel to alter course. I thought about Desmin's comment about "someone picked up our pot, stole from us." Perhaps that was how Cory and he made their exchanges of cash and coke. Perhaps I was motoring past another cache of their drugs and money right now. Visions of the morning sun rising on me frantically trying to free a buoy line from my prop kept me straining to see in the dark.

An hour and a half later, I cut the engine. The depth gauge read over one hundred feet. I hauled the quahog boat up close, and stepped in. The bilgewater was cold against my feet, and when I flipped on the cabin light, I saw it was tinged red with Desmin's blood. I tied one cinder block to his ankles, and the other to the dog's body.

Before heaving them over, I knelt beside Desmin, looking through his pockets for something that could help me find Cracker. In the upper pocket of his shirt I found a crumpled yellow slip, which looked to be some sort of bill of lading. "ACE Van Lines" was the company name at the top. Borenson had said Desmin had a regular job in addition to the quahogging, and Desmin himself had said come Saturday, Cracker was going to be "one happy trucker." There was a Warwick address on the yellow paper.

I heaved Desmin over the side, feeling watched every moment, half expecting a Coast Guard boat to come crashing out of the darkness, white lights glaring. Back in the *Spindrift*, I towed Desmin's boat another half mile. I retrieved my two guns and dumped his rifle overboard. I pulled my dinghy up and secured it to the sailboat, then checked the quahog boat for additional flotation, Styrofoam under the seats, but there was none. Desmin Lowe had lived dangerously. Using a rusty hatchet I found in the toolbox in his little cabin, I chopped open the roof to make sure no air might be captured there, then put two big holes in the wooden hull.

The oversized outboard on the stern took it down remarkably fast. The line to the *Spindrift* snapped bar-tight. A wave slapped the bow around, and suddenly the *Spindrift* was listing hard to port. The quahog boat was dragging it down on the quarter. I clambered up the stern ladder, my heart pounding, suddenly convinced that I was going down with Desmin.

But I chopped the line with the hatchet in time, and his boat sank into the black water. I was alone on mine, the sweat on my face already cooling in the ocean breeze, my first killing accomplished.

18

Ellen's funeral was at eleven the next morning. I awoke at the mooring in Newport as the sun rose. I had spent a fitful hour dozing, and I wanted a good look at the boat before heading off. I put on my bathing suit, dove in, and did a slow crawl around it, my bruised ribs sending bolts of pain throughout my body. But I had no choice; I needed to make sure I had washed the blood off sufficiently in the dark.

Even though I had done a thorough job, when I climbed back on board and headed below deck I could smell him. I spent an hour sponging off every square inch, but still the smell was there. Whether it was there in reality or just in my imagination, I didn't know. Along the way, I found the bulletproof vest I had stowed away. It amazed me that I had not thought to wear it the night before—what else was I forgetting?

I packed it along with the automatic in the backpack, and put the sawed-off shotgun in my dive bag. I left the portholes open, and took the first launch out.

By the time I reached home, I had stiffened up so that every step was excruciating. I showered, took four aspirin, and had a cup of coffee. In the mirror, I saw a big bruise on my chin where he had clubbed me with the gun butt, and my sides were mottled black-and-blue. My eyes had big thumbprints underneath. I looked like a man who had spent the last twenty-four hours stumbling-down drunk. I decided to complete the image, for the sake of the police who were sure to be there. I downed a full tumbler of scotch. Better they think I had spent the night in a self-absorbed drinking bout than start asking if I had been in some sort of fight.

I left my car in the funeral home's parking lot and rode alone in the first limo. When I approached Geoff and Sylvia at the church, he shook his head wordlessly. Apparently, whatever connection I had made with Geoff at the meeting with the mortician did not include sharing our grief publicly. I stood alone in the front left pew; they stood in the right one. I could see Sylvia's lower lip trembling, and I stepped back and watched the church fill. Ellen's other relatives stared, their hostility barely contained: Jenny, her younger sister; Burt, her older cousin by a year; her aunt Cynthia; and all the others. My lack of tears probably further deepened my culpability in their eyes. But I felt far away from them, found myself impatient with the funeral ritual. Holding Ellen's body moments after her death had brought the truth home to me—I didn't need this ceremony to grind in the finality.

A number of business acquaintances came, including Geena and other members of my staff. I was surprised to see Derby standing near the back, talking with Leon Gotting, another photographer. His head was down close to Leon's ear, and I wondered if he was describing how I had blackmailed him. When he looked up, his eyes seemed to lock on mine, and I nodded, but he gave no indication that he noticed.

Just before the service was to begin, Nick came in. He walked slowly up the aisle. His head and hands were bandaged, and he winced as he blew his nose.

"You don't look well enough to be here," I said, as he moved in beside me.

"I'm not," he said. "And I never will be." He apparently registered the hostility from Ellen's family, the cool speculation from my acquaintances. As the minister stepped to the pulpit, Nick said quietly, "What the hell have you been doing to yourself? You look worse than me."

Afterward, as they lowered the casket into the ground, I noticed Derby and Nick talking. It was the first time Nick had stepped away from me that afternoon, and now I saw him looking back at me, his eyes hard.

Detective Swampscott had joined the funeral procession, and when we started back toward the cars, he walked over and shook my hand. He wore the professionally sympathetic expression of the undertaker. "I want to extend my condolences," he said.

"Looking for faces that match the Identikit?"

He nodded his head. "It happens often enough that we always check."

I saw Nick striding away from Derby now, his pace too fast for his condition. I turned back to Swampscott. "Thanks again, Detective."

"We'd like to talk with you some more."

"All right," I said, but stepped away from him to head Nick off.

"What're you doing?" Nick said, in a barely suppressed whisper. "Derby told me you forced him to supply coke." Nick's grip on my arm was still strong, but his eyes looked hollow, feverish.

"Go home, Nick. You're not up for this yet. There's a cop right behind me."

"So? Maybe I'd be doing the right thing telling them. Jesus, you were really in on something with those guys?"

"What do you think?"

I waited.

He met my eyes, then turned away uneasily. "I don't know. If not that, what then? Why did you buy it?"

"I can't go into it."

Fiercely, he whispered, "Well, that's too goddamn bad. Look, I'm sorry I broke down on you when you came to see me. I know you're going through shit. But I'm going to grab that cop and we're going to talk all this through, and this bullshit is going to end now."

I grabbed his arm as he started off, and he yanked it away. He started to say something, then he looked past me. I turned to find Sylvia behind me.

She lifted the black veil and said, "Riley, the family is coming back to the house."

"Sylvia, I—"

She shook her head calmly, and I realized she was heavily sedated. "No, Riley, I'm not inviting you. I'm just taking what little opportunity I have to hurt you in some way. You were once one of us." She looked at me almost wonderingly. "You're drunk, and feeling sorry for yourself. Well, self-pity is all you're going to get, mister. Crawl back to where you came from. You're a brutal man, Riley Burke, a brutal, selfish man."

Geoff took her elbow. "Come on, let's go."

"I just wanted to say that," she said, in mild protest. "I don't ever intend to speak to him again, I just wanted to say that."

Nick touched the back of his head gingerly, and winced. "Jesus Christ. Let's get out of here. I took a cab, so give me a ride back and tell me the whole thing on the way. Then I'll decide what I tell the cops."

We didn't speak until the limo driver dropped us off at my car. Nick leaned back into the seat and closed his eyes. "Talk to me."

"How would you handle it again, if you had the chance?" I asked.

"I can't think of a more useless speculation."

"But you have. What did you come up with?"

He shrugged. "The kind of revenge stuff you'd expect. Blazing guns, winning the battle. All that shit I should've grown out of by the time I was eighteen. Thank God I'm old enough to know better."

"That's why you tried to fight the gunman with the billy club."

"Look what it got me."

"You're here."

He looked sharply at me, but apparently saw no rancor on my face. "I didn't do anything to deserve it, particularly. I was just lucky. And she wasn't. That's all."

"So forget luck. Answer my question—what would you do differently if you had the chance?"

The shrug again. His voice sounded bored. "Change the direction. Not sit there waiting for them to make a move."

"And how would you do that?"

"I don't have a clue."

He was silent for the next few minutes. When I arrived at his house, I turned off the ignition and faced him.

"You do?" he said. "You know how to find him?"

"I can't go into it if you're going to go to the police. Nick, if I don't take care of this my way, I'm as good as dead. I can't rationalize this away."

"Why not use the police if you have ideas?"

"Because I was responsible. Me. I involved the police before, and maybe they did their best, but that doesn't change the fact that Ellen's dead."

"So it's revenge. Straight revenge. You intend to kill them."

He nodded his head. Slowly, he said, "I can understand how you would feel that way. But can you actually do it? That's the question. This isn't the Wild West, and it's not Vietnam."

"It is to them. And now it is to me. Understand, they're going to try to kill me, and maybe Rachel."

He cocked his head at me. "You think so? All this publicity, all this attention, you think they're still coming after you?"

"Yes, I do."

"Let me help. I'll keep an eye out for Rachel."

"I've got that covered," I said. "An off-duty cop is sticking with her."

He stared straight ahead, and his voice was tired when he spoke. "What was I thinking? I'm the guy that let them kill Ellen."

"You fought to save her, practically unarmed. It's not like that."

"Sure it is. It's just like that. But you can't stop me. Get off your goddamn horse, Riley, and remember they shot me, not you. I'm going to help look after Rachel, and that's it."

I bit back my argument. He was right, of course. I couldn't stop him. So I put my hand out, and said, "Thanks, partner."

"So what leads do you have?"

I told him about Alicia, and my plan to work it back through her: either she might have a link directly back to Cracker or she might be able to help me find the person who originally stole the coke, and from there I might find a way back to Cracker.

I didn't refer to Cracker by name, and I didn't say a word about killing Desmin Lowe. Nick was my best friend, but I wasn't willing to confess murder to anyone.

19

Nick said he would call Rachel later that day, and I left with his promise that he would keep what I had told him to himself. At home, I found the red light on the answering machine blinking. The first message was from Borenson, and as I scrolled through the following calls from reporters and acquaintances offering condolences, I thought about my next step.

My first reaction was to ignore his request to come down, but then figured I'd better at least put in another appearance with the Newport police. I wanted to track down Cracker through the ACE Van Lines lead myself, but if I didn't keep helping the police work through Alicia, they might get suspicious and want to talk with Desmin Lowe again. And if they found out he had disappeared, sooner or later they might show up at my boat with a court order and forensics team.

Yet wearing a wire in against Alicia could land me in the same spot—if one of Cory's customers *did* lead the police back to Lowe, then the police would probably be showing up just a little later.

I had to warn Alicia somehow, but not scare her off. Before attempting that, I needed to know more about her. She was so full of inconsistencies I couldn't figure how she might react. What I really needed was to talk with someone who knew her.

And that answer was possibly supplied by the last message. "Ah, Riley, this is Evan McArthur. Just wanted to get back to you. I did hear from Jack Reynolds this morning. He did remember the name of the young prostitute."

I couldn't believe it when I first heard him. I rewound the tape and listened again. ". . . Linda Noel. That's Linda Noel. Hope that helps."

The launch driver.

I was stunned. The impression she gave me was of such an earnest young woman, I had a hard time conforming that with my idea of a prostitute. Although I should have known better; most of the hookers in the Tenderloin district had been capable of playing dozens of roles.

Still, I had a hard time seeing it.

But perhaps her being involved with Cory for a long time might explain why she would be willing to come up to the dock while we were fighting with Cracker. It was consistent with what everyone said of his powers of persuasion that she would risk herself to save him.

Perhaps it said still more about her.

Either way, since Alicia and Cory had once been lovers, there was a good chance Linda knew Alicia. Borenson had not said anything to me about her knowing Alicia—and therefore maybe that was her secret. The danger in going to her directly was that she might tell the police. And if it came out that I had lied to them about Cory and Alicia's relationship, Borenson would have some very hard questions for me.

But there seemed to be no choice, I decided. I would go to see her after the launch service closed.

I called Borenson and made an appointment for noon the next day. He said he wanted to be in the room when I called Alicia. When I pointed out there was no guarantee she would be home and that it might be a wasted trip, he said, with heavy irony, that it was the only way he could "guarantee" the batteries in the recorder were fresh. I brushed past his sarcasm, saying we could talk about it later. He let it drop, perhaps remembering that just a few hours ago I had buried my wife.

Soon after I hung up with Borenson, Rachel called. "Are you sitting in your house alone?"

I told her I didn't want to talk.

"Riley, do we deserve this somehow? I can't believe that I somehow caused Ellen's death. That's just not right. I didn't do anything worth that, neither did you. Could you come over?"

"I can't."

"Yes, you can. Come to my house, check out my guards, whatever. I want to talk to you, I'm in this with *you*."

I started to push back harder, then decided I was being unfair. She really *didn't* deserve the way her life had been turned upside down. I told her I would be there within a half hour.

Sheenan opened the door. "Somebody gave you a good clip on the chin," he said.

"I stumbled last night."

Sheenan holstered the gun he had been holding alongside his leg. A younger man with bulging muscles wearing a gray cutoff sweatshirt walked into the foyer and said, "I've stumbled like that more than once. Found tomato juice, lots of pepper, and about two shots of vodka first thing in the morning does wonders." He adopted a quick look of concern as he put out his hand, saying, "Mick Caruso. Sorry about your loss."

"Don't kiss his ass, Mick," Sheenan said.

Caruso acted as if Sheenan hadn't spoken.

"Hell of a thing," he said, shaking his head. "Hell of a thing."

"I'm going to sack out," Sheenan said disgustedly, and faded off.

"Guy's fresh as a rose, isn't he?" Caruso said. "Rachel's in her bedroom. I think she'll be right out. You shouldn't mind Sheenan too much. He's a grouchy old bastard full time, but he's good at what he does." Caruso took a rubber ball from his back pocket as we stepped into the kitchen and began squeezing it, the muscles in his right forearm as sharply defined as steel cables. "Hired me, didn't he?"

"Are you with the Boston police too?"

He laughed. "Not likely. I'm my own man. Sheenan couldn't bring anyone else on the force in on this—he's going against orders. This is pure vendetta, and they don't go for that."

"So no one knows we're doing this?"

He made a derisive noise. "At best they're going to drive by the apartment a few more times a day. You've got to understand—nothing's happened in *Boston* so far."

A gun appeared in Caruso's left hand. "Not bad, huh? Sheenan's got this place rigged like a goddamned arsenal."

"Cute. But the guy I have in mind won't take the time to watch you play with a rubber ball."

"We can accommodate that, too." Caruso slipped the gun back behind the refrigerator. "Exercising and this kind of game, keeps me occupied. Some guys, this type of duty, they sit down, watch TV, fade out. Not me."

I had no doubt he was telling the truth. Caruso had a quick, nervous energy, but he walked with an easy balance that I suspected came from martial-arts skill. The entire time he talked, his eyes flitted between me, the doorway, the windows, constantly taking it all in. Now they shifted to Rachel as she joined us in the kitchen.

"Mick show you his kitchen trick?" she asked lightly. "Sometimes it's like first grade in California. We do drills, and I have to hide under the bed and call the cops. We're having all sorts of fun, right?"

"Right you are, ma'am," Caruso said. To me, "She's bored."

"That's one of the reasons I invited you here, Riley. At least you won't talk about me as if I'm not standing right here."

"Uh-oh." Caruso stepped out of the room.

"It's a joke to him," she said. "It's a damned joke. I'd say I wanted to get rid of him, except he helps the time pass, and he really is so confident. He figures he can handle anything. These days that's kind of an impressive quality, don't you think?"

I nodded.

"I'm chattering, I know. And you look awful. Look, sit down, okay? I haven't had any lunch. I was going to open a can of soup or something. Will you join me?"

"Coffee will do."

"Soup," she said decidedly. "You're in my home, I'll make the culinary decisions. You look like you need it."

She took a beer from the refrigerator and filled a mug. I tasted it, and watched the stiff set of her shoulders begin to loosen as she moved around her kitchen, heating the soup, toasting bread. She buttered the toast and gave it to me on a heavy stoneware plate. I nibbled some, mainly to be polite, and found I was ravenous. She glanced at me as she was pouring the soup and put two more slices in the toaster.

"Where were you last night?" she asked. "I called. I didn't leave a message on your machine, but I did call."

"I didn't want to talk with anyone."

"And not now, I suppose."

"Not really." I thought about my telling Ellen how we needed to communicate more. Now it sounded so futile, like so much psychobabble. What could words change? I watched Rachel's hands as she laid out the bowls of soup and the silverware. She wore a clear lacquer on her short, trim nails, and now her hands seemed to reflect her own confidence returning, as she folded the cloth napkins quickly, as she poured the rest of my beer in the mug and walked over to rinse the bottle in the sink.

"So tell me what's going on," she said.

I sketched the police version of what I was doing, telling her about how Alicia had joined me on the boat, and how I was going down to Newport to wear a wire against her. As I spoke, Rachel's eyes began to focus on a spot just over my head.

"I wouldn't trust her," she said, her voice remote.

"Of course not."

Rachel shook her head, as if to herself, and said, "I can't believe this. I haven't even met this woman, and I'm jealous of her. I know this is the wrong time to discuss this—but you don't feel anything for me, do you? You never did."

I felt exasperated. "I apologize for leading you on that night, Rachel. But otherwise, I think I've been clear enough. I like you, I feel protective of you. But no, I don't love you, I don't even want to have this conversation right now."

"I don't deserve this."

"Who does?"

"Maybe Ellen did."

Cold anger swept through me, replacing any thought of explanations. "What the hell is that supposed to mean?"

"I don't _know!_" She practically shouted the last word. Caruso stepped quietly into the room, took in the situation with his quick eyes, then backed out.

"I do know this," she said intensely. "Cory was a selfish man. I could tell it the instant I talked to him—he had those good looks and he expected everyone to fall over themselves to help him. Well, damn it, Ellen was cut out of the same cloth."

"Ellen is dead." I stood up. "She's my wife, and I buried her this morning."

Tears slipped down Rachel's cheeks. "You'd better go."

Sheenan appeared as Caruso led me to the door, and bared his yellow-toothed smile. "See you later, heartbreaker."

At one in the morning, I was sitting across from the launch service parking lot, waiting for Linda to tie the _Dauntless_ off for the night and head home. I had rented another nondescript sedan in Providence, and had brought along a big Thermos of coffee.

I had already gone through half the coffee, waiting for her, thinking about Ellen. My eyes felt gritty and sore. The caffeine and nervous energy kept me on a kind of high. I had listened to punk rock on the drive down from Providence, the volume cranked up as far as the speakers in the rental car could take. The music was primal and abrasive, and I had used it to feed some of my anger toward Rachel. I knew there was some truth to what she had said about Ellen, and yet her comment had infuriated me.

A half-dozen people walked up the dock into the parking lot about twenty minutes after the hour. Several were women. I was looking at one who looked a bit like Linda heading toward the Wharf when I heard the chatter of a small engine being started, and I saw Linda riding out of the parking lot on a moped.

Following her at a discreet distance wasn't easy. The traffic was minimal, and she made frequent turns through the winding streets. Luckily, she didn't have far to go. She passed the police station, went on past the hospital, took a left, and pulled up in front of an apartment building. I drove by and parked a block down. As I walked back up, I could see her rolling the moped into a narrow alley and chaining it to a drainpipe. She glanced my way as she hurried up the stairs, then did a quick double take, her straight hair whipping across her face as she apparently recognized me.

"Linda," I said, starting up the stairs behind her. "Just give me a minute."

She pushed open the glass foyer door and slapped the door buzzers. "Open it!" she cried, and I stopped in my steps. She reached into her anorak, and I heard the jingle of keys.

"Easy, easy. I'm not going to do anything to you. Look, my hands are in my pockets."

She turned, one hand out in a defensive manner. "Back off," she said. "I don't want anything to do with you."

"I bet Professor Judd Streeter said the same thing at first."

She blanched.

"You've been with Cory a long time, haven't you? And the police don't know that." I stepped up to the stairs, my hands in my front pockets as promised. I didn't realize her leather-covered key chain was actually a spray container of Mace until she fumbled with the safety guard over the trigger button. The one shot of liquid she let off hit my palm as I lunged forward and wrenched the container and keys away. She cried out and backed against the door, her arm up to cover her face, elbow in to protect her stomach.

I unsnapped the key ring from the Mace and handed the keys back to her. "I'm not going to hit you, Linda. No matter what." She took the keys.

"Now, what's it going to be? Do we talk, or do I go to the police? Tell them about the blackmail scheme, the sixteen-year-old prostitute."

"I wasn't a prostitute!" Her lips trembled. "Besides, I was practically another person then."

"Maybe so. But the police think that you just happened to know Cory slightly from working in the same harbor. As far as I'm concerned, that means you're lying. And I want to know why."

"Let it go, will you? Just let it go."

"My wife was killed. I'm going to find out who's behind it and why."

"Oh yeah, your wife," she spat out. "You were with that other woman, the blonde—don't give me how you're going to make it all up to your wife now." Linda unlocked the door, but I held the knob firmly. She jabbed me in the belly with her right elbow and tried again to push open the door. I held her at arm's length, trying not to hurt her—and she landed a solid kick against my shinbone. Her shoulder under my hand was all tightly coiled muscle and bone, and I felt as if I were being given a beating by a small, strong child. I let her go, and tried to act as if her kick was not as excruciating as it really was.

"I guess it's not going to work, Linda. I'll call Borenson and let him deal with you. Four people have been killed so far, and I don't want you, me, or Alicia to be next."

She hit the doorframe with her fist, rattling the glass, as I reached the street. "Don't tell them," she pleaded. "Just leave us out of this."

"Say it—who do you mean when you say 'us'?"

"If I tell you, will you promise to drop it with the police?"

"Not for that. But if you help me, tell me everything you know, I'll do everything I can to keep you out of it. And that's a promise. Now, is Alicia the other half of 'us'?"

Linda said miserably, "Yes. And when Cory was alive, he was too."

"Thanks. Now, what else?"

She shoved the door open. I caught it just before it slammed, and followed her up to her third-story apartment.

20

Her apartment was surprisingly large, a big one-bedroom decorated in soft grays, blond wood, clean white walls. She apparently noticed me taking it all in, because she said, "Not bad for a water taxi driver, huh?" She closed her bedroom door, and I turned on the kettle and went over to her door and listened, thinking she might have gotten cold feet and decided to leave by the fire escape.

But she was out a few minutes later, having changed out of the anorak into a dark blue sweater. She hurried past me to the bathroom, and when she came out the tendrils of hair framing her face were wet. "God, it feels good to have some of the salt off."

I looked at her more closely. She was much prettier than I had realized. Her skin was flawlessly smooth; her eyes were blue-gray. With the bulky anorak gone, the image I had of her being rather shapeless changed. She had a lithe, firm body.

She nodded at the stools around the kitchen island, and I sat across from her. When she flicked on the light, I saw her wince. "Jesus," she said. "Somebody hit you, didn't they?"

I shook my head, saying that I had stumbled the night before.

"Uh-uh. Somebody hit you. I know what that looks like."

"How?"

She looked at me more closely. "When did you last sleep?"

I pulled back. "What do you know about the man who attacked Cory on the dock?"

She shook her head. "Nothing, really. Look, I did know Cory very well once, but we haven't been close for years."

I thought of the way Alicia distanced herself from him the same way, and said, "How about you fill me in on him? How'd you end up in that blackmail scheme at sixteen?"

She pursed her lips. "Long story."

"I've got the time."

"Why should I tell you anything? I don't know who killed Cory, but I do know the type of people they are, and taking a knife or gun to a short launch driver wouldn't give them a second's pause. If I told the cops what happened, and if the guy who did all this was arrested, *and* made it to trial, I would have to testify. And then Alicia and I are dead. Maybe immediately, if he has friends. Or when he gets out of jail in a few years, he'll get us on the street. I'm twenty-two. I don't figure buying it before I'm twenty-five is what I expected out of life." She walked over to the refrigerator and took out a bottle of wine. "Want some?"

"Sure."

The wine was good, and I think just the action of sharing it with me relaxed her. "So, what is it you want me to do?"

"Tell me about you, Cory, and Alicia. What happened after you left me and Rachel on the *Spindrift*. I'm looking for a way to trace the person who killed Cory and my wife by finding who stole the coke. Also, I'd like you to pass along a message to Alicia for me."

"What good will that do? If you go tell the police this stuff, they're going to want to know how. It's not like you can just say 'none of your business'—they're not going to take that for an answer. Either way, I end up talking to them, testifying, then I'm right in the position I told you I want no part of."

She reminded me somewhat of Alicia, and I was curious about the incongruities in her personality: the toughness juxtaposed with her apparent naiveté. "Tell me about your background with her and Cory first. Starting with Professor Streeter."

She made a face. "How'd a nice girl like you end up in a photo like that?"

"Something like that."

She pushed the hair back behind her ears. Her skin was naturally fair, ruddy now from all the time in the sun. Her eyes were watchful and steady. "Okay," she said slowly. "You'd have to go back about six years. That's when I first met Cory. I was sixteen, sitting in the bus station in Boston, wearing a leather jacket I hoped made me look tougher than I was. I had thirty-two dollars in my pocket, and I knew that wouldn't even buy me a room for the night."

"Where were your parents?"

"New York. Not the city. Binghamton. Where I figure they still are." She looked at me. "You'd probably like them—they're very normal-type parents, to look at anyhow. Except my dad liked me more than he should, touched me in the wrong way, let's say. My mom didn't want to listen, said I misunderstood. He came to my room and did it the night after the candles and cake for my sixteenth birthday. And I just lay there and blubbered. But the next day after class, I saw this tough-looking leather jacket, and I thought about putting it on, and buying a knife, a switchblade or something, and coming home and killing them. But I knew I wouldn't do that, but I could buy the jacket. So I did, and with what I had left, I bought a ticket on the next bus out of New York State. And that's how I found myself in the Boston bus station, with the pimps in black capes inviting me to dinner, telling me that I was the sweetest little thing they'd seen in the past month."

"Cory was a pimp?"

"Cory was a 'social scientist.' That's the name he gave himself, but mainly it meant he liked to play with people. See how they reacted." She leaned forward. "He had money—his family was very well off. Let's put it this way: he had a dorm room at Thorton, but he had an apartment in Boston too, okay? But he got bored really easily, and he had this professor who was not going to pass him on the basis of his smile, *and* he saw a way to make himself some real money. His own money. And he wanted to give it a try."

"What was he doing at the bus station?"

"Oh, he was dragging all right. He was looking for a girl like me. And we're there to be found. Virtually any day of the week, you can go to a bus or train station and find girls like me, running from something.

"You've got to understand something about him—there was this really upbeat energy about him. Everything was a lark. And that made him better than those pimps, because he wasn't going to turn a razor blade on you, but worse, too, because you really could fall in love with that guy. He was a dream come true for looks—you've seen him. I'm pretty smart, but after a week of his attention, I would've walked into a liquor store with a gun if he had told me to. The whole time, he was talking about hustling people like it's some great profession, he had it wrapped up in so many philosophical ribbons. Taught me how to dress, how to talk. He was full of ideas. Then he'd take off for school, and leave me alone. I got so I was totally dependent on him. After about a month of this on-again-off-again, he hit me with this plan to make some money so we could get married, but there was just one thing I had to do."

"Streeter."

"That's right. I cried and cried. But he would get so dejected, say that he understood, but he thought *I'd* understand how you had to be tough to get what you wanted. And so on. Eventually, I said yes. And it was as awful as you could imagine. Judd reminded me of my father when he touched me, and it made me want to scream. Yet he was so sad, too. I never expected Cory to put the photo in the paper. When Judd killed himself, I just went catatonic. The police couldn't prove we had blackmailed Streeter, but they were able to send me back to my parents. My dad left me alone for a couple of months, but one night the door opened, and I just pushed past him and was gone.

"When I got back to Boston, I found Cory had moved Alicia in. He said that I really was too young. That she was a couple of years older than me, and that made her a woman. I was devastated. I cried and made scenes, and yelled at them outside restaurants. I got a job working tables on Newbury Street, and rented an apartment with a couple of other waitresses for a few months, until one day Cory says to me that he'd bought a huge water bed, and maybe I should move in with them. I was there within the hour, blew off my roommates, to be with my kinky little family."

"And Alicia went along with this?"

Linda poured more wine for herself and me. "It didn't start as a natural thing, for either of us, but it worked out that way. You've seen how beautiful she is." Linda's eyes didn't falter from mine. "You have to understand, neither of us thought we had a lot of choices. Cory pulled it all together for us and made it an adventure. He had been kicked out of school, and his family disowned him after that Dean Reynolds told them what he and I had done. It was like the three of us against the world."

"Where was Alicia from?"

She grinned. "Maryland. Prettiest girl in her high school, got pregnant, but with the coach, not with the team captain. Cory picked her up, made some decisions for her, and paid for the abortion. And so he had his little team. We were three hustlers. He'd tell us we didn't have to have sex with anyone, that we were working cons with him. And usually it would work that way. We all worked for a convention service. I expect you've been to some event at the Hynes Auditorium or something, and there are all of those good-looking young men and women to show you around."

"Sure."

"Anyhow, that's how I'd meet the guys. I was only sixteen, seventeen then, so sleeping with me could mean real jail time for them. I'd leave the door unlocked, take off my clothes, and before anything happened, Cory and Alicia would burst in. Her with a camera, him with a gun. She'd take the shot, throw a robe around me, and out we'd go. He'd stay behind with the gun and 'negotiate' for a 'settlement fee.' The police never had a clue, which just kind of confirmed our faith in Cory. We did that scam for a couple of years, until one of the marks got the gun away from Cory and beat him so bad we had to sell the car to pay the hospital bills.

"That's when Cory decided to go into coke. At first he just sold it to strangers, people in bars and so on. All this right in Boston. Money was coming in hand over fist, and Cory was generous enough to let Alicia and me sleep with him, and help him spend his money. Then he got ripped off. Customer pulled a gun on him in an alley, said he'd blow his head off unless Cory gave him all that he was holding."

I sat forward. "Tell me about that."

She shrugged. "I doubt it was the same sort of thing. See, he wasn't being careful then. Just doing business with whoever had the cash. The guy in the alley was a tough black dude—and Cory's face was bleached white when he came home. The guy had cut the buttons off Cory's shirt while talking to him. Held a gun with his right, a straight razor with his left. Sliced those buttons off, while telling Cory to give him the snow quickly, that he was clumsy with his left hand. Cory was shaking all night. He lay there between us looking at the ceiling. It wasn't just the guy in the alley, understand—he owed money to the supplier, and if he didn't come through he was in deep trouble.

"Next morning, he woke us up early and sent us out to hock the jewelry we'd bought. He sold off our second car at an incredible loss, and then counted up what cash he'd stockpiled and whatever we had. He sold what little coke he had left at bargain-basement prices, calling people on the phone to unload it. He had just enough to cover his loss. Then he grabbed the two of us by the hair, screaming that we were going to have to go to work again, that he wasn't going to run all the risk by himself."

"Back to what you were doing before?"

"New wrinkle. We were to find reliable customers, 'clients' he told us to think of them as."

"I didn't think finding customers for coke was any too hard."

"It's not. Finding safe, steady customers, who thought of him as Superfly—afraid of him, dependent upon him—that took some work. Get it? Carrot and the stick. He wanted me to work my way into some guy's heart, get him to buy me some coke, and make the introductions. 'Hey, I know a guy named Cory who can help you with that.' Before the guy knows it, he's half in love, he figures coke has helped him be a stud. By the time I fade out, Cory is his friendly supplier *and* Cory knows enough about his affair with me to blackmail him if he wants. You understand, the guys we were supposed to go after usually were pretty successful, a lot of them married. So Cory's got his hands on them in a couple of ways. So all he has to do is just call them, tell them his shipment is in and he's looking for their cash. They say they don't want to buy, Cory uses his old blackmail skills to convince them it'd be in their best interests not only to buy, but to buy more. Safe, just the way he liked it."

"And that's what you did?"

She glanced away. "It's not a time in my life I'm proud of. Anyway, it was just a couple of months, and I was out."

"What happened?"

Linda spread her hands on the table. Her nails were well bitten, but otherwise she had very nice hands. "Let's just say the long-term hustle wasn't what I was cut out for. This wasn't just a one-night con. I had to try and make them love me, like with Judd Streeter."

"You fell in love with one of them."

She nodded. "Alex was an engineer at one of those Route 128 high-tech companies. When Cory found out I was planning to break away, he took care of that with a few choice words to Alex. Gave him some questions to ask that I couldn't answer. But it was enough to bust me loose from Cory." She smiled briefly. "I got out the leather jacket, hit the bus station again. And that's how come I'm in Newport. I decided I liked the ocean while living in Boston, so I went right to it down here. Got a job as a waitress. Got this one almost two years ago. Taking a few courses here and there." She gestured toward a full bookshelf with her chin. "And all those self-help books. Learned a lot. Do stuff I like to do, like give kids swimming lessons."

"You're not lonely?"

She shook her head. "Being alone like this for a few years has been good. It's like I've had a chance to look at myself and say, 'Who do *I* want me to be? Not my father, not Cory.' And it's funny sometimes how much that seems like another life. I teach these kids, and sometimes I look at their daddies when they come in to pick them up and think, 'This is the type of guy I've black-mailed,' and other times I see them in a different way and figure there are guys who'll hire a sixteen-year-old hooker to slap her around for fun, and there are guys who won't—and you can't necessarily tell which is which by looking at them. But the good guys are out there. And I teach the kids too, I teach them about drownproofing—you know what I mean, when you relax into the water facedown, and then let the air in your lungs bring you to the top, and you take a breath?"

"Part of every scuba course."

"That's right. Well, when I teach them that, I think that no matter what kind of life I've led before, one day a kid might not drown because of what I taught him. And the concept of it is good too—that if you can take it, if you can survive, then there can be good things afterward. Like my life has been here in New-port."

"No other guys like Alex?"

"Not quite. I haven't been a nun entirely, but really, I'm in no rush. And now that I'm not dressing to pick guys up, I'm not having to fend anybody off, believe me."

"I don't," I said, smiling.

She smiled back, looking up at me from under her lashes, and my sense of her being somewhat asexual vanished.

"Hey," I said.

She laughed. "It's handy stuff to know." She blushed slightly.

I changed the subject. "Do you know who Cory's customers are now, and how Alicia fits in?"

"No clue as to his current customers. I've been out of it for over three years. I know Alicia kept up with it for some time. When I moved down here, they tracked me down, and we kept in kind of a loose touch. It's not like I hated them, even after what Cory did to me and Alex. I just didn't want to live the way they did anymore."

"How did they end up down here?"

"Visiting me. Cory liked boats. He needed a front job, and I guess he was able to work out some sort of arrangement with a supplier down here that he figured would be better than the one up in Boston. So he moved down here about a year ago and got an apartment. Though he went to Boston all the time, so I figure he still had most of his customers up there."

"What sort of arrangement with a supplier down here?"

"I don't know exactly. Maybe Alicia does. Something to do with being on the water—he was able to use his job somehow."

"Showing boats? Was the coke coming in off of boats?"

"I made a point of not knowing. But that's probably true. It's in the newspaper all the time, stories about the stuff being flown in from the south up to Maine. The offshore trawlers pick it up, bring it back here. I do know that he worked out some sort of arrangement where he didn't have to meet with his supplier face to face. Those guys scared Cory." She met my eyes. "You figure they're the ones who killed him and your wife."

I nodded. Desmin's boat almost certainly was part of the distribution plan. Perhaps he picked up the dope from the trawler, and he and Cory had some prearranged swap. Desmin had made a comment about me stealing one of his lobster pots. "Did Cory have access to a boat?"

"Yes, a Boston Whaler. It had one of those canvas dodgers that covers the bow. With coke, the money is the bulky object. Either way, that would be enough to cover up the load. It's not like Cory was really big-time. He was pretty conservative in his way. He wanted to keep his customers in line, make good money, live the way he wanted to. He had lots of women."

"All tied into the drugs?"

She shook her head. "No way. I'm sure he had one or two

working after I left. Alicia and he broke up right when they moved down here. She moved in with me for a few weeks, then got her own place." Linda stared at me as she said this, her eyes defiant. But she colored slightly. "He'd have other women just as treats along the way. Some of them were real stunners."

"Alicia said he was snorting a fair amount of coke himself lately."

She nodded. "That was my impression too. Like he was going to crash. I don't know if he thought he was invincible or if he couldn't stand the pressure of all the cons . . . or maybe it's just simply that he had such easy access to so much coke. She tell you about his gambling?"

"Yes."

"Do you think it's possible he was simply killed because of a gambling debt?"

"Could be, but I don't think so. Why would they stick him under my boat? Tell me, did he contact you at all the day before he died? Were you planning to pick him up at the dock?"

"He called me. Said he was scared, that he needed a place to stay and whatever cash I had. It was like that time back in Boston—he was caught short and his supplier wanted his money. He said he couldn't turn the real estate around fast enough. I told him to forget it, that I didn't want any part of it, that I was living without that kind of nonsense any longer." Linda gestured at her apartment. "You know how hard it is to make a home like this on what I make? This is my . . . my nest, this is what I think about when I think about getting my life in control. I didn't want to have to worry about men with guns. Even though Cory kept saying there was no way they could know about me, I didn't believe it." Linda took another sip. "He called me at work, and said he was really scared, he said he wanted to stay on one of the boats in the harbor. Wanted me to tell him which ones were never occupied, figured he could lay low for a couple of days. Said that if he could make it for a few days, he might be able to buy a lot more time afterward. I don't know why."

"So did you help with that?"

She shook her head. "Not until the end. When he called me at work that last time, he said he had talked to a friend and had permission to use the boat, to not give him an argument when I saw him waiting on the dock. I didn't really believe him, but at that point I agreed to meet him."

"So that wasn't just chance when you came by?"

"Well, it was a regular stop anyhow. But it wasn't clear to me at first what you had to do with it."

"What happened after you let us off?"

"I convinced him to go in and get the finger taken care of."

"He didn't argue?"

"A bit, but he agreed. At first, anyhow."

"At first?"

"Once we got back to the dock, he started back on wanting to go back to my place."

"Which boat did he want to stay on that night? Who was his friend?"

Linda shrugged. "I don't know. I think that may've been pure bull anyhow, because he knew if he saw me face to face, I would have a harder time saying no. He said he really wanted to go back to my apartment. At that point, with him sitting there with a broken finger, I gave in."

"And?"

"So, I gave him my key. He said he was going to take a taxi, but I guess he actually walked to my house. Took him about a half hour, probably."

"And he spent the night?"

"Of course," Linda said, with forced lightness. "I bandaged up his finger, then helped him feel better. He said all sorts of nice things which I didn't believe, but you know how old songs can be your favorites if you haven't heard them for a while. He stayed all the next day, and then we crawled back into bed, and that's when Alicia let herself in. She still has my key."

"Did she care?"

"You know, that should be a dumb question." Linda touched my hand. "After all our time together, you'd think she couldn't care less. But she did. She was upset. Not screaming and yelling, but she was hurt. Hurt about all the other women he was going out with, now hurt to find us in bed again together. I snapped back that she *wanted* me to take him in, and she says not like *that*, and so on and so on. Cory got into it at first, and then I lost it. I told her to take off and she did, but not before she said she was going to get us. She ran out crying, and Cory ran after her yelling, 'Don't do anything stupid! Don't do anything stupid, you bitch!'

"Then I kicked him out. I was sick of the both of them. Can't you see that? Wouldn't you feel that way too?"

"Sounds like you were a better friend to them than they deserved."

"Well, I don't know about that. If I could've held my temper another six hours or so, Cory might still be alive. At least I wouldn't feel so guilty, and distrustful of Alicia."

"Why? What does six hours have to do with it?"

"Dawn. I don't think they would've done it in broad daylight, with all the people around."

"Who wouldn't have done what?"

"I looked out the window to watch him go—it's kind of a habit I formed early on. Only this time, I saw a guy get out of a truck and put his arm around Cory. It was across the street, but even under the light out there, I could see Cory's face looked scared as he looked back at my window."

"You were worried for him."

"Oh, I knew he was in trouble." Linda's voice was shaky. "I knew he was in trouble bad."

"Why didn't you call the police?"

"That's a habit that doesn't come naturally to people like me."

"But still, if you thought it was his life . . ."

"Weren't you listening?" Linda cried. "Alicia said she was going to get back at him! She was angry enough—maybe she knew how to get back to the supplier."

"Did you recognize the man?"

"I don't know. It could've been the guy on the dock, but I don't know. It was too far away. Understand Alicia, please. She stayed with Cory even longer than I did. It was easy to fall in love with him, and I've used all those books to help me out of it.

And I could always look in the mirror, see that I was pretty, but not gorgeous. A woman like her grows up with . . . expectations, thinks she's owed a real love. And sometimes she just couldn't take the reality, you know?"

"So you think she called the man who took Cory away. You think she's in this pretty deep."

"I don't know," Linda said miserably. "I know that he's dead. And I can't help but wonder if I'm in control of my life after all, when things are turning out this way."

21

Linda admitted that she was the one who had pointed me out to Alicia in the bar. "The habit of giving her what she wants runs deep with me. I worked it out of her that she wanted to sell you Cory's address book of customers, or maybe even broker the coke herself."

"That's what she told me."

Linda nodded slightly, her eyes looking past me. "Who knows? It could be true." She suppressed a big yawn. "Jesus, I've talked more tonight than I have in the past month." Her half-smile was faintly mischievous. "I must like you," she said. "And given my background, that means either you're slime or my taste is improving."

She stood up and stretched. "Don't try to answer that. I'm going to bed now. Have you booked a room someplace?"

"No." I stood also. "Thanks for all you've told me. I do need one more thing."

"The message to Alicia?"

"Right."

"Tell me at breakfast," she said, yawning again. "No hotel, and I guarantee you there's no launch service to your boat now. Sleep on the couch." She picked up the Mace I had put on the counter. "I *do* like you, but if you come in my room tonight, I'll blind you with this."

I laughed shortly. "It's a deal."

I lay down on the couch and closed my eyes. She went into the bathroom. My exhaustion swept through me, and I was almost asleep a few minutes later when she covered me with a blanket and whispered, "It's me. My taste is improving."

She awoke me around nine o'clock, and offered me the use of her shower. I stood under the steaming water and used her pink razor to scrape the stubble from my chin. I put my clothes back on, and then explained over a quick breakfast what I wanted her to say to Alicia.

"I feel funny about this," Linda said. "I don't want to be lying. Even though I don't really trust her, I still know her a lot better than I know you."

"Tell her the truth. Just make sure you do it away from her apartment—it may be bugged. They were trying to get a warrant to tap her line, and they may've succeeded by now. Tell her I was lying when I said I had the coke. But I do have enough money to make it worth her while if she can get me that address book. And what's most important, she should take my phone call at noon when the cops are listening in, so we can try to get their attention off her. And any other time, if I use the word 'coke'—instead of 'chocolate,' which is the word she used for it last time—then that'll be her cue the police are listening in."

"Secret agent man."

"Uh-huh. She should work herself out of it, say she was just blowing smoke, that she's read the articles about Ellen, that she's scared to be involved, and she didn't really have any address book, that was just something she said to get my attention."

"Anything else, Captain?"

"Ask her for some safe place for me to meet her this weekend, preferably out of state, and I'll go there and we'll talk. Tell her to bring the address book. I'll make it well worth her time."

Linda said, "Where I come from, you pay couriers."

"What do you want?"

She looked at me appraisingly, then said, "Dinner. Dinner in the restaurant of my choice, when this is all over."

"You've got it. Flowers and champagne too."

"Like a date," she said. "What a nice idea."

I looked out the window as she putted away on her moped, standing in probably the same spot she had stood when Cory was being abducted. She said he had been hustled into a truck. Most likely Desmin's, I figured. Or maybe Desmin's reference to Cracker as a trucker related only to his owning a pickup truck— but that didn't seem likely. I made a mental note to ask her if she remembered anything else about the vehicle, if it had any lettering on the side, anything that would match it up to ACE Van Lines, the name on the receipt I had found on Desmin's body.

After she rounded the corner, I drank some of her tea and read the paper. I wanted to call Nick to see how it was going at Rachel's, but I didn't want any phone trail on record from Linda's apartment that could be linked to me. As I looked around her carefully arranged apartment, her desire to restructure her life was apparent in little phrases stolen from car bumpers, bits of wisdom from clichés like "Today is the first day of the rest of your life" to those more indicative of her dark-edged humor: "If you love something, set it free—and if it doesn't come back, hunt it down and shoot it."

Nick would love the last one, I thought. I recognized her need for them, though. When I first became a civilian again, I found

myself putting a particular emphasis on the rituals and accouter-
ments of my job: the good clothing—including for a brief period
suspenders and bow tie—but also the office, the car. I read auto-
biographies of self-made men; more than one "inspirational" book
held my attention as I figured out how to make the life I wanted
for myself.

Her books were more specifically focused upon self-help, cur-
ing problems. I looked them over, titles full of words like "em-
powerment," "choice," "determination." Under a stack of gothic
romances—turned spine-in—I found a three-ring photo album. I
felt a prickly bit of shame for being a snoop when I flipped the
cover open, but that passed immediately when I saw who was in
the lead photo. Cory. It was a good shot. He was looking over
his right shoulder, his eyes very direct into the camera. Handsome
boy with an arrogant mouth. The photo should have been in the
lobby of some summer-stock theater. Then prints of boats, Newport Harbor, the other launch drivers, random shots with a Po-
laroid. A few pages later, there was one of Alicia, those eyes of
hers arresting. The next page had a shot of the three of them.
Cory's eyes were on the camera, and Alicia and Linda were mugging it up, their cheeks pressed against his. They all looked at
least a couple of years younger, and they seemed to be at a party.
Even with all the reasons I had to hate Cory, I had to admit to
myself that his grin was infectious. He knew how to paint himself
the rogue, Cory did.

The doorknob rattled, and Linda walked in. "Put that down."
She strode across the room and tugged at my arm. "Just get out."
Her voice had a dull quality, and she was breathing quickly, shal-
lowly.

"What's the matter?"

"Go." Her skin was pasty.

"Linda," I said sharply. "What's happened? What did Alicia
say?"

She took the scrapbook from my hand and threw it on the
floor. "Get out!"

I touched her shoulder, and she tried to hit me. I caught her
wrist and said, "Enough of that. Now what did she tell you?"

Linda struggled to be free briefly, then her face crumpled, and she held my arms tightly, keeping me rigidly away as she started to cry. There was nothing girlish or affected about her tears. She let out a keening cry, and then shut her mouth as if sound were dangerous.

"Tell me," I whispered.

She nodded, but it was a moment before she spoke. "I was just so angry coming home, seeing you looking at that picture. It's like you brought this all on us, even though you really didn't. I know you were here last night. I waited up a long time, thinking you might come in to me. So I know you didn't cut her. You're not the one who killed my Alicia."

My heart felt as if it were knotting upon itself. Linda described what had happened in a flat, emotionless tone after her crying ceased. She had let herself into Alicia's building and apartment, using her own key. The place was torn apart, and she thought for a second Alicia was stripping the place to move. Then she saw the smashed glass. It was from a glass egg, a beautiful piece that Cory had bought on a whim for Alicia a few years ago. Now it was smashed in front of the fireplace, and bloody footprints led away from it into the bedroom. "I followed them," Linda said. "I didn't want to, my whole body started trembling, but my legs kept moving me, as if I didn't have any choice. Alicia was half sitting up on the floor, leaning against the bed, her robe pulled open. Her eyes were wide, and I've never seen her so scared."

Tears rolled down Linda's face again. "That's what's so awful. She could be a tough girl, she'd seen a lot. But if you knew her like I did, you'd know how soft, how sweet, she could be. And I can't, you know, tell myself that she didn't know what was happening. Her hands and arms had cuts, she must have tried to keep him back. She knew, right when he was stabbing her in the chest, I don't know how many times, she knew he was killing her, and damn it, she was so scared."

22

Linda was worried about fingerprints, even though she had wiped the doorknob off on the way out, after finding the body. She thought that was all she had touched then. But maybe she had left prints during an earlier visit.

"When was the last time you were over there?"

"A couple of months."

"Have you ever been fingerprinted?"

"No."

"How about the neighbors—would they know you?"

"I wouldn't think so. And I don't think anyone saw me today. *I* didn't see anyone."

"Did Alicia have a scrapbook like this, with your photo?"

"No. I was the soft one as far as things like that, you know, between Cory and Alicia."

"You say she lived with you for a few weeks. Will any of her old bills have your address?"

"Not likely. She probably didn't file a change of address for that short a time, and besides, you don't understand how she lives. She buys with cash. It's hard to get a credit card when you haven't ever held a straight job."

"Did she have an address book?"

Linda wiped her eye with the back of her hand. "I've got to start using the right tense, don't I?".

I waited.

"No, I don't know if she had an address book. I just don't know."

"How about Cory?" I said. "Do you think he really kept one?"

"He used to. Simple black binder. He'd make up nicknames for his customers, usually kind of insulting ones, and then whenever he called he'd use the nickname, saying it was safer in case the line was bugged. Bullshit stuff, you know, just one more way to keep them in their place. He transposed the last couple of digits on the phone numbers so that in case the police got hold of the address book somehow, between the nicknames and the wrong numbers, it wouldn't be useful as evidence."

"Do you think she had it?"

"I don't know. I guess she could've gotten hold of it easily enough. I didn't see anything like that lying around, but then again, I wasn't looking."

I put my arm around Linda's shoulders, and she let me pull her close.

"What do you think?" she said.

"You'll probably be okay, for a while anyhow. The police might find old prints, but without yours on record, I don't see how they could make a match. And we probably have some time before she's found."

Linda winced.

"I know you don't want to think of that," I said. "But it's something we've got to figure in."

"I realize we do. It's just that I'm not sure we do have so much time. I was upset, and I wiped the knob, slammed the door, then ran. It made that kind of hollow bang—like maybe the bolt didn't catch."

"And you didn't go back."

"I was *scared*, goddamn it." She pushed away from me.

"Easy. I just needed to know." I looked at my watch. It was ten-thirty. Borenson would be expecting me within an hour and a half. For all I knew, a cop could be standing over Alicia's body at that moment.

Linda drew her hair back severely as she paced back and forth across the living room. "I don't want to go to the police any more than before. You promised me you'd keep me out of it."

Thoughts rushed through my head as I watched her. Borenson would be suspicious if I didn't show up. Doubly so when Alicia was found. Linda and I could provide alibis for each other, but that certainly wasn't going to ease his suspicion. And if the newspapers picked up on it, and outlined Linda's past relationship with Cory, then Cracker might well go after her. Did Alicia's death mean she had been working all along with Cracker and something went wrong? And where was he at this moment, and what was he going to do next?

"Linda, do you have any idea how long she had been dead? Did you touch her?"

"I felt her at the throat. To see if there was any chance."

"Was there any warmth?"

"She was cool, but not completely, no. It's just like she had . . . stopped."

"And the blood?"

Linda's voice was barely audible. "It hadn't dried."

"Have you told me everything? Is there any way he might know about you?"

"I have no idea," she said. "Alicia could have said something about me. Particularly at the end."

I had to figure he would be coming for me or Rachel next. Linda, maybe.

Rachel.

My guns were in the car. If he was waiting outside, then I was stuck. I wanted to call Rachel right then, but again, I didn't want the phone trail.

Linda stopped in front of me. "What are we going to do?"

"You've got to come with me. I can't risk leaving you here."

She bit at her thumb and looked around her apartment, her haven, then back at me. "No, you can't. I don't have any choice."

The automatic was still under the passenger seat of the rental car, within easy reach. I picked Linda up at the front door and we drove over the Newport Bridge. In Wickford, I stopped at a pay phone, called the ACE Van Lines number on the receipt I had found on Desmin, and asked for the dispatcher. The receptionist put me through, and a few minutes later a man said hurriedly, "Talk."

"Hey, cowboy," I said, pitching my voice to mimic Desmin's. "Cracker in yet?"

"Who's this?"

"Who the fuck you think? Lowe."

"Dez? Where the hell you been? You sound weird."

"No shit. Cold took me off at the frigging knees. Anyhow, Cracker in yet?"

"Yeah." The man's voice held a nervous edge. "Look, I don't keep tabs on Cracker. He came in, said he needed to borrow the pickup, I let him have it."

"When?"

"When did he come in?"

"Are you deaf?"

"Last night. He brought the load in. He was looking for you then too. What, you guys doing some hauling on the side?"

"That's none of your fucking business, cowboy," I snapped back.

He continued in an aggrieved tone. "Hey, listen, I don't want any trouble with you. But I can't leave your job open if you're not going to show. I mean, I got people I report to, and they walk in the warehouse, see all the shit stacked up on the floor, and the forklift sitting there without a driver, they start asking questions. Now look, just tell me, are you working here or not? 'Cause if you're not, I've got to get somebody else. I mean, shit, you didn't even call me, you didn't answer the phone when I called your house—"

"What do you mean, he was looking for me 'then too'?"

"I mean he was looking for you yesterday, and he was looking for you this morning. *He* couldn't get you on the phone either. He looked pretty pissed off. Now I don't *want* to know what you guys are doing, I really don't—"

"Cowboy," I said quietly, "shut up."

He did.

"Now, real slow—when did you see Cracker last, and where did he go?"

"This morning," the man said defensively. "He was waiting for me, waiting for *you*, first thing this morning, around seven-thirty. When you didn't show, he took off, then he just stopped back about an hour ago. Hell, he should *be* at your place by now. Aren't you at home?"

"That's where he was headed?"

"I guess—he took the pickup."

"Got it. And cowboy?"

"Yeah?"

"I quit."

Twenty minutes later, I pulled off Route 95 into Warwick.

"What're you doing?" Linda asked.

"I need to check something out. I should be back within a half hour," I said, pulling into a doughnut shop parking lot. "Could you wait here for me?"

"Why?"

I slipped the shift into park, and turned to face her. "Because I asked."

"I'm not big on blind faith, Riley. Is this your idea of taking care of the situation? Getting me out of town, then dumping me at Dunkin' Donuts?"

"I'll be back. Promise."

"Unless something happens. Think of it this way," she said, tucking a leg underneath herself and leaning close to me. "If you don't come back, sooner or later he may come after me. So maybe I'd like to know what you're up to, so at least I'll know where to send the cops."

She had a point. Borenson would be able to figure that since I was in Warwick, maybe Desmin had more to do with it all than I admitted. Whether he could find Cracker from there was questionable.

"Tell Borenson if I don't come back," I said. "He'll put together where I went. And I'll leave a note under the driver's seat of this car, give him what I know."

"Why not just tell me?" she said, her eyes hurt. "Don't you trust me?"

"A half hour, Linda." I leaned across and opened her door.

"You bastard," she said wonderingly. "You really don't."

Driving past the dirt driveway of Desmin's house, I looked for some sign of the pickup truck for ACE Van Lines. The high brush hid the view from the road. I drove around the corner and scratched out a quick note:

Lt. Borenson, Newport Police:

Don't waste time looking for Desmin Lowe. I killed him last week, and sank his body off Brenton Reef. He was in the car, he was one of the men who killed Ellen. If you're reading this, I didn't succeed with the second. His name is Cracker, last name I don't know. Works for ACE Van Lines. My take is that Cracker trucked the coke up into Rhode Island, and Desmin handled local distribution and collections somehow on Narragansett Bay, using his quahog boat. Cory was one of probably a few local dealers, and he either tried to cheat these two or someone else stole it from him and left him to make the explanations. Cracker was doing his enforcement when I stepped in, and you know the rest.

Good luck,

Riley Burke

I hesitated for a moment, thinking maybe I should add some sort of explanation to help Linda out when Alicia was found, but I figured the less said about her the better. They had no reason to link her with the murder, and they might never find out about her previous relationship with Cory and Alicia. She had the sense to place an anonymous call to the police if I didn't return.

I took my backpack from the trunk, got back into the car, pulled on the bulletproof vest, and covered it with a light sweatshirt. I loaded the sawed-off and threw extra ammunition into the sweatshirt belly pocket.

After exchanging the note for the handgun under the seat, I walked around the block and started up the driveway to Desmin Lowe's house, the backpack over my shoulder.

23

Once inside the hedge that shut out the neighbors' view, I pulled the sawed-off free. The window Desmin had climbed through was still open wide. I walked around the back of the house first, keeping close. A window fan buzzed on the second floor, and I kept turning to look at it, expecting to see a face to go with the sound.

I walked around to the shore side. Desmin's Harley was still there, but his big Ford pickup was replaced by a yellow one with "ACE Van Lines" emblazoned on the side.

Apparently Cracker had left. But I needed to make sure.

The door had a bright new-looking keyhole plate, and I thought of the stories I had read about police using small battering rams to break down the reinforced doors of drug dealers, and decided I would go in through the window Desmin had left open. There was a plastic milk basket near the propane tank behind the house, which gave me a foot or so of advantage as I pressed myself up on the sill, leaned forward into the room, and did a quick roll back to my feet. I swept the short gun muzzle across the room. Not a sound but the fan upstairs and my breathing.

Cheap veneer furniture. A poster of a fuelie dragster tacked over brown paneling. Beer cans scattered across the floor, a coffee table turned upside down. The huge new television set had been kicked in. I walked around the broken glass into the next room. Waist-high stereo speakers, the cones sliced open. A partly dismantled motorcycle engine lay on its side.

Flies buzzed in the kitchen. The floor was covered with broken plates and glasses, flour, and drenched with the contents of the open refrigerator: milk, beer, orange juice, jelly, spaghetti sauce. A brown streak on the wall led down to a piece of steak and a splatter of beans. It looked as if someone had swept the plate off the table in a fit of rage, perhaps triggering the rampage in the rest of the house.

A small room off the kitchen was apparently Desmin's little library. From the ripped-apart pages on the floor, I gleaned that his taste in reading material ranged from religious pamphlets— *Bring Jesus into Your Heart!*—to *Hustler* magazine.

Upstairs, I went into the room with the fan, which was apparently Desmin's bedroom. It was a shambles. The mattress had been cut open, and the stuffing was strewn across the floor. The bed was shoved into the middle of the room at an odd angle. A King James Bible was pinned against the wall by a big sheath knife, the blade shoved through the spine of the open book.

Is that the knife that Cracker used on Alicia? I thought.

But there was a sheath strapped over the right bedpost; apparently Desmin kept it within easy reach. Where the bed had been, there was a square of floorboards pulled away, leaving a hiding place about the size of a small suitcase.

Desmin's clothes were on the floor, the dresser turned over, the cheap mirror smashed. I could envision Cracker working in a rage, the fan turned on to cool his sweat as he searched for the coke. Probably he gave up after finding the hiding place. Found the empty space, and nailed Desmin's Bible to the wall. Must've seemed a pretty poor substitute for Desmin—and dirt-poor as a substitute for me.

That night, Desmin had been genuinely frightened by his partner's impending visit . . . and his belief that I had the coke also seemed genuine. So I doubted he had double-crossed his partner.

But Cracker wouldn't know or care about the details. Desmin had failed him.

Alicia must have failed him, too.

I ripped the note I had written to Borenson into tiny pieces and tossed it out the window like confetti as I hurried back to pick up Linda. I pulled up to the phone booth near the entrance and called Sheenan. Since he was a cop, I doubted he would withhold information on my behalf no matter how good a shot he had at Lenny's killer. So I told him simply that Borenson had called me and said a woman I had been talking with beforehand had just turned up dead.

"Who?" he said with sharp interest. "How's she tied in? How'd he do it?"

"I'll tell you what little I know when I get there. I just wanted to be sure you two are on your toes."

I got through to Nick almost immediately and told him about Alicia, letting him assume I had heard the news through the police. "Look, I figure he may be heading up to Boston. I've told Sheenan, but you should stick it out at the agency, or stay someplace with a lot of people. Don't go home right away, all right?"

"Like hell." His voice sounded distant, as if he was frightened but trying to control it. "I'm going to Rachel's."

"No. That's exactly what I don't want you to do."

"Sorry, buddy. He scared the hell out of me, and that doesn't sit any better with me than it would with you."

He hung up.

24

On the way to Boston, I pushed the rental car up over a hundred during much of the stretch between Providence and the ramp to Route 128. Luckily, I was warned of the one speed trap by a driver across the meridian who flashed his lights, allowing me time to slow to the fifty-five limit. It was a nerve-racking trip. Linda and I had little chance to talk, since I had to concentrate hard to maintain that speed as well as keep an eye on the rearview mirror for a pickup truck with Cracker at the wheel.

As we passed through the last toll on the Mass Turnpike into Boston, I said to Linda, "We've got a dilemma."

"What's that?"

"What to do with you. I'm going to Rachel's place, because I think that's where Alicia's killer will show up. He forced Ellen to give him Rachel's full name—it should be easy enough for him to find out where she lives."

"Why don't you move her, then?"

"He could simply follow us. We might as well take care of it while we're ready."

"How're you going to do that, advertising man?"

"I've made arrangements."

"You have, huh? Hope they're good."

"Look, I need to know right now where you want to go. If he's watching Rachel's apartment, my walking up to her door might be just the incentive he needs."

"To kill you on the street." Her eyes were steady. "So with that in front of you, what's the dilemma with me?"

"Obviously you can't go with me."

"Why obviously? Taking me up to meet your girlfriend might be too awkward? Don't worry, I can keep a secret. The fact you spent the night at my place will stay with me."

Exasperated, I said, "Don't be stupid. You can't walk up the street with me for just the reason you said. He might try to kill me there. I'm armed—that's what I want him to try. I can't have you there too." We took the Copley Street exit and drove past the library. "Right now, what are you going to do? I don't have any more time."

"Pull over."

I stopped the car, and she gestured toward the subway entrance. "I'm headed to the airport. I'm going to use a credit card this time, take a plane. You can come with me. You walk in, put the card down, say the first city name you like. It's easy." She touched my cheek. "Come on, Riley, I'm just getting to know you. Don't go die on me. Just leave."

I shook my head. "I can't."

"Yes, the fact of the matter is you can. You just don't know it." She shook her head. "Never mind. Give me this woman's name, number, and address."

I scrawled the information out on the back of an envelope and handed it to her. "Go on now. Find a cop at the airport, and talk with him about anything at all until the flight leaves. Call me just before you get on the plane, and once you get there."

Her mouth twisted. "Story of my life," she said. "Two guys that I really go for: one's a creep, the other thinks he's a hero. Both get themselves killed."

Rachel's apartment was only three blocks away, and I parked just as Nick got out of his car directly across from it. After taking off the silencer, I started up the street with the automatic in my belt, hidden by the sweatshirt. I had the sawed-off wrapped in a light coat.

Nick's back was to me, and I didn't want to call attention to him, so I kept quiet as he walked behind a brown UPS van double-parked in front of her building, and simply followed a dozen steps behind. He nodded to the uniformed deliveryman. "Hot as a bastard, isn't it?" he said, as the two of them stepped into the foyer. His voice had a nervous, strained quality. I'm sure mine would have sounded the same.

The outside foyer door was closing slowly.

"Think so?" the deliveryman asked.

A green Chevy pulled up behind me, with two men in the front seat. The driver was a big man with curly black hair.

I dropped the coat from the sawed-off, cocked it, and had it in the driver's face before the car rolled to a stop. He cried out, shielding his head with his arms. Broad face, panicked eyes, the guy was in his late forties. Not much time to see him, but enough to know he wasn't Cracker.

I had almost killed an innocent man.

Before I said any words of apology, I heard the deliveryman behind me say, "You're going up to 8D? I've got something here for you."

The friendliness in his voice was something out of my nightmares. I swung the shotgun around just as the outside foyer door shut, cutting off whatever answer Nick made to Cracker.

I heard the car door opening behind me but ignored it, my

limbs feeling leaden, aware that I could never move fast enough if Cracker's intent at that moment was to put a bullet behind Nick's ear. Through the glass I saw him take what looked like a huge pistol from the package he had been carrying, then I recognized it as a machine pistol, an Uzi or something. Nick's back was to him; he apparently was unlocking the door.

I couldn't cut loose with the shotgun with Nick there.

I froze.

That's when they hit me. Suddenly my knees buckled, the shotgun was pulled from my hands, and I found myself on the pavement, the heavy voice to go with the knees in my back saying, "You're under arrest, fucker." He snapped a handcuff bracelet around my left wrist and tried to tug my right behind me.

I dug my shoulder into the sidewalk and yelled, "Get off! He's on his way upstairs, he's—"

Something hit me in the back of the head, slamming my face into the pavement. I tasted blood. "Shut up, asshole!"

"Cuff him, Lew!" The voices of both cops were shaky. I saw heavy black shoes in front of my face, and when I tugged my arm away again, the standing cop shuffled back and kicked me in the side. He said, "Will you look at this cannon? I thought we were fucked."

He kicked me again.

I tried to explain. The one on my back slammed the back of my head and said to the other one, "Genaro, help me cuff him, he's fighting me."

"Motherfucker! You pulled a piece on cops." He kicked me in the head.

A woman's voice called out, "Hey, what are you doing? Leave him alone!"

"Jesus Christ," the one standing said. He raised his voice. "Just move on, lady."

"Police!" she called, and that's when I realized it was Linda. The automatic was digging into my belly. I yanked my right arm away and dug for it.

The cop on my back pulled at my elbow and snapped, "Hey, Genaro, help me!"

"He's going up the stairs," I said. "He's got—"

"Shut up!" Genaro roared, and kicked my shoulder.

"Hey!" Linda cried, only a few feet away now.

"Miss, look, we *are* the police, and we're on the job right now."

I drew in a deep breath.

Genaro cried out.

I put an all-out effort into twisting underneath the surprised cop on my back. Genaro was clutching his groin, and Linda was already running up the street. I swung my elbow back and clipped the cop across the chin. Probably the blow did no more than jar his vision for a half-second, but that gave me enough time to pull the pistol from my belt and jam it into his gut. "Gun, partner!" he screamed.

Genaro reached inside his sportcoat jacket, and I yelled, "I'll kill him!"

He hesitated.

"Now get off," I said as calmly as I could.

"You're making a big mistake, mister," Lew said.

"Move! Right now."

He did.

I stood quickly, then backed to the apartment door. "Drop your guns," I said.

"No," Genaro said, a heavyset man with a double chin and frightened-looking eyes.

"Not me," Lew agreed.

I figured Cracker had almost a minute on me. No time to argue with these two. I said, "Apartment 8D."

"What about it?" Lew said.

I backed against the outside door, into the foyer.

"I told you. The man who killed my wife is on the way upstairs now. He's got one of those small machine guns."

"Bullshit," Genaro said. "Drop the piece, mister."

"Genaro," Lew said, warning. To me, "Explain."

The inside door was locked, of course, but it was glass.

"Not enough time," I said, and turned to smash the door with the gun butt.

"Genaro, don't!" I heard, and the glass splintered and crashed to the floor in front of my eyes. He had opened up on me.

In the distance, I heard a woman screaming—Linda, I think— and then it was as if a great fist had punched me in the back, and my body slammed through the remaining glass.

25

Glass pebbles under my cheek.

Cold marble floor.

Hoarse voices. "Is he down? Is he down, for Chrissakes?"

I'm still alive, I thought. I couldn't draw a breath at first. *My lungs. Are my lungs hit?*

"You dumb fuck, Genaro, I told you to hold it."

"He had a piece, for Chrissakes!"

I sipped air, then rolled onto my back, took in some more. *The vest. The bulletproof vest.*

"What if what he said was true?"

"Let's check him out," I heard, so I let two rounds off into the ceiling.

The noise was incredible. I scuttled back to the elevator, pushed the button, and waited on my butt, the gun pointed toward the front door. *Don't make me kill you, you stupid bastards,* I thought. When I tried to say it, nothing came out but a croak.

The elevator tone sounded.

I turned the automatic to the opening doors.

Empty.

Rolling in, I hit the button for the eighth floor, and as the elevator doors started to slide shut, the cops rushed the entrance.

"Back off!" I yelled, and pointed the gun to the ceiling so they could see I was not forcing their fire. The sliding doors began to close.

Genaro leveled a huge gun at me, a long-barreled revolver, probably a .45. But Lew hit his arm as it spoke. The sliding doors touched, and inside the metal blossomed a jagged hole, and there was a sharp tug at my left arm. Blood coursed out of my biceps, and I dropped the automatic and doubled over.

It felt as if white-hot metal had been pressed into my skin, but when I pulled back the rip in my shirt, it looked no worse than a deep scrape, and the bullet was embedded in the wall behind me. I could still move the arm fine. My left hand was shaking, but all the fingers worked. My every breath was painful; the impact of the bullets that had knocked me through the door had probably bruised or cracked a few ribs.

Under the circumstances, not so bad.

About to get worse.

Passing floor five now.

Cradling the gun in my left hand, I ejected the clip and replaced the two spent cartridges.

The elevator doors opened just as the machine gun began to chatter.

Over it, I could hear a man's guttural cry suddenly extinguished.

As I ran down the hallway toward Rachel's apartment, one of her neighbors, a middle-aged man holding a coffee mug, stepped out to look toward her door.

Until he saw me. "Jesus God!" The mug shattered on the tiles as he hurried to lock his curiosity away.

Her door was locked, too.

Shoving off against the opposite wall, I placed a solid kick over the knob, and then I was into the carnage. Cracker had Rachel by the hair, his gun at her neck.

"Drop it!" I yelled.

"Riley!" he boomed in a friendly voice, a voice that belied the horror around him, a voice a salesman would use for his favorite customer. "*Thought* I saw you downstairs. Now *you* put the gun down, or I'll cut her fucking head off."

Caruso's body was splayed out on the floor.

Sheenan had been blown up against the wall. His face was stark white, and when he saw me, he croaked, "Finish it."

"This is your talent, huh?" Cracker said. "Soft, the both of them. Neither would shoot through your buddy over there."

Sheenan slid down the wall, dead.

"It's finished, dad," Cracker said. To me, "Now, where's my shit?"

"Oh God!" Rachel cried. There was a splatter of Sheenan's blood on her cheek. "Give him what he wants, give him what he wants!"

Nick was on his knees in the kitchen. He had a gash over his right eye. "I had to let him in," he said. "He had that thing at my head, I had—"

"Shut up!" Cracker said.

"There are cops downstairs," I said.

Cracker pushed Rachel's head against the wall, his palm flat against her temple. "You're fucking with me again," he said warningly, as if I were a disappointing child telling foolish stories.

"Riley!" she cried.

"Now drop the gun!" Cracker roared suddenly. Gone was the drawl. His voice was flat, cold. "You'd better come through right now or I'm going to just take you all out and call it a loss. Now what's it going to be?"

"Cracker, you so much as scratch her, I'll kill you." I aimed the gun at his face. "The police are right behind me. You can't win. Put it down, we'll all get to live. Now."

"Bullshit." He shook his head. "You're a liar, buddy. There is some weird shit going on around here, and you're right in the middle of it. But that chick I cooled this morning told me you had the coke, and *she* wasn't lying, not with what I was doing to her. You can count on that. You know my name—Dez set me up, huh? You working with him?"

I shook my head. My aim settled just below his jugular. I said, "No. But I did cut his throat, tow him in his boat offshore, and sink him."

That made Cracker pause. He began to grin again. There was something about that grin that was different, something that I almost did not recognize, then suddenly it was obvious—he was scared. "Seems I made the same mistake about his wife," he said to Rachel. "He's hung you out." His trigger finger whitened.

I crouched, extended the gun slightly, telegraphing that I was about to shoot.

He snapped the Uzi toward me, away from Rachel. I squeezed the trigger.

His shirt moved high on his left shoulder.

The little machine gun spat bullets over my head.

Easy, I thought. *Do it right.* Behind him, Nick dove for the gun behind the refrigerator. I squeezed off another one. It was a solid shot, right into Cracker's chest.

He coughed once, and dark streaks of red slipped down his chin, but he stayed on his feet. He looked at me as if he were perplexed, and a bit embarrassed. I shot him again. It rocked him, but he held the Uzi in both hands and steadied the chattering fire in a sweeping arc. I lunged off to the left, thinking I might have another chance for a shot . . . but I was just a little too slow.

His fire was upon me.

I don't know how many bullets punched into my body, into the vest, but I was lifted right off the floor. My head bounced hard against the wall. It was Nick who finished him off, who stepped out of the kitchen with the gun and put it to Cracker's temple. I saw the revolver kick in his hand twice before I passed out, thinking that Sheenan had his revenge after all, his preparations had paid off.

26

There was a period of haze, filled with small, excruciating moments on a texture of white linen. Through a kind of osmosis I understood I was in a hospital: antiseptic smells, a man who cried plaintively for a nurse, the clink of bottles, the squeak of rubber-soled shoes on tile. A man wearing a white lab coat touched my forehead with medicinal-smelling hands and said to someone else, "Bullet was tumbling—damn thing skipped, hopped, right along the top of his skull. Lucky, considering."

I dreamed Nick was sitting between me and the window. Only instead of the window in my room, it was in a van, and the city rushed by outside. He had a bandage around his forehead, and spoke into my ear, slowly and carefully. Whenever I struggled toward understanding him, it drifted away. But later it would seep back clearly: "We told them nothing about the other one, Riley. Rachel and I told them nothing about the one you said you sank offshore. Do you hear? We said nothing."

Sometimes Desmin himself sat in the chair in my room, seawater dripping on the floor, his lips blue. "You're home, cowboy," he said. "Surprised Cracker, for sure. Me too." He threw his head back and laughed, showing me his wound.

When I vomited, it felt as if I were being stabbed repeatedly in the back and chest.

There was blue sky out the window when my focus settled on a young woman, and I slowly pieced together that she was upset. Why, I could not remember, not until her name fell into place: Linda.

I guess I said something, because suddenly Linda's face was above mine, her expression considerably brightened from that of a moment ago. "Welcome back, Riley," she whispered. "Listen, I told them how I knew Cory and Alicia. I told them I found her, got it?"

"Miss, get away from him," I heard, and saw the policeman, Genaro, striding into the room.

She turned back to me. "Tell me you're overjoyed to see me, then ask for a lawyer—okay?"

"Overjoyed and lawyer," I said, closed my eyes, and was gone.

A day later, I was sitting up drinking juice when Tom Windon ushered in a large man wearing a beautifully tailored summerweight suit and a great shock of white hair. The big man looked at me with an expression I can only describe as bemused as Tom argued with the uniformed policeman outside my door about why both of them needed to see me.

"Genaro said only one lawyer was coming," the cop said. "Not two."

"What difference does it make?"

The cop looked back at me balefully. He had stepped into the room after the doctor left that morning to say he would have blown my head off had I pulled a gun on him. "The difference is, I haven't got a reason in the world to do this guy a favor, and if Genaro said one lawyer, he meant one lawyer."

The big man handed over a business card by way of identification.

The cop's face grew slack, and he waved them in. "Screw it."

The big man's smile broadened as he closed the door.

Tom said, "That's amazing. You actually had him scared."

"Scared only of the inconvenience I could bring upon him, I'm sure," the other lawyer demurred.

To me, Tom said somewhat nervously, "Riley, glad to see you're up. Listen, that woman Linda didn't have to push so hard. I mean, she's practically been camping out in my office since the day before yesterday. I would've been up to see you even if you hadn't asked, but I had to take care of Nick first. The cops have been all over him. I got him a terrific local attorney, Sam Benoit. As she said, both of you need criminal lawyers, not a contract attorney like me." He paused—for effect, I realized. "Let me introduce Larson Mitchell."

Tom's face fell a little when I failed to react. I guess every profession has its heroes. "Larson flew up from New York on the shuttle yesterday and has been on the phone and pulling stuff together like you wouldn't believe."

"Only what I could glean from the reports Tom was able to get hold of, as your attorney of record," said Mitchell. "And I have a few friends in the media. They're already having a field day—'Enraged Husband Kills Drug Dealer'—but that's not important. You tell me what actually happened. Particularly as to how an off-duty cop ended up getting killed."

I told the story I had been mulling over since Linda had woken me. I kept it simple. I had lost my head for a few days, had purchased two guns off a man at a bar—no, I did not get a name—and had tried to do some investigating of my own. That Linda had provided me with some background, and when she found Alicia dead, I had come back to Boston to help guard Rachel. Throughout the explanation, I tested the image I wanted to create for the police: a man who had tried to take the law into his own hands for a few days, with very little success. It wasn't much of a stretch. I made no mention of Desmin Lowe, since I figured the police would assume his disappearance was a result of a falling-out with Cracker.

"Why didn't you call the police?"

"Sheenan was the police. I called him."

"Off-duty."

"So? I had no way of knowing the killer was on his way. Sheenan was on duty when he said the police couldn't wait around for something to happen. Now, how about your telling me what's been going on while I've been unconscious."

Mitchell looked at me intently, then said, "All right. I'll tell you what I know from both angles, good and bad, then you fill in the blanks. The bare bones of the situation have been outlined by your three friends, Ms. Linda Noel, Ms. Rachel Perry, and Mr. Nick Daniels. Noel came forth saying she knew Cory Dearborn sold coke and had been intimate with Alicia Nadeau. Both she and Ms. Perry confirmed that Cracker Beauregard was the man on the dock who attacked Dearborn."

"That's his name? Cracker Beauregard?"

"Actually, Roland Beauregard was his real name, but he was known to hurt people who used it. He was a long-distance trucker, and from the shipping records at the Rhode Island distributor with whom he worked, the police have confirmed he was in the area during the attack on Dearborn, your wife's murder, and the Nadeau killing. They found a cache of cocaine in a bottom dresser drawer in a sealed crate—those big wooden boxes shippers sometimes use when they're trucking up small loads from multiple sources. Presumably, he could have had a whole line of local dealers like Dearborn up the Eastern Seaboard. If he did, then perhaps there's some double-cross there that you were mistakenly pulled into. I expect Beauregard's concern was to make sure future shipments weren't going to go awry, as well as to recover the stolen coke and enforce his control. Anyway, physical evidence puts Beauregard at Miss Nadeau's apartment, and there isn't much doubt he killed her."

"So did the Newport police send the Boston police after me?"

"At that point, Newport had just found Nadeau's body and you were late for your appointment with Borenson. He asked the Boston police to check for you at Ms. Perry's apartment. Their report says you pulled a sawed-off shotgun on them—and they acted the way cops do when anyone points a gun their way. The police are going to want to know how you got guns registered to a Mr. Keiller. He said he sold them to a Carl Jorgensen, for cash, without providing any sort of paperwork. The physical description he gave doesn't look a bit like you, and so far, even though Keiller is facing some minor legal trouble himself for selling guns in that manner, he is sticking to his story."

Into it now, Mitchell pulled up a chair and said, "But that's small. What we need to do is focus upon the background of Cracker Beauregard. And on the fact that a respected policeman and his associate were killed because his brother police officers screwed up—'if only they had helped you along instead of shot you in the back,' and so on. The fact that you were saved by a bulletproof vest provided by the Newport police hurts their credibility—it reinforces the idea that the Boston police screwed up, crossed wires with Newport. And of course, there's the unfortunate UPS man. His body was found in a warehouse near North Station this morning. Poor bastard had a bruise on the back of his head—he was apparently knocked out, stripped of his uniform, and then stabbed to death. Two of the wounds clearly match the knife found on Cracker Beauregard, and there were traces of the driver's blood on the knife. As well as blood from Miss Nadeau down in Newport. All in all, you're in pretty good shape." Mitchell smiled encouragingly. "Of course, we can't get cocky. It could swing the other way. Boston is a liberal town, so vigilantism won't be so well received. You did pull a gun on two policemen. Very serious item there."

"What can you tell me about Beauregard?"

Mitchell leaned forward, rubbing his hands. "We're quite lucky there. Nobody's going to cry because he's gone. The police turned him up right away on fingerprints. He's about two years out of Starke Penitentiary in Florida. In for assault, which was actually a watered-down rape charge. Miami woman. He's been a suspect in two murders there already, both drug-related. Dropped because of insufficient evidence. But there's ample evidence with the UPS driver, and Miss Nadeau. With her, it looks like he took his glove off, maybe to touch her to see if she was dead. Then he reached out to brace himself against the bedpost when he stood, leaving us with a fine set of his prints."

Nausea swept over me. "You're right, Mitchell, we are lucky there."

He put his palms up and shrugged. "I'm just packaging it right."

Windon said to me, "It's critical that Larson make everyone in the jury box focus all their animosity on Beauregard."

"_If_ we get to trial," Mitchell said. "There's going to be an investigation, and a hearing, of course, but I'll do everything I can to show the prosecution that it would do the police more damage to go to trial than to let this die."

I hoped he could make good on his plan. Because I assumed if it came to a long trial, a police forensic team might go over the _Spindrift_, and if they found traces of Lowe's blood, I was going to have some very difficult questions to answer. "Let's go to it," I said.

Mitchell turned to Windon and said, "Thanks. This promises to be an interesting one."

Windon looked embarrassed, knowing he was being dismissed. He handed Mitchell a file and said, "Okay. . . . You're in good hands, Riley."

"Thanks, Tom."

He left.

Mitchell hitched his chair closer. "Okay, the key is publicity. Or more to the point, the threat of it. Lucky for you, I have a reputation for being a publicity hound. And the police have a very embarrassing case on their hands here. There are reporters stacked up downstairs, and that's a leveraging point for us right now, presented right. You see, this is an election year, and the DA is not going to want to come down on the side of a drug dealer, not over a respected businessman who avenged his wife's death. Better for everyone if this simply goes away, meaning they let you walk, and you in turn don't generate any more headlines."

"And how are you going to stage that?"

"First off, their attention is on Nick Daniels, and that's just fine with me. He's given some interviews already, and freely admits that he shot Beauregard in the head, killing him."

"I don't want Nick, Rachel, or Linda to get into any trouble over this. Perhaps one attorney should represent us all."

"Absolutely not. The two women won't run into anything serious. It's best for them and you to break this up into pieces. Nick's going to undergo some scrutiny—he actually killed the man—but he will almost certainly get off with justifiable homicide."

"How's he taking it?"

Mitchell shrugged. "I haven't met him. The interview read as if he just did what he had to do in an extraordinary situation. It's not something most of us could do, but from what I read he sounds as if he's all right."

I rubbed my temples, feeling an excruciating headache coming on. "Beauregard would've killed me in another second. Nick was in the National Guard—he's never seen action like that before. It's not easy living with shooting someone, no matter how justified." I thought of the shudder of the knife through Lowe's neck, and felt sickened. Now that it was over, I was exhausted, and weak. I fought to keep my head clear.

"Speaking of which," Mitchell said, "go over your own military background for me."

I outlined my service record while he took copious notes. Finally, he flipped over to a clean sheet of paper on his notepad. "Now about the two women. Linda kicked a policeman in the balls. What exactly is your relationship with her?"

That took me half a beat. What I felt for her mainly was gratitude for the loyalty she had shown me, for whatever reason. "You could say we're friends."

"Well, are you screwing her?" He put his palms out again. "Don't look at me like that. You'll be asked worse. It'll clarify things for me."

"No."

"How about Ms. Perry?"

"No."

"Never?"

I told him about our argument on the *Spindrift*.

"All right. I'll tell you what I'll do," he said comfortably. "I will talk with your friends. Again, I'm certain Nick is going to get justifiable homicide. The gun he used was registered to Sheenan, and he did not assault a cop on the way upstairs. His own gun, which Beauregard had taken away, was registered. That's the difference between you and him, and it's not inconsequential. Anyhow, once he's settled, they're going to look at you very hard. The question is whether Nick and the two women have anything on you that could hurt us. If so, I need to know it as soon as possible, so I can try to contain it or at least minimize the damage."

I told him they had nothing that would hurt me.

"You're sure? Don't even start to tell me how you trust them— let me tell you, *everyone* turns when you put them on the stand and face them with criminal prosecution. *Everyone.*"

"I'm sure."

"All right. Now, there's a lot the police don't know yet. I believe they have a line on someone down in Rhode Island who may have been working with Beauregard."

Mitchell's tone was casual, but his eyes were watching me carefully.

"Who?"

"You were asked to point him out."

"In Borenson's lineup? Which one was he?"

"A rather large fellow. Bald. Had a home in Warwick. Owned a quahog boat, which has disappeared also. Know him?"

"I remember there was one in the lineup who was bald. Lots of freckles on his forehead?"

Mitchell shrugged. "Hard for me to tell. I've just seen a mug shot." His voice still smooth, he said, "Now, Riley, you wouldn't be bullshitting me, would you?"

Meeting his eyes, I said, "It'd be stupid of me, and I'm not stupid. Maybe I've acted that way for the past week, but I had reasons."

Mitchell tapped at his teeth with the pencil, thinking. After a moment, he seemed to shake himself into the present. "Interesting, Riley, damn interesting. I don't know that I believe you completely, but I think I have enough to short-circuit this right now. Let's get started."

He had me place a call to Nick at the office by way of introduction, and then Nick set up a conference call with his attorney as well. "If I can work it the way I intend, I'll be back to you, Sam, in an hour or two for a meeting with the DA," he said to the other attorney.

Then he put a call in to Genaro and arranged to have him come down to take a statement. The policeman apparently pushed back, saying he wanted me down at the station. "You can have it here and now," Mitchell said, "or I'll have a doctor's report ruling that it's impossible to move my client for at least a week or more. It's your choice."

Mitchell put the phone down with a satisfied smile. "Thirty minutes."

The cop outside knocked on the door, then leaned in. "Company's here," he drawled.

"Right past all those reporters," Mitchell whispered to me. "Now you just do what I say."

The two detectives I knew as Genaro and Lew walked in. Genaro looked angry. Lew's expression was wary, but he said in a friendly tone, "How's the arm?"

I nodded to him. "Thanks for the nudge."

"Enough of that," Mitchell said, looking at me frostily. "Read him his rights, gentlemen. Then I've got a press conference to attend."

An hour later, Mitchell left with the police for a meeting with the assistant district attorney. It had gone much as Mitchell had predicted. Mitchell had let them persuade him to meet at the district attorney's office before holding a press conference. They convinced the ADA at home on Sunday that it was worth his while to come in. Genaro looked defensive as well as angry as they left, with Lew telling him to shut up.

I settled into a half hour or so of troubled sleep, and awoke feeling sticky and angry myself. Sitting up caused fresh bolts of pain, but it was not too bad walking slowly into the bathroom. The doctor had said that I had several hairline fractures in my ribs, and bruising, but nothing compound. It would be several months before the pain subsided completely, he figured.

In the mirror, my face was pale and heavily stubbled. I started to wash my face, and the warm water felt so soothing that I buried my face in the bowl, regardless of the bandages, and then began to scrub with a soapy towel. I ignored the pain movement brought, instead stripping down to wash thoroughly. It was not so much what I had done that made me feel unclean, but what I was willing to do to get away with it.

27

My guard was called off by evening visiting hours, soon after Mitchell came back from the meeting with the ADA. "You keep your mouth shut and you'll be okay," Mitchell said. "The incident in the lobby becomes a 'mishap,' and regardless of the noises they made about a weapons charge, they're not going to pursue it. To the extent the ADA can direct it, the media attention will shift more to Nick, as I explained before. They want it to go away, so it will. I expect we can clear all this up in the next few weeks, but you can sleep well tonight, knowing you're no longer under arrest."

I thanked Mitchell, and he went off, dreaming of other deals, I presume. Rachel and Nick came in immediately afterward. She looked washed out. I doubted she had slept much in the past two days. She stood beside my bed and said formally, "How are you, Riley?"

"Doing all right. How's your head?"

"Fine." Her posture was rigid. I reached out for her hand, and she backed away slightly. I let my hand drop, and asked Nick the same question.

He touched the bandage over his forehead and said, "Seems I can't let a week pass without a new wound."

I thanked them both for their help. Rachel looked at me coolly. To Nick, I said, "You know, the courts and press are going to be all over you for a while."

He waved that away. "The guy was a murderer. He was trying to kill us."

I looked at him closely. Nick seemed flushed, a bit full of himself. It made me feel better—at least he seemed to have regained his self-esteem. I thought about how he had cried when I visited him in the hospital. The idea that he had been cowardly up in Manchester was entirely his own. Yet I could understand his need to redeem himself; my own acts of revenge were perhaps no different.

Rachel's color deepened. "For God's sake," she cried. "Listen to the two of you. Three men have been killed in my home—I've been covered in their blood. All to avenge Ellen? What about me? And you, Nick, I don't know what to think. You talk as if killing that man was like climbing a mountain or something. It wasn't a sport, for God's sake."

"Rachel," I said warningly.

She returned her attention to me.

"I can't sleep, I can't eat. You used me. His gun was at my neck, and yet I saw you were going to shoot. I saw it and so did he."

"Come on," Nick said. "Riley drew fire to himself."

"It doesn't matter. He didn't do it to save me. It was for Ellen. He wanted a chance to kill that man for her, or die himself."

"Damn it, Rachel, there's no way you can know that," he said.

Her angry eyes were fixed upon mine. "Tell him, Riley. Tell me."

"It was the only chance I saw." I knew her reaction was due as much to jealousy as to anything else, but I couldn't help but feel angry. Just what the hell did she expect? "It was the only way out. I'd do it again. He wouldn't have let any of us out of there alive."

"For her," she said bitterly. "Thanks for the clarification. Guess I'd better start taking reality a little more seriously, shouldn't I? It's not as if you lied." She fumbled through her purse and came up with an airline ticket. "So. I'm quitting, of course. I'm going to treat myself to a vacation—London sounds nice, appropriately dreary for my mood. Why should I compete with sunshine in the Bahamas, right? Goodbye, gentlemen, it's been a pleasure."

"Rachel, you might run into trouble with the cops on that one," Nick said. "If you take off—"

She reached out abruptly, as if to strike him. Nick flinched, then grew red-faced as she simply placed her finger against his lips. "Shush. I don't work for either of you anymore, am not in need of your advice, and do not intend to ask the police for permission." She looked at me. "And I don't presume you're going to report me, are you?"

I shook my head.

"Well, how about that," she said. "You're finally thinking of me." She left the room.

Nick sat beside the bed and touched his forehead gingerly. "You think maybe you could've lied just a little? Would it have hurt?"

I listened to the sound of her walking away. "Yes, I think it would have hurt," I said. "That's been my experience."

"So when do you walk out of here?" Linda asked, a few minutes later. "I hear you've got the best legal talent available. It can't be long." She put a vase of roses beside my bed and gave me a swift kiss. I had the sense that she was somewhat embarrassed in front of Nick, but braving it out. She was dressed simply—jeans, a pink oxford shirt, a simple gold bracelet on her sunburned wrist—and she looked terrific. I introduced her to Nick. They had seen each other that first day at the police station, but had not met. I too felt awkward.

My feelings for her were a bit more than just gratitude, but I shied away from thinking of her as anything more than a friend—that capacity just did not seem to exist in me any longer. She was a survivor, that I knew, and I empathized with the earnest effort she was making to re-create herself.

"I understand you're Riley's prelegal defense," Nick said, smiling. "Pushed on Tom Windon to make sure he got the best attorney. And a good thing too, seeing as I was so busy explaining myself to the police I didn't do all I should've."

She waved that away, but she seemed pleased.

"And you'll be all right as far as kicking that cop?" I asked.

"They were kind of scary, right afterward. But I think I'll be fine."

"Good."

She sat down in the chair Nick had vacated. "Listen, the police in Newport got hold of me yesterday on the phone. They want me down to ask more questions, and I'm going to see them tomorrow. They wanted me yesterday, as a matter of fact, but your attorney was helpful there." She glanced briefly at Nick, but continued. "Anyhow, I did get from them that Alicia's apartment was turned upside down, but they haven't found Cory's notebook. So they're out of luck so far as finding out who stole the coke initially."

At that moment, Ellen's father walked in.

He looked curiously at Linda, angry. I realized he might be assuming she was Rachel. I introduced Linda and explained briefly how she had helped me.

She stood and reached out for his hand. He ignored it. She stepped closer, saying, "I'm very sorry about your daughter."

"Save it." He twisted a rolled magazine in his hands. To me, he said angrily, "I can't thank you people for doing what you should've done before my baby was killed."

"I understand your feelings for me. But Linda and Nick just found themselves in the middle of this nightmare, and they've helped. If it weren't for them, Cracker Beauregard would still be alive."

"You don't understand my feelings for you," he snapped back. "You've been my son-in-law for ten years, damn it. Now I see you, and I want to hurt you, I want to punch your goddamn face." He scowled tiredly and rubbed his face. "But I know you wouldn't have done what you did if you hadn't loved her. So I came down to . . . to *acknowledge* that." He walked past the foot of the bed and stood at the window, looking outside at the city below, at the Charles River shining in the fading evening light. He tapped his leg with the rolled magazine and ignored us for a minute or so. Then he said quietly, "It's as if Sylvia is gone now, too. She just says it's beyond her, that we're too old to take this." He turned to me, and his voice turned harsh again. "I want you to tell me about it. I want you to tell me what you found out, and about killing him. Maybe it'll do something. Maybe I can give it to Sylvia, maybe it'll give her something to hold on to."

He threw the magazine down on my lap. It was a copy of *New England Monthly*, opened to a full-page ad. "She's still alive there. In those ads. Still laughing, still beautiful. I guess no one told them she was dead."

Nick said, "That ad was probably placed with the publication over a month ago."

"It's all right," Geoff said. "Opening the magazine and seeing her like that was a shock, but it was worth it to see her face again."

Thinking of how I had clung to the smell of her perfume, that first night alone in our house, I picked up the magazine to see the jewelry manufacturer's ad she had shown me a month ago—seemingly years ago—of her sitting at a dinner table with a white-haired man apparently in his mid-fifties.

It was as if someone punched the air out of me.

She was reaching back to fasten the clasp on a gold necklace. Her expression captured the moment beautifully: she was letting her husband know she was delighted with the gift, while managing to catch the eye of the young blond waiter with a mischievous glance, as if to say, "Can you believe the extravagance?"

The waiter was Cory Dearborn.

28

Linda and Nick bent over my lap to look at the ad. "She looks beautiful," Nick said sadly.

I watched Linda's face. "She does," Linda agreed, and then her face paled instantly. She kept her head down over the photo for a moment, her hand on my shoulder in a gesture that probably appeared consoling to the other two, but her nails dug in sharply. "I didn't realize how pretty she was. I was so upset. That time at the police station."

I was stunned. How could I not have recognized him? I thought I had the first time I saw him on the dock, but then had dismissed it. Immediately I gave myself reasons: it was such a bit part in the ad, his features were not that clear, I had only glanced at the ad . . .

I had not been paying enough attention to Ellen. Though her reasons, the words she gave me, were different, she had shown me the ad. On some level she had to have been trying to make me see, but I had tuned her out, irritated by what I saw only as vanity.

"I've got to go," Linda said.

"Stay a bit," I said. "I need to talk with you."

"I can't."

"Do you need a ride somewhere?" Nick asked.

"No. I've got to go." She looked at me, her eyes frightened.

"Linda, stay."

She stepped out the door and was gone.

Nick shrugged. He had the faintly embarrassed look of a man standing in the middle of someone else's marital dispute. He apparently had not recognized Cory. Of course, his only reference would have been the newspaper photo.

My head ached, and I felt as if I might be sick. I closed my eyes briefly, wondering where Linda's fear was coming from. Had she been hiding the fact that Cory and Ellen knew each other? Or did she think I had?

Geoff had been following the exchange, and I expect to him it looked as if I was pleading for her company. He looked disgusted. "I just don't understand you, Riley. I guess I never did."

"You look like hell," Nick said to me. "Maybe we'd both better go, Geoff."

Geoff nodded shortly. "I've got nothing else to say."

He reached for the magazine, and I pulled it back. "I want to keep this," I said. "Go ahead, Nick. Geoff, stay a moment, and I'll tell you what you wanted to know."

"You look beat," Nick said warningly.

"I'm all right. Go ahead."

Nick touched Ellen's father on the arm, nodded to me, then left. I waved Geoff to the chair beside me.

As the night fell upon the city outside, I told him the steps I had taken to avenge his daughter's death, including the killing of Desmin Lowe.

"Lord. My Lord, you did it, Riley," he said wonderingly. "Any other circumstance, had you told me this, I would be repelled and frightened by you." He looked past me out at the night. "But it does change when it's your own blood. Vengeance does bring some sense of . . . *order*, anyhow, doesn't it?"

I thought of the shudder of the knife through Lowe's neck, of Rachel's words, of Ellen and Cory looking at each other in the magazine, and shook my head. "Maybe with a little distance, it might. But not for me now, no. It was necessary, or at least I thought it was."

"Of course it was." He looked at me afresh. "You took quite a risk telling me this."

I hated to bring him back into the uncertainty. "It looks as if I'm not finished. You didn't recognize his picture from the paper, not in this context. But this waiter in the ad is Cory Dearborn, the man found under my boat, the one I tried to help out on the dock. Until you showed me this ad I had no idea Ellen knew him."

"What?" A wave of emotions swept over Geoff's face: shock, disbelief, anger. I recognized them all, having wrestled with them myself for the past few minutes.

"Just what are you saying?" His voice was thin, and he gripped the bed rail. "That can't be right. You're mistaken. Your partner just said that ad would have been sent to the magazine over a month ago."

"That's right. And given three to four weeks to do the production, that's at least two months ago that Ellen knew Cory."

Geoff's face grew mottled. "Damn you! Damn you, don't try to place the blame on her—"

"Maybe I'm wrong, Geoff. But it's a hell of a coincidence. The way she reacted when she first saw his body, I thought it was just because of the awful way he looked." I thought of the whiteness of her face . . . and the fear in her eyes later at the police station, the constant trembling. "It doesn't look good."

Leaving the hospital was uneventful. I didn't sign out; I put on my jeans and Geoff's sweater, and simply left with him as if I were another visitor. We went directly to the garage elevator, avoiding the lobby in case there were still any reporters. He gave

me a ride home. I told him I was going to go through her files
to find out which agency handled the ad.

"I can help," he said as we pulled into my driveway.

I shook my head. "Won't take long."

"Call me when you know," he said. "We can talk about what
we need to do next."

"No. I'll take it from here. If I find out where the photo was
taken, I'll leave the file in Ellen's dressing table upstairs. Go to
the police with it if something happens to me. Otherwise, just
stay out of it. You can't discuss it with Sylvia, and you can't be
running out to help me without explaining it to her. And I've
involved too many people as it is."

He nodded tiredly. "Even if I were younger, I don't know if I
would be that much help. I couldn't have done what you did to
those two dealers. No matter what I felt, I wouldn't have been
capable of it." He stared at me. "How could you? Maybe growing up the way you did . . ."

I got out, angered by the implicit accusation, that my growing
up a bastard had brought all of this upon his family; that I was
therefore the only one capable of straightening it out.

I ignored him when he called out, "Tell me about it when
you're done." He drove off as I walked upstairs in my empty
house to the room Ellen had used as an office, to find out things
I did not want to know.

There was no file under the jewelry manufacturer's name, "Stardust Memories." I ended up flipping through virtually all of the
folders before finding the ad. The agency was Providence-based,
a relatively small firm that did good work. I knew the owner well
enough, Jerzy Towle, but I was reluctant to bring any attention
to the ad by calling him. Besides, I found what I needed in the
second unpleasant shock of the evening. It was in the form of a
copy of the photographer's release.

Derby Tucker had taken the photo of Ellen and Cory.

29

Hot anger pulsed inside me like a fever.

My .22 was only a single-shot varmint gun, and though I thought it unlikely that I really needed a gun for defense, I figured it would help jog the truth out of Derby.

It took me about half an hour to reach his building. All the lights were dark, and it looked just like what it was—an old factory at night. The names outside the door seemed to be for small independent businesses. Good chance we would be the only ones in the building, assuming *he* was there. There was no answer when I pushed the button for his loft. No intercom crackle, no tape of a barking dog. Through the narrow pane of wire-meshed glass in the door, I could see that the elevator was down. Naturally, the door was locked. I backed away and looked up at the window from which Derby had leaned, seemingly months ago. It was partly open. In the moonlight I thought I saw a faint gleam inside the window. I called his name. No answer.

I decided to wait for him inside. After going back to the car for a pair of light cotton gloves, I found a piece of hemp in the narrow alley behind the factory. I knotted the line around a brick and tossed it up to catch the lowest rung of the fire escape so I could pull the counterbalanced ladder down. Knowing that it could appear that I was burglarizing the building, I left the .22 behind a dumpster. If the police arrived as I was climbing in the window I might be able to make a case for waiting in the apartment of an old friend. But no way would they ignore a gun the second time around, no matter how good Mitchell was. I would just have to think of something else to scare Derby into the truth.

But those concerns proved to be a waste of time.

The gleam I had seen from the ground turned out to be the streetlight's reflection off Derby's bald pate. His eyes bulged unnaturally, and not because of me. He was slumped chest-down across an armchair just inside the window, his chin caught in such a way that he seemed to be looking at the vacant lot below. I climbed in. There was a neat round hole in the back of his head. Blood had trickled out of his ears. With a kind of numb sense of abstraction, I noted that it must have been a small-caliber bullet not to have left an exit wound. I stood in the gloom waiting for my eyes to become accustomed to the darkness. My heart tripped along inside my fractured rib cage, and I moved away from the window abruptly, realizing the target I was presenting. *Think, damn it.*

Derby must have been running to the window to escape when the bullet took him down. The flat gunpowder smell lingered in the air. I touched him with the back of my forearm. Still warm.

The clouds parted and the moonlight brightened outside. Going back down the fire escape now would leave me so vulnerable as to be suicidal. Of course, staying there was not too safe either. I cursed myself for leaving the gun down behind the dumpster.

It was a big loft. The noises of the city outside, the dull rumble of traffic and the muted sound of horns blowing, made it impossible to tell if there was any other sound in the loft. The elevator was down, but it was an automatic elevator, so that meant nothing; the killer could still be with me. Or he could have left ten minutes ago.

The windows on the other side of the room were covered with the heavy black curtains. I took a long-bladed knife off the magnetic strip over the stove and started around the loft. In the back, I found an open window behind one of the curtains. I leaned outside. There was a foot-wide ledge that went around the building to a dormerlike roof. The killer could have left by there and climbed onto the roof, or have used the fire escape on that side, or simply crawled into the window of one of the other lofts on the same floor . . . or maybe Derby had simply left the window open for the breeze.

Then I noticed the padlock to the big closet where Derby had kept his coke was gone, and the door was ajar. I walked over to the open door and listened. Nothing. Inside, the closet looked as dark as ink, until I reached out with the knife and realized Derby had overlapping black curtains there as well.

I took a deep breath, and put my left hand up in front of my face and tucked my elbow in to protect my chest as I passed through them. Inside, the darkness was total. There was a strong chemical smell. I fumbled around until I found a wall switch. A red light glowed, and I found myself in a simple little darkroom. I ran my hand across the black-painted surface. Plywood. On the wall opposite the door was a wide three-drawer file cabinet with a row of binders along the top. To my left was a print stand, a light table, and a rack of boxed chemicals. The sink and developing trays were along the brick wall. The place made me sad in a way that seeing his body had not. His death was scary. Seeing this place reminded me of the man, reminded me he had recently purchased the loft, and had probably built the darkroom himself for small jobs and developing contact sheets.

I opened the file cabinet. The specific assignments were labeled by ad agency in Derby's neat handwriting. Inside were model releases, contact sheets, negatives or color slides, and prints of the photos selected, presumably. The file under my agency filled almost a drawer, and I thumbed through it quickly, remembering almost all of the projects over the years as if I were reading a private journal.

Under Towle's agency, I found the "Stardust Memories" file and took the set of plastic sleeves with color slides over to the light table. I found a model release stapled to Cory's photo, and was puzzled to see the name Brett Thomas. Then I remembered Linda said Cory had used a pseudonym with the convention service; the same was apparently true for his modeling.

It made me sick at heart in so many ways, standing there, using a magnifying glass to study the dozen or so rolls Derby had taken to arrive at the selected photo. They were mainly variations of the man/wife/waiter shot. In some, Cory was clearly involved; in others, just a passing waiter, face unseen. There were also a few of the candid shots most photographers end up snapping throughout a long day. In this case, of the crew setting up the "restaurant," of the stylist bending over the "husband," biting her lower lip in concentration as she applied a brush to his cheek . . . and the ones I was searching for and dreading.

Cory had his arm around Ellen and she was laughing, her eyes aslant to him, her lips mere inches from the line of his jaw. She had his suspender in her left hand, tugging. His mouth curved—apparently he was making some joking remark to Derby, his hand out, *Don't take the picture, man, her husband will kill me.* The shot after that, they kissed. In the one after that, it was Ellen who waved Derby away. Cory was looking past her. Maybe I was reaching, but I believe the camera had captured her in a moment of shame, of loneliness.

I shuffled through the rest of the plastic sleeves, perhaps on some level looking for a photo showing that my wife had not cheated on me. How that picture would have been composed was beyond my imagination, yet that was what I hoped to find.

The binders along the top of the cabinet caught my eye. They were labeled "Derby's Debaucheries" and dated by year. There was something familiar about them, and then I realized with unpleasant certainty that they were the same make as the photo album in Linda's apartment. I started with the one farthest to the right, the one dated for last year, and found Cory in several photos. They appeared to be party shots. Although I didn't recognize any of the other people, the background looked vaguely familiar. Cory was in the next year back, and one shot included a woman, face turned away from the camera, who might have been Alicia. Three years back, I found the exact same shot of Cory, Alicia, and Linda that was in Linda's book: the three of them mugging it up for the camera.

My hands were shaking. I ripped the photo out of the notebook and laid it on the light table with the others. I opened the drawers again, and ran through the files quickly, looking for the current-year negatives. As organized as Derby appeared to be, I had no doubt he waited until the end of the year before making his selections for the photo albums. I found the file, brought it over to the light table, and started running through each sleeve. Then in my haste I slid them all across the table and ran my magnifying glass across the colors of Derby's most recent loft party.

My worst suspicion was confirmed. The slides were dated just last month—it was the loft party which I was not able to make, but to which I had blithely sent my wife and best friend. In a sequence of three photos, Nick stared jealously at Cory, who had his arm around Ellen. In the last photo they were less than two feet from each other, Nick's face was contorted in ugly rage, and Cory was apparently saying something to him with a half-amused smirk on his handsome face.

What else did Nick know?

I shattered the light table with my fist, wanting darkness, wanting no more answers at that moment.

I expect I was making a lot of noise at that point. The first realization I had that I was not alone was when I heard the snick of metal on metal. I whirled and shoved the knife through the blackout curtain.

It bit into wood. The door was locked—what I had heard was the padlock being snapped shut. I shoved the curtains aside, drew back my foot, and kicked the plywood door. The whole wall flexed, but the door held. The room filled with the sharp smell of gasoline. In the red light, the floor under me turned darker.

I kicked the door again. It gave slightly, and then there was a scratching noise, and light flickered underneath the door, and I scrambled back beside the file cabinet. I called out once just as flame whooshed under the door and climbed the ceiling in a bright orange sheet. The heat rolled over me like a wave, singeing my hair, taking away my breath.

The flames were licking the boxed chemical rack right beside the door, and there was a trickle of liquid fire making its way toward me. Grabbing the heavy three-drawer file cabinet, I wrestled it catercorner away from the wall. Taking the knife, I pried at the corner, where the plywood was butted against a two-by-four.

The blade snapped.

I slammed my shoulder against the plywood, and got nothing—it flexed like the door, but did not break.

The door itself was fully engulfed in flames now. I had the briefest of thoughts that I might break through it when it was sufficiently weakened by the fire, but then flames seared my left calf, the pain just as intense as if I had knelt on the electric range in my kitchen. I hit the wall again, and bounced back against the corner of the heavy file cabinet. It lifted slightly and fell back near my foot.

Breathing was now close to impossible, and my eyes were streaming. The weight of the cabinet just barely registered in my head, and then I grasped it as my salvation. I stepped into the fire and wrenched the cabinet so one side was facing the door. Back against the wall, I stamped my feet and beat the flames from my pants leg, roaring with frustration and pain. I threw myself at the top edge of the cabinet. It lifted, but not enough.

I hit it again.

Same result.

I yanked the bottom drawer open, pulled out the files, including all of the remaining negatives for the "Stardust Memories" shots and the party shots for the past few years, and threw them into the flames near the sink. Bracing my foot on the back wall, I shoved the top edge of the cabinet with all my strength.

It tipped, balanced, then crashed through the burning door, blanketing the flames momentarily. I jumped over it into the middle of Derby's loft. Flames billowed out of the darkroom. I half walked, half crawled over to the window. The blinding pain that coughing caused my bruised and cracked ribs made me expect I was bringing up blood. I touched Derby's arm, and even through the glove, enough heat had radiated from the fire to make his skin hot. The chair was beginning to smoke.

Below me, the ladder rattled down toward the ground, and I watched Nick run away, rifle in hand.

30

The lights of Nick's house were blazing. I held the .22 alongside my leg as I quietly made my way to the back door. It was much the same as hundreds of other visits—we had long had the kind of relationship where one could walk into the other's house unannounced.

Seeing him hurry down the fire escape was going to change that.

Recent memories seemed full of hidden meaning now. Derby and Nick talking at the funeral—had Derby been blackmailing him? And Nick shooting Cracker, the gun snapping up as it belched flame—was Nick simply eliminating an embarrassing partner? Why hadn't he killed Rachel and me right then too, with

Cracker's gun? Had he thought he wouldn't get away with it? Or was there some residual feeling toward us? The more I pulled at it, the more questions I had. Had Nick killed Alicia too? Did Ellen know he was involved, and if so, was that why she had risked everything to drive down and talk with me? And the question that pulsed behind all the others—*why was he doing this to me?*

His Jaguar was in the driveway, but the big Suburban was gone. The back door was unlocked. Inside, I listened but heard nothing. Bearing in mind that that was all I'd heard in Derby's loft too, I moved cautiously through his house, the .22 held at my waist.

I did not know if I could kill him, in spite of everything.

I found myself hoping that he was in the house and that he had a gun. That he would come after me quickly, and I could leave the decision to my reflexes. The habit of thinking of him as my friend was juxtaposed with thoughts like being ready to make a head shot, since I was carrying such a small-caliber gun.

I looked immediately to his key rack in the kitchen. I knew he kept separate sets for each vehicle and both boats. The Jag and dive-boat keys were still there; the keys for the Suburban and his sailboat, *Dark Dancer*, were gone. The thought that he was therefore heading for Newport struck me immediately, but then, I told myself, this was no time to count on Nick's characteristic orderliness. The house was a mess. There were still dishes in the sink; the living room had magazines thrown about, beer bottles on the coffee table, on the television. The bedroom was worse, with the bed unmade, and a stale animal smell, as if he had not opened the windows in weeks.

There was a large closet to the left of the window, and a light glowed from around the door. Inside, the big closet smelled strongly of gun oil. There was a Remington shotgun propped up in the corner, and a big S&W .45 handgun on the shelf. I had thought he had only the one gun, but then there was a lot about Nick that I obviously didn't know. How long, I thought. How long has all this been going on?

Beside the handgun was a box of .22 cartridges.

I had the same ammo in my pocket.

Up the elevator he had gone, ostensibly to talk with Derby about the latest development, the ad showing Cory and Ellen. Maybe he was as shocked as I was upon seeing it. If so, he was a hell of an actor. But then, he had to be.

When Derby opened the door for him, Nick must have leveled the rifle at him. Derby had run to the window, to the fire escape, and when the little rifle cracked out, Nick had taken care of that particular problem. The elevator returned down automatically, and he would have been down himself with the photos in a few minutes, except I showed up. Perhaps before he could plant some evidence linking me. He knew I had a .22, and I had told him that I had stayed up with it the night after Cory had been found. All it would have taken was a call to the hospital to find that I had already left. He could figure that once I saw the ad the police could logically assume I had tracked my way back to Derby, as I had.

But it didn't make sense, I thought. Framing me for Derby's death could so easily go wrong. First off, I might have an alibi. And the police would be able to tell my gun hadn't been fired; surely he knew that.

I felt stupid. Surely he did—it was just that his next stop probably would have been to kill me. With my own rifle, if he could manage it. If not, he could shoot me with his own, then fire a round from mine into the phone book or something, and walk away with the spent bullet, leaving a fired rifle and suicide note beside my body for their investigation. He probably had always intended to burn Derby's place down, unless Derby just happened to have gasoline in his loft. No, I expect my arrival just pushed his schedule ahead, so he changed plans. Innovative, Nick was. It had been one of his assets as a business partner, I thought, as I began to feed shells into the Remington.

After loading the S&W .45 revolver, I used the phone on the bedside table to confirm that Rachel had made her TWA flight to London. She had. Next, I called the launch service number. The young man who answered there said Linda had just gone out on a run, to try back in forty-five minutes.

All the time I was sitting on the bed, I found myself getting more and more anxious. I had plenty of good reasons, yet it was not until I put the receiver down that I identified exactly what I was feeling: it was as if Ellen were watching me. Not some mystical connection, not as if she were standing in judgment, or defense, she just seemed *there*.

I could smell her. Her perfume, rather, that scent I had tried to capture that first night alone. I looked about the room, the dresser, and then back to the bedside table drawer. Under a hand mirror there was a small bottle of her perfume. And a Baggie, a zip-up Baggie filled with white powder, with cocaine. The silver mirror reflected the rigid set of my face, the tightness of my mouth, eyes blank even to myself, as I turned it at an angle to the table lamp. Traces of coke dusted the surface, and I could see my wife bending over that mirror, looking into her reflection one too many times, with my angry partner waiting over her shoulder for his turn.

I dialed the launch service number again. Linda was still out. "When do you close?"

"One-thirty."

About two hours.

Hurrying down the stairs with the guns, I thought about my options. If he was just driving away, leaving the state, heading for California or Mexico, then there was not much I could do other than notify the police. But I felt it was more likely he was heading down to Newport. The coke was presumably stolen there, perhaps it was hidden there. The keys for *Dark Dancer* were gone.

A possibility struck me. Both his vehicles had car phones. After going out and moving Ellen's Jeep a few blocks away, I went back to his kitchen and took the keys for his Jaguar, put his guns on the floor of the backseat, and took off for Rhode Island.

I rejected the idea of calling the Newport police. I told myself a full investigation would be inevitable, and I would almost certainly be linked with Desmin Lowe. That I would have to tell them about Ellen's relationship with Cory, and I had no desire to share the details with the newspapers. That I couldn't be sure Linda wasn't involved more than she had said, and I needed to think *someone* wasn't lying. . . .

But what it really came down to was making him explain. I didn't want to hear about it through the police, through reports and testimony. In his own words, I wanted to know why my best friend had tried to murder me.

31

Just before Providence, I used the car phone to call Nick in the Suburban. I had wasted time trying to persuade a string of operators to identify his location. They assured me they could not help, and even if it were technically possible, the information would be confidential.

"Nick," I said when he picked up. "You never had a problem following through before. You left before the job was done."

Silence on the line. Then, "Riley?"

"That's right."

"Whoa. Voice from the grave. Where are you?"

"In your Jag," I said, with an eye to the clock. For all I knew, he could be heading west from Boston on the Mass Pike, or just about to step out of his truck at Logan Airport for a flight to Europe.

"My car?" He sounded surprised.

"Got any objections?"

"Hell, no. Who am I to complain? Blow the horn for me, though. I'm a bit more suspicious than you might've realized."

I did.

"Heard it," he said. "You are alone though, right? Because if you're not, you should be. I want to talk about the guy you took for a boat ride."

"I'm right here."

"If the cops are listening in, you're going to jail too."

"They're not."

He paused for a second. "First, how'd you get out?"

I told him.

"That big-mother file cabinet? Jesus. Did you know it was me locking you in?"

"I had a pretty good idea."

"You didn't yell much at all. You're a John Wayne kind of guy. Thought for sure I'd get some begging. Anyhow, did I hear you right, that you cut that quahogger's throat? How do you figure it, Riley? We're just two guys who own an ad agency, then this."

The plastic phone creaked under my hand. "Cut the charade, Nick. Why did you do this?"

He was silent for almost a full minute. I held back and waited. When he spoke, his tone was earnest, as if he was confiding a secret. "Not as much of a charade as you might think. It's not like I'm a raving crazy, though I know what I've done fits the bill. Funny how it is, Riley—you can do murder, and still feel like essentially the same guy. Different too, of course. Kind of above it all, like I'm floating a few feet off the ground." He laughed. " 'Course, that could be the coke. Sometimes I feel like I can just as easily walk through a door as open it. But most of the time, I feel like just the same guy. Eat the same food, wear the same clothes, you know. Makes me wonder, was I always headed for some sort of violent destiny? I mean, could you go back to my childhood, and something my father said one day set me on this path? Or did my mother hold my peepee or something?"

"Nick. Were you working with those two? Did you have them kill Ellen?"

"Of course not." He sounded affronted. "They shot me in the head, for Christ's sake. Ellen would be alive today if you and Datano hadn't reduced me to throwing sticks."

I couldn't trust my voice. I turned the phone to speaker, and put it down. My heart was pounding inside my chest. I wanted to hurt him. There I was in his car, his pride, this English racing-green Jaguar, which smelled of good leather and a faint touch of his after-shave. Real wood dash. Compact disk player. He treated himself so damn well, I thought abstractly. I said, "She is dead, you're up to your neck in all of this, and I want to know why."

"Hell, I'd never have hurt her no matter how angry I was. Even though she didn't love me. She said you came first. When she took off with the rental car, I was sure she was going to tell you about our affair. She had talked about it those nights when you were down in Newport, when I was up in Manchester. She acted as if I had leprosy, and even though she didn't know I had killed Cory, she was beginning to ask questions, I could see she was beginning to scratch at it. Too much coincidence, she said. She wanted to come clean about our affair, said she didn't want to lie to you anymore."

He sighed. "It worked to my advantage that she died, I'll admit. I've wanted this conversation, you know that? Didn't think I was going to have it—maybe that's why I was feeling depressed before. Look, buddy, pal, fucking friend and partner, you *stole* that woman from me. I felt sorry for you, damn it. You were this goddamn stiff when you first came into the agency business. You scared people and didn't even know it. I mean, Christ, you were this bloody vet, this guy people would shrink from when he walked into the room, we all knew you'd killed people. And then you told me about how you grew up. It was like having a Doberman pinscher rub up against you—you damn well pet it if it wants you to, but otherwise you'd just as soon it went away.

And I befriended *that*, I helped you along, and you came out and stole her away."

"That was over ten years ago." I was stunned.

"I haven't been stewing on it all that time, don't flatter yourself. It was working with you every day, the king-of-the-mountain assuredness you put into every gesture, every word. Who do you think you are? You're just a bastard kid of a whore, but you walked in and *told* me you were going to take Ellen out—you didn't ask. Our whole business marches to your step. You threw out clients you didn't approve of, you just counted on me to fall in line like a good soldier. I never signed up for that. I'm stronger, you damn well know that. I could push you through a wall."

Speeding the Jaguar up another ten miles an hour, I kept an eye on the radar detector. "Do I? Where are you, Nick?"

He snorted. "I might as well be honest—I'm just about to hit the Connecticut border. No, sorry, it's the New Hampshire border. Son of a bitch, what am I saying? I'm sitting in Kenmore Square right this minute, under the Citgo sign. Confusing, isn't it? Shame you can't call the police, since you know I'll tell them about the quahogger. Murder is *inconvenient*, isn't it?"

"Tell them what little you know."

"Oh, more than enough. Scuzzy biker house in Warwick, right? Desmin Lowe."

My silence let him know he had scored a point. He said triumphantly, "Murder, partner, murder one. Cut his throat, man. You've got balls, I'll give you that. Must've made a mess. Maybe we could share a cell and I can fill you in on how little you know. You didn't know your 'best friend,' you didn't know your wife. Ellen and I talked about it in the sack a few times. I don't owe you any explanations. Figure it out yourself."

The clock read twelve fifty-five. I was passing through Warwick now, and figured he had about twenty minutes on me. If I picked the speed up, I would certainly be able to trim that down some, giving me a chance to catch up if he was indeed heading for Newport. Big if.

"You're enjoying yourself," I said. "Don't give me this line that you don't want to talk. Does it start with Susan leaving you?"

" 'Does it start with Susan leaving you?' " he mimicked. "Fuck off." He hung up.

I tapped the launch service number immediately. The young man answered.

"Is Linda in?" I asked.

"Yeah, who's calling?"

"Riley."

"Hold."

Silence.

One full minute passed. Finally the young man got back on, and his voice had changed from agreeable to somewhat defensive. "She's gone out again. Bye."

"You said she was just there, damn it."

"Yeah, well, I told her."

"Tell her to keep away from Nick. Tell her to go to the Charthouse bar, and wait for me."

"Got it."

Nick called me back. "Okay, you're right. It did start with Susan. Bitch said I was insecure, self-absorbed, boring. *Boring.* Can you see that? You know, doing what I do for a living, that's like a crippling thought. I guess it's been eating at me. I went out with a lot of women the past few years, but none of them really did anything for me, not until this winter when I started making love to your wife again. You want details? Number of times, orgasms, the way she twisted her fingers in my hair, what? What do you want to know?"

"She left you, too," I said, injecting a coolness into my voice I surely didn't feel. "Ellen would have hated you for the fear you're showing now. She had enough of it herself, but she despised it in others. I suppose you had fallen in love with her completely."

His bitterness was not masked by laughter this time. "Like

without a parachute. I'll tell you the truth, I was ashamed of myself. I had a hard time facing you at work. But that made the sex even more exciting. For about three months, we couldn't get enough of each other. Then the same thing as with Susan—'Let's break it off, okay, hon?' Oh, Ellen had more class than that, she talked the good talk, sat on the bed with my hand in hers, eyes on mine, very frank. All came down to the same thing. She was bored."

I waited.

"What, am I boring you too?" He paused. "Guess expecting sympathy from you isn't too reasonable. And I am reasonable in my own way. Then Derby invited all of us to his studio party late this spring. Remember? You, me, Ellen. You backed out at the last minute, shoved the two of us into a car, said, 'Go have fun.' Frankly, nothing would have made me happier, but Ellen had other plans. I honestly don't know if she'd ever had an affair before me. But that night, maybe she wasn't exactly looking for it, but when Cory Dearborn walked up with that big white grin of his, she was ready. Derby comes up, starts talking about them doing a shoot for him, though I had no idea they did it until I saw that ad in your hospital room. I just about shit.

"Dearborn was a model, you know. Not that he did that much of it—he used it mainly for contacts, for finding chumps like me and you. Steady supply of pretty girls to play with and help him out. Anyhow, you're back at the office pounding away on the computer, I'm watching Ellen fall for his line. I felt as if I had become you. Wearing horns. Only what could I do? Go back to you and say, 'Hey, pal, somebody's beating your time, and it's not me'? Strange mix of feelings, let me tell you. I wanted to rip his head off, because I could tell he didn't care about Ellen worth a damn, that he was just trying something different, this beauty who was six, seven years older, see what she knew. And I could see she was really going for him.

"Anyhow, halfway through the evening, Dearborn turned the charm on me. He had that talent, he made you want to talk. Made *me* want to talk, anyhow. He introduced me to this beautiful woman, Alicia."

"Alicia?"

"That's right, buddy, Alicia. My God, what a doll, wasn't she? See, I could forgive Cory that night at Derby's party, because he introduced her to me, and she introduced me to coke. I mean, I'm an adult, I've had a few lines before, and I've gone to bed with my share of models. But it was nothing like this, nothing like this quality, and not with a woman like her. We spent time together, we had this short thing, must've lasted three weeks, a month. I was half crazy about her, sexually. I didn't feel about her the way I did about Ellen, but you don't know what that snow can do for you, do for a man. Maybe *you* don't need it, but Alicia and Queen Snow gave me scenes I've never acted in before. I knew she was a kind of prostitute, and I was going down the tubes, ripping through my savings, running to Cory for cocaine. But it was the slide of my life."

All the time he was talking, my arms and shoulders felt heavier, my body felt as if I were being shoved deeper into the leather seat. Not just from what he had told me about Ellen, but from realizing how blind I had been to what was happening around me. I buried the gas pedal in the carpet as I came out of the entrance ramp to Route 138 toward Jamestown, the island between Newport and North Kingstown.

"You killed Alicia," I said dully. "Not Cracker."

"Oh, it was him, all right. I just about had a heart attack at the funeral when Derby told me you had been sniffing around for some dope. Then you admitted you had talked to Alicia. I called her, wanted to know if she had said anything about me. She said no, that she wanted to hold on to every card she had, that she had gone sailing with you, that one minute you were a virgin, no white powder on you, the next you were claiming to have it. She thought herself a wheeler and dealer, Alicia did, thought she was tough. But she wasn't, not anywhere near the degree she thought she was. See, the thing that confused her, and probably everybody involved, the police, Desmin, Cracker, all of them, was the way you stepped in to fight for Cory. People just don't do that to help a stranger out, not unless they've got something at stake. Me, I believed it when I saw it."

"You saw the fight?"

"Sure did. From the parking lot. When you said you were heading down to Newport that night, I called Cory's answering service. When he called me back, I told him I wanted to meet him on my boat that night, that I wanted to put some serious money, fifty thousand, down on some coke, that I was tired of nickel-and-diming it. He was desperate for cash then—as I knew he would be, since I had ripped him off myself, wearing a big scary Richard Nixon mask—so he agreed we would meet at the launch to go out to the *Dark Dancer* and make the transfer. Which was a laugh for me, because I knew he had nothing to transfer, he was running scared from his own suppliers, and therefore he *had* to be planning on ripping me off, or knowing him, pulling some blackmail scam. Any case, I figured it would be a perfect time to let you three introduce yourselves—you, Cory, and the enforcer. I didn't know his name at the time. In fact, I thought it would be Desmin Lowe, not this Cracker, who showed up."

"You were working with them? How?"

"Naw. Look, a lot of this stuff I just did as I went along. I saw Ellen and Cory in Wickford one day, right after Alicia had broken it off with me. Probably Cory pointed out a new target for her, a new chump. I just kind of snapped—I *refused* to be in this position anymore. I figured the hell with him, and the hell with you and Ellen. It took some figuring, but I decided Cory was my first target. And if you separate him from his dope, what's left, right?

"So I bought myself a quahog boat, and kept it in Jamestown. A fast mother, with a one-fifty outboard. I acted like a digger, and followed him out early one morning when he was picking up the lobster pot with his coke and getting ready to drop his cash. With me barking at Cory behind the mask, with the shotgun right in his face, he proved to be a fountain of information. Not only did he hand over both the cash and coke, but he told me about the operation—seems they traded the coke and cash that way to avoid dealing with the danger of a face-to-face hand-over. Dearborn said Lowe had a couple of dealers who picked up within Narragansett Bay like that, which was good for me, because I bet the first place Lowe and Beauregard turned was to the other dealers. But best of all, he gave me Desmin Lowe's name."

"So you called Lowe."

"That's right. Just after you left the bar. I said I was the gen-
tleman who had ripped off Cory's shipment of coke and cash, and
I was willing to sell Lowe the coke back for the full price, just to
keep from placing an anonymous call to the police to describe his
operation. I would, of course, be keeping the cash."

"In other words, you set Cory up in a way most likely to
enrage his suppliers."

"That's right. And told Lowe where Cory would be right about
ten o'clock. Just to see what would happen. If I was lucky, I
figured, he might take both of you out."

"What about Rachel? You set her up too, placing us all in the
same place at the same time."

"Bad luck. I assumed you were going down alone."

"So how did Cory end up under my boat?"

"That took some doing. The next day, I waited outside Alicia's
house, then managed to follow her when she went out that night.
I figured Cory might want to see her. A bit of a gamble with all
the women he had, but sure enough, she led me to your little
friend's apartment. Then she came storming out, and a bit later,
so did Cory. And there I was with a gun under my coat. Step
this way, Mr. Dearborn, your cruise awaits."

I cursed myself. Linda had said that a man with a truck had
abducted Cory, and I had jumped to the conclusion that she meant
a pickup, not even thinking of a big enclosed vehicle like Nick's.
"I'm going to take a break," I said. Since he knew where she
lived, it was more critical than ever that I get through to her.

"Remember Mr. Lowe."

I hung up and called the launch service.

"You again?" the young man said, when I started to leave Linda
a message about Nick. "Take a hint. I gave her your message
about meeting at the bar. She doesn't want anything to do with
you. She's got to work, and as a matter of fact, so do I."

"Tell her to stay away from Nick, to not be alone—"

"No, I don't do this stuff, work it out yourself." He slammed
the phone down.

. . .

When I dialed it again, it was busy. "Goddamn it!" I jammed Nick's car into a lower gear, and took small pleasure in listening to it wind up to redline as I shot up the Jamestown Bridge before upshifting. The phone sounded.

"Get this," Nick said. "Cory was blubbering all the way on the drive over to Jamestown, and as we headed out in the quahog boat. I planned to simply drop him over the side, tied to some weights. Maybe alive, maybe dead first, I wasn't sure. I had developed a powerful dislike for this kid. He not only took Ellen away, but he had only to snap his fingers and Alicia was gone too—this glorified dock boy! When he found out that his affair with Ellen was part of the reason I was dumping him, he said, like he was amazed, 'Ellen? You're doing this for *Ellen Burke?*' So I blew him away. Ka-boom. Then, I figured, why am I doing you two favors? I admit, right then I wasn't thinking too straight. I rowed into Newport Harbor, and when I saw the *Spindrift* was dogged down tight, I dropped him underneath your boat. Figured both of you had some tough explanations for each other."

I shook my head. "How did you expect to get away with all of this?"

He laughed shortly. "Doesn't look like I have, does it? But I would've except for that ad. You took care of Lowe, I took care of Beauregard. Now, I frankly don't know where the hell I'm going to go. I guess I'm going to see my face on one of those TV shows, those 'most wanted' things. Get somebody handsome for my role, will you? Have them make me look like some master criminal who pulled off a major drug heist, not some psychotic, okay? Even though the truth is I just did what I felt like. I can't say it all makes sense. But I'll tell you this—I am tired. I'm all burned out." He intoned, "And miles to go before I sleep."

"Why Alicia? Did she figure out you killed Cory?"

"She didn't even seem to *think* of the *possibility* I had ripped off Cory myself," he said. "Didn't even occur to her. It infuriated me. I mean, I was running this whole thing, and the last thing I wanted was them to figure it out—but I could barely speak, I was getting so pissed when she was talking to me on the phone about how *you* seemed to be controlling something, how *you* got real heavy with her at the end, and there was something about *you*, she thought, that made you capable of pulling off a scam—and the most, the *most* credit she's going to give me—and this is a woman I screwed I don't know how many times—and all she's willing to credit is the idea that I might be helping you."

"You set her up. For that, you set her up?"

His voice over the miles managed to convey a defensive kind of pride. "I made another phone call. Got Beauregard this time, said I was you . . . and that I was scared shitless, that I wanted it all to end, and that though I *indeed* did not have the coke, a young lady by the name of Alicia Nadeau from Newport had approached me, saying that she had the list of Cory's customers and she had a good idea who had the stuff. That I would sit it out with my girlfriend Rachel, that once it was all over, please never bother us again, goodbye, put the phone down."

"Jesus."

"Taught that redhead to dismiss me," he said flatly. "Just think, the whole time he was doing it to her, he was probably telling her that you sent him along. I expect your name's being bandied around hell quite a bit these days."

"You're proud of yourself."

"Wouldn't you be? It's a lot to accomplish. I had to move fast. Had to take risks. Most people don't have that. Most people don't have the balls to make their payback."

I charged up the steep incline of the Newport Bridge. "Nothing we did to you deserves this. Nothing."

"I never said it was fair. Look, Riley, you want to understand it, it's this simple: I found it was something I could do. I was all churned up, heading for another month-long depression, and then I took some action that most people couldn't even conceive of— and it felt good. Going through the day like a normal nice guy, but knowing inside what I was capable of. *You* know what I'm talking about. Hey, it's been a good chat, but I've been sitting here watching people wander off, and it looks like Linda's the last. She's coming this way. And you know what?" His voice was light, playful. "I just took a couple lines a few minutes ago—and I don't feel tired at all now."

I heard him yell, his voice distant as if he was speaking out the window. "Linda, got a minute?"

I heard a muted voice, but couldn't recognize what she had said.

"Run!" I yelled. *Would she recognize his truck in time?*

Nick said, "Riley's been trying to get in touch. Ah, come on, give him a break, he's on the line now, just have a seat for a minute, talk to him. What can it hurt?"

Again I bellowed into the phone, as I pushed the Jaguar into a power slide through the exit ramp. The futility of it was obvious; my yell would be no more than a tinny scream inside his car, one that he could silence with the palm of his hand. I called to her again.

"Riley?" Her voice was crystal-clear.

"Linda, get out of the truck! Get away from Nick!"

"What—"

I heard the sounds of a struggle. A muffled scream. There was the sharp sound of a slap, the plastic clunk of the phone being dropped. Linda cried out. I beat my fist against the dashboard. "No!"

I could hear Nick's ragged breathing, but she was silent. "Jesus, she was a tough little piece," I heard.

"Damn you!" I raged, alone in his car, hurtling toward the waterfront area, only minutes away.

"She's still breathing," he said, his voice clear in the phone now. "I know you're following me. I'm going to put her in a sail bag and take her in my dinghy out to *Dancer*. Now Riley, I want you to understand something. You could call the police now, and they would find me, pick me up, put me in jail perhaps. You could do that. But then this little girl wouldn't be breathing. Because the first sign I think anyone but you is approaching the boat, I'm drowning her like an unwanted kitten. Weighted bag, over the side, and she might have enough air trapped inside to understand you'd failed her. So don't do that, Riley. Don't fail her. Meet me at R2 off Brenton Reef—that's the whistle—in one hour."

"No," I said. "I can't make it that soon. Give me time. I just got into Jamestown, it'll be fifteen minutes before—"

"One hour or she goes over the side. That's all."

32

The Suburban was parked in the almost empty launch service lot. No one was around. Sunday was an hour and forty-five minutes gone, and everyone sane was in bed.

Fifty-five minutes left to my hour.

The mutter of a small outboard was briefly audible, and I hurried down the launch dock with the shotgun and .45 to see an inflatable dinghy heading out under the bright moonlight to a sloop as familiar to me as my own: *Dark Dancer*. The dock moved under my feet; it was a windy night. Nick lifted something large and white over the stern, but clouds moved to obscure the moonlight before I could be sure it was a sail bag.

There were two launches beside me, one tied outboard of the

other. I jumped into the one farther out. No key. I hurried up the stairs to the office of the launch service, and was about to kick the door in when I noticed the red light glowing just inside. Under the eaves I saw a high-intensity lamp and a megaphone-like speaker—an alarm system. Sweat poured down my already slick back and arms. If the alarm had sounded, Nick might have carried out his threat within seconds of my foot hitting the door.

I heard the rumble of the Hinckley's diesel, and backed away, thinking fast. The ramp to the dinghy dock was protected by a high metal fence. I could get past it, but chances were good that most of the outboards were chained. On the dock to the left were a number of big cruisers and sailboats, and access to them was also protected by a fence. Breaking into one of those, finding a key, and getting it started would take too much time. Better to drive around to the Fort Adams side, where I would be closer to the *Spindrift*, and maybe there I could break free a boat without wasting too much time. Then I noticed the catamaran.

I remembered it well—it was an older Hobie that saw constant use around the harbor. It was tied off against the dock to the left, with about ten feet of water separating it from the outside launch. The wind gusted up just then, whipping my hair back, cooling me, as I checked the time.

Fifty minutes left.

I stepped across to the outside boat, placed my foot on the rub rail, and jumped, the guns stretched out in my arms. I splashed into the water about a foot away from the hull, but managed to hook my arms around it as I went down, keeping the guns dry. After sliding them on board, I hoisted myself up, gasping with the white-hot response from my ribs. Rolling to my feet, I raised the big main and cast off. I pulled the roller-furled jib out, backwinded it so the boat slowly fell off, and suddenly we flew out of the docks into the harbor. I hiked out as the windward hull lifted from the water. My weight was not enough—I had to spill wind and head up to get her to settle down. This kind of speed was something I was not used to under sail. Before I knew it, I was at the mooring where *Dark Dancer* had been. I came about and began a fast series of tacks to Fort Adams.

The ride through the crowded harbor took all my skill as the catamaran hissed along at over ten knots. Moored boats would suddenly appear out of the dark. Twice I touched mooring floats, and the second time almost pitchpoled as I overcorrected with the rudders and the knife edge of the lee bow dug into the black water.

My last tack took me adjacent to the stern of *Dark Dancer* as Nick made his way out of the harbor under power. The catamaran was moving a good three knots faster than *Dancer*, but Nick was able to head directly into the wind, as I, of course, could not.

But maybe with a steady hand and some luck, I could bring this whole thing to an abrupt end.

I slipped the .45 from my belt and wedged it under my leg.

"Looking good," he called over the roar of his engine. There was a quick ratchet noise. "Twelve-gauge," he said. "Six-shot. One for you, one for her. Four more to make it messy. Keep going—you've got forty-two minutes."

He was past the Fort Adams buoy by the time I turned into the wind beside the *Spindrift* and stepped on board. Minutes later, I too was bounding straight into the wind under power, my body missing the freedom of the fast sailing boat in a way so elemental that even in that circumstance I could acknowledge it, even as I tried to save the woman, and kill the man.

Once out of the harbor and into Narragansett Bay, I grabbed a chart and tapped into the loran a course to the R6 bell, and from there to the R2 whistle. The distance was short, but without a chart and compass, it would be easy to go wrong at night.

I checked my watch. Twenty-five minutes left. At this speed, it was going to be very close. I had the power poured on; *Spindrift* was hunched down in the stern. Better that he see me coming from a distance, I decided, and snapped on the running lights before setting the auto steering.

Below, I dried what water had splashed onto the guns with a paper towel. I selected a five-inch carving knife from the drawer, wrapped the blade in a dishcloth, and tucked it behind my back.

Back on deck, I checked the time and speed, and cut the inflatable dinghy free. It slipped away quickly into the night. *Spindrift* picked up another knot, but I had to push away the feeling that I had let go of an option. Ideas like sending the *Spindrift* ahead the last few hundred yards on auto steering while circling behind in the dinghy, or rigging some sort of diversion with it, had been cropping up. But they all had an unrealistic ring; I could conceptualize them, but no way could I actually see implementing them without including a scene of Nick turning casually to Linda and shooting her. I had to get on his boat, I had to find a way for him to let me aboard.

As I passed the R6 buoy, I heard the gong buoy ahead, and beyond that, the R2 whistle. I went up to the bow and peered ahead. The sound of my diesel was remote from this far forward; I heard instead the rush of the water below as the *Spindrift* lifted up into the heavy swells, crested, and slid down. The sad moan of the whistle sounded again. The sense of being alone, of being in a strange and remote place, filled me. I stared into the darkness, willing my eyes to provide some insight into what he would have waiting for me.

Five minutes before the hour ended, I went back to the wheel, disengaged the auto steering, and laid the shotgun and revolver on the seat. I had a clear view of the deck, but now that the moon was again obscured, I couldn't see more than a few feet beyond the bow.

Just as my loran sounded, *Dancer*'s white deck and snapping mainsail jumped out of the blackness like a magic trick. Nick had turned on his spreader lights. His boat was a half-dozen lengths away, tied off to the R2 buoy with doubled lines, her bow pointed into the wind.

Linda was encased from her neck down in a large sail bag, and perched on the cockpit coaming. Her head was angled back, showing the white of her throat. Her hair whipped against the sailcloth. Apparently the drawstring was pulled tight behind her.

She turned her head down. I saw him release a fistful of her hair, and she spoke.

I cut the power and swung *Spindrift* parallel to *Dancer*, keeping the screw turning just enough to maintain away. With the engine noise suddenly abated, I could hear Linda clearly, hear her attempt to maintain control. "He says to tell you that if you try to come on board he'll shoot me. Big surprise, huh?" I saw the barrel of the shotgun move behind her. He was well protected, having retreated halfway down the ladder leading to the cabin.

"How're you doing?" I said.

She shrugged, exaggerating it so I could read her through the bag. "Been better."

He shoved at her with the gun, and she cried out as she tried to regain her balance. I tensed, ready to jump in, but the *Dancer* rolled on a swell toward the port side, helping her out. "All right, you bastard," she said, over her shoulder. "Never been worse."

That made him laugh. "Hey, Riley, don't you just love a girl with *spunk?*" He kept the laughter going, hamming it up. "A girl with spunk" had always been one of his favorite clichés.

"You've got our attention," I said.

"So I do, so I do. Now then, what about you take one of those guns of mine, put it in your mouth, and pull the trigger. Or I blow her head over to you to ask why not."

"Riley, you know the minute you're dead, I am too," she said.

"Ah, isn't that nice," he said. "She's being noble. Come on, *I* took a shot in the head. Give it a go."

"This is your plan?" I said. "Look, let's try for a little reality here. You think you can kill me, and the police are going to leave you alone, you'll be able to go back to work, and keep snorting coke and spending the money? You can't believe that. So this comes down to you and me. And here I am. Let Linda take the *Spindrift*, and it'll just be the two of us."

"Makes some sense. That it does. But who says I'm doing this to make sense? If I was going to do that, I wouldn't have hooked Cory's body to your keel, right? I would've dumped him in the deep blue ocean. But I wanted to make a statement."

"Which was?"

"Isn't it obvious? That Ellen was a whore. That you were a cuckold with twelve-point horns. Not exactly in control the way you thought. Like now."

"Nick, be a man. You keep strutting about how tough you are, you've got muscles packed all over, and still you're hiding behind Linda. Take me on directly."

"You don't give the orders here, ace. Understand? And I'll 'take you on' in my own time. Now, what I've got lined up for this little rendezvous here is damn simple, starting with you dumping your weapons. All of them. Or she goes over."

I pretended to think about it, then, slowly, "Okay, we trade. Let her go, and I'll throw away the gun." I held the Remington up. It was useless at that distance anyhow, and if he stood, I might be able to line up a clear shot with the handgun.

"Oh, you're going to bargain with me, are you?" He shoved her overboard. "How about I establish the stakes?"

Linda fell forward, and I jumped up on deck and brought the shotgun up to my shoulder. I almost fired before realizing she was still tied to the boat. One end of a line was wrapped around the genoa winch, the other to the sail bag's handgrip. When the *Dancer* rolled down, Linda was at face level to the sea; when it rolled back up, the line pulled her abruptly against the hull. She called out once, then gritted her teeth as she again slammed up against the hull, hard. A wave splashed into her face, and she started coughing. Nick was well hidden; all I could see of him was his hand over the cockpit with a knife over the line. At that distance the shotgun pattern would be so broad I would hit her too.

"This is the trade," he called. "The shotgun over the side, now, or I cut the line, and she drowns."

"Here," I said, throwing it into the air so he could see it. It splashed a dozen feet away from Linda.

"Now the handgun." He released a foot of line, and suddenly Linda's head dropped underwater. The rolling boat brought her up briefly, then plunged her below. "Don't waste Linda's time telling me you don't have one."

I threw the .45 away.

"Anything else?" he called.

"No. I swear to God, no." I kicked my shoes off. He would be able to shoot us at his leisure, but I could not just stand there as she drowned.

"Keep your pants on," he said.

I hesitated.

He stood and fitted a handle into the winch, then cranked Linda slowly up to the coaming. "Matter of fact, if you and Ellen had both been able to do that, you wouldn't be here today." Water streamed from the bag as Linda coughed and strained against the hull. "I'm going to let your friend drain a bit while I take care of one more piece of business. Bear with me here, guys."

He started the engine and edged closer to the whistle buoy. The bow lines sagged. He cut the power, hustled forward, took out a telescoping boat hook similar to mine, and slid it open to full length so he could snag a small, brightly colored lobster pot buoy. "Bet there's something tasty down there, what do you think?" He hauled the line up, hand over hand, the thick muscles in his chest and arms rippling through his short-sleeved shirt.

A normal enough lobster pot came up, but he took out a heavily taped plastic garbage bag. "Take a guess," he said. "This hide-in-the-open system worked well enough for Lowe and Dearborn. I figured, why fix what wasn't broken? Dropped my own little pot. Coke and cash to go. New life after this, pal. I'm rich in a modest kind of way. And I won't have to waste any money buying coke, and I don't have snort it off Cory's hand on the days he's feeling like the pope."

"All those people dead, for this?"

He looked surprised. "Weren't you listening? This is just the gravy. The look on your face right now is the meat." He threw the empty pot and line back overboard. After dropping the bag down into the cabin, he said, "Now, raise your main, buddy— we're going for a sail." Leaning over to the port side, he released a line that suddenly snaked all the way up to the bow chock and to the buoy, and then the *Dark Dancer* was free. She slid back in irons briefly, and Nick took the wheel, swung the stern around, then headed off the wind as the sail began to fill.

From the vantage of my deck as I yanked off the sail cover, I could see clearly into his cockpit. As the *Dancer* began to heel to port, he cut the engine, locked the wheel, and then swung Linda inside and freed the line from the genoa winch. She looked half dead, and I was as surprised as he when suddenly she released a kick through the bag, apparently hitting him in the chest with both feet. He staggered back, tripped over the seat, and would have fallen overboard if not for the safety lines. The *Dancer* heeled more in the breeze, and I lost sight of Linda as she slid down toward him.

"Get into the cabin!" I yelled, jumping down to the wheel and shoving the throttle forward. *Spindrift* lunged ahead, and I put her over hard, aiming to ram the *Dark Dancer* amidships. Their struggles apparently had knocked his wheel free of the lock, because the *Dancer* headed into the wind, abruptly leveling off. Nick's cocky expression had disappeared, and the rage that must have been with him at all times knotted his face, revealing the ugly, self-pitying man underneath. He grabbed Linda by the hair and slapped her viciously, and then he saw me charging ahead.

"Fall off!" he cried, then heaved her with incredible strength up to the Hinckley's beam, right where I was heading. He bent down and came up with the shotgun and let go a blast across my bow. A fast snap of his hand, the gun was cocked again, and he was on deck pointing it at her head. "Your choice!"

She was crying now, but even under the strange lighting, I could see she was furious, the cords in her neck standing out, her anger feeding the tears. That she was still fighting filled me with a perverse exaltation. I spun the wheel over, put the engine in reverse, and crabbed sideways over to the *Dancer*. Nick kicked a bumper tied to the rail over the side.

He said, "Scratch my hull, buddy, you die." But the pretense of humor was really over. He was flushed, apparently unnerved at how close he had come to actually going overboard. "Get your butt over here and fend off."

I ignored him and let the *Spindrift* hit with a jarring impact.

"Shit!"

"Linda," I said quietly, "we're going to find a way tonight. You hear me?"

"Sure I hear you, I'm not deaf." Linda shook her head, to clear the wet hair from her face. She said, "Tonight's your night, Nick."

"Shut up! Riley, get your sails up, and follow me out of here.

You come abeam, you start your engine, you do any fucking thing I don't want ..." He nudged Linda with the gun. "Well, you know the rules."

I backed off without a word, letting my hull screech along his, leaving deep white scratches. His reaction was very interesting. He raged and shoved at the stanchions on *Spindrift*, with little effect. But he did not shoot. He could easily have killed us both, yet he hadn't. And even when I had almost rammed him, he was careful to shoot across my bow. Though I had no doubt he intended to kill us, he apparently preferred not to have any shot pocking the hulls of the *Dark Dancer* or the *Spindrift*.

And if that was true for the boats, then it was probably true for our bodies.

33

We beat into a steady seventeen-to-twenty-knot wind for about an hour and a half before the wind died down to ten knots. After setting the auto steering, I did what I could to prepare the boat for Nick. In addition to the knife in my belt, I hid four steak knives about the cabin and two in the cockpit. I made sure the two life vests would come free easily from their stern racks. And I loaded the flare gun and put the two remaining meteors in my back pockets. Each supposedly would climb to about two hundred feet and burn for a little over five seconds—I, of course, had a much shorter, horizontal range in mind.

The wind continued to die. Seven, four, two knots. Just over fourteen miles out south from Brenton Reef, *Dark Dancer* turned into the wind and I heard her engine start. "Furl your sails," Nick called. "Then turn on your spreader lights."

I complied with his instructions. He swung the *Dancer* up behind me, with a bow line already through the chock and the bitter end looped back onto the pulpit. His lights remained off. Apparently he felt vulnerable throwing the line to me; perhaps he was afraid I'd hit him with the boat hook. I'd already rejected it as a weapon. Although a rigid tip extended two inches beyond the hook, unless I had an opportunity to jam it into his eye, I probably wouldn't be able to do much damage. The whole thing was hollow, designed to be buoyant and compact: two aluminum tubes fitted into one like a telescope so that it could be extended from five feet in its collapsed state up to twelve.

Better to put a flare into his chest at point-blank range, I figured.

I snagged the line and hauled the *Dancer* up, keeping crouched low so that Nick couldn't shoot me without also chewing up the deck.

"Your little friend whispered in my ear that she'd like to join you." Nick walked Linda up to the bow. She was free from the sail bag, but her hands were tied in front. Nick had the shotgun at her head, and I could not use the flare gun anyway, since she was in the line of fire.

I helped Linda climb on board. I gave her arm a squeeze, and she lifted her bound hands up, saying, "This is carrying fear of women to an extreme, wouldn't you say?"

"You're dangerous, you know that."

Nick turned the shotgun directly on me. "Drop that pole. Where are the flares?"

"What?" I asked, stepping back so Linda would follow, maneuvering us both into the cockpit.

"Get up here," he snapped.

I held Linda's arm. She waited. We were easily within his range, and apparently at the end of the line. If he didn't shoot now, I figured my little theory was correct.

I put my hands out, and let my voice shake, which was easy

enough to do. "Calm down. Look, you want the flares, they're down below as usual. You want me to get them?"

"No. I want you to get up here and lift your sweater. You had enough time on the boat to remember them. Now get up here." I shook my head.

He stepped on board quickly and jammed the shotgun against Linda's chest. "Now or later," he said. "You want to make the decision for her?"

I threw the flare gun onto the seat cushion.

"Partners for all these years—I knew you'd be resourceful."

I included the meteors, figuring they were useless without the gun, and he would find the knife if he searched me. Then he had me pull the toolbox out of the port cockpit locker and open up the cockpit hatch down to the engine. He knew right where I kept everything, and I took some comfort in his apparent failure to remember the knives. Then again, I hadn't figured out a way to use them without getting Linda and me shot.

"Take a screwdriver, get down there, and take the hose off the cockpit-drain through-hull valve." He dug into his pocket and handed me a rusted and broken hose clamp. "Put that around it first, then take the good one off and hand it to me."

So he intended to sink us. The hose was as thick as my wrist; once I pulled it off the valve, seawater would flood the boat. But he apparently was thinking in terms of the boat passing some sort of police inspection afterward, meaning he did not have his own suicide in mind.

Good.

I crawled down into the tight compartment. The engine smelled strongly of oil, and it was too dark to see the through-hull valve clearly. Looking up at Nick, I noticed the handle of the boat hook just over my head, where I had laid it on the port cockpit seat. "There's a flashlight in the bin just forward of the galley," I said dully. "One of you get it and aim it down here for me."

He looked at me suspiciously, but indeed the angle was wrong for the spreader lights to do any good. "Okay, Linda, I've got something for you to do for me, too. While you're doing it, re-member all it would take for me to fill that cabin with shot is to pull the trigger." He reached into his pocket, pulled out two Baggies, and tossed one to each of us. Coke. "Put those in your pockets."

"No." She looked at him defiantly.

He started toward her, and I said curtly, "Linda, remember what you tell your swim class. You can get through this."

Nick laughed derisively. "You can't really, but do what I say anyhow."

I pocketed the dope. She stared at me, but shoved the coke into her jeans. It was awkward for her to do with her bound hands, but nowhere near as awkward as it would be for her to stay afloat. I hoped she understood my message and was prepared. She went below.

"Okay," Nick said to her. "Push that little red button by the stove. See it? Good."

Apparently he planned a propane explosion for us as well.

"Now turn the burners on, but don't light them." His voice rose. "Leave the cabin lights off! Okay, now come on up."

He sat down carefully, opened the stern locker where the propane tanks were stored, and twisted the knob; I could hear the hiss of the escaping gas down in the cabin. I figured it would take a few minutes before the gas made its way past the stairway that closed off the engine compartment from the main cabin.

The flashlight snapped on. Linda was now standing on the cockpit seat on the starboard side, her eyes fixed on me. The light washed over the engine. One of my three batteries—the one mounted a foot and a half up and to the side of the driveshaft— was missing the cover of its plastic case. I remembered I had taken it off when I was working on the engine at the mooring, seemingly months ago.

"What's keeping you, Riley?"

I yanked the drain hose off.

Under the flashlight beam, seawater gushed out in a silver fountain. My instinct was to jam something in the hole, to stop the flood, but instead I rested my knee against the base of the battery box and said to Nick, "You're screwing up."

"That so?" He had the flare gun in his belt now, and he gave it a pat. "Seems to me you're the one whose boat is sinking, who tried to make a run with your little chick—"

"—who runs below, gets his flare gun, and what? Trips on the stairway? Just panics and lets the flare go off inside the boat, causing a propane explosion? You figure you can shoot one into the cabin of my boat from the deck of the *Dark Dancer*, huh? Pretty farfetched, isn't it? The leak, propane, and flare all going wrong at one time?"

"So what? Murphy's Law. That's the way it goes on boats, you know that. The Coast Guard sees examples of it all year long. Besides, they won't have more than a few pieces and an oil slick to check."

The water sloshed just under my knee now.

"And if they find our bodies with a residue of cocaine in our pants, you think that'll be enough. Guilty couple die while sailing away. Justice served."

"Something like that." He put the gun directly on Linda. "You first. Get below."

I could smell the propane now. The water was over my knee. "What about when they find your body? Won't that throw off your little scenario?"

He grinned. "You threatening?"

I shook my head and pointed to the black water slopping just inches from the top of the battery box. "I told you. You're screwing up. What do you think is going to happen when the water hits the battery and everything shorts out?"

Even in the bad light, I could see his face go slack. He looked over at the cabin, and the gun barrel moved between me and Linda. I reached over my shoulder, took hold of the boat hook, and swung it in a whistling arc down onto the gun. "Jump!" I cried to Linda.

But he pulled the shotgun away and was bringing it to bear on me when she went for it. He punched her in the chest with the butt, then swung the barrel around to her face as I scrambled up into the cockpit. I shoved the boat hook up over my head, parallel to the cockpit sole. It lifted the barrel just enough; flame brushed Linda's hair, but the shot went over her head. I looped the hook around and shoved her to the rail myself. She lost her balance, then kicked off, turning her fall into a dive.

Nick pumped the gun fast, and I used the boat hook to shove it back against his chest, then swung the handle into his groin. Nick cried out, and I slapped the pole against his head. But the lightweight aluminum wasn't enough to put him down, and he butted me in the face.

Grit of kinky hair, hard bone. A cracking noise, horrendous pain. My nose was broken, and I felt my knees buckle.

It was pure luck that I was able to deflect the gun one more time. I jumped overboard. I dove as deep as I could, but the boat hook's buoyancy brought me back to the surface. I kicked away on the surface, my shoulders hunched, waiting for the shot. But Nick had apparently decided to get clear of the *Spindrift*. I heard the engine of the *Dancer* racing, and saw it backing away.

I called out to Linda.

No answer.

The *Spindrift* blew.

There was a muffled *crump*, then a huge billow of orange flame ripped the cabin roof and deck right off. A blast of hot air laden with debris swept along the water's surface, and I ducked below again, hoping for God's sake Linda was doing the same, and would answer me when I surfaced.

34

But she didn't. I thrashed about the surface, yelling her name. The flames from the boat made the water come alive; orange light reflected off the swells. Minutes went by as I waited in the cold emptiness, lifting and falling, calling for her at the top of my lungs.

I lost it finally. All of it came up like bile. Cursing rage, beating at the water with my hands, beating at the sea as if my anger would be enough to propel me across the water to kill my former friend. I was alone. So damn alone. His treachery, Ellen's, my own inability to see what was happening to us. All the people killed around me. And now Linda. She had told me she could survive anything, and under the pressure of Nick's gun, I had held on to that statement like a talisman and pushed her overboard with her hands bound.

I fell back into the water, exhausted. The sound of *Dark Dancer* grew louder. The *Spindrift*'s fire was roaring close to the waterline now. Sometimes I would lose sight and sound of her altogether in the heavier swells.

I was down in one of the troughs when I made the connection: Linda had gone over just a little earlier than me, and even though the wind was dead, the swells were strong enough so that the boat was drifting quickly—and with her bound hands she was surely using the drownproofing technique, so that most of the time she would be underwater, and at least several boat lengths away from me.

The chances of her hearing me were therefore virtually nil, but she could still be alive.

After snagging the boat hook on my belt, I began swimming parallel to the *Spindrift*. Every ten breaths, I stopped to look in the direction of the flames, using the boat to provide a backdrop of light. The water was cold, and I was fast becoming chilled. Neither of us would last long at this rate. The sixth stop, I saw something. Waited down in the trough, came up, saw nothing. Again. Nothing. Third time up, two swells away, her head lifted out of the water, then she went back down.

The pain in my ribs and from the broken nose just let me know I was still alive as I sprinted a dozen fast strokes over to her. It was too dark to see her expression as she came up, but when I grasped her shoulders, she said, simply, "Hands."

"Float on your back." Pulling her arms back over her head, I towed her along, and used the knife I had tucked into my belt to cut the line.

She tread water, her face white in the moonlight as she took a few deep breaths. "I knew you'd find me. I just took that one breath at a time, telling myself it didn't matter if you came on that one or the next, or a hundred later—you'd come. Thought I heard you, and called out once or twice, but mainly I just breathed." She kissed me, then murmured, "Don't worry, I won't panic," as we slipped a few feet underwater. I hugged her, finding a core of warmth through the touch of our cold skin that denied being fourteen miles from land, with no boat, and Nick only minutes away. We floated slowly back to the surface and tasted air, then turned to face *Dark Dancer*.

She was between us and the *Spindrift* now. A powerful flashlight swept back and forth in an arc from the bow. The beam flowed past once, then snapped back, finding us. The flashlight beam jerked as Nick moved back to the stern to take the wheel. The *Dancer* changed course slightly, bearing down right on us.

"We can't hide," Linda said, her teeth chattering audibly now. "He's going to just power up and shoot us. Even if we managed to, we'd die out here . . . what, within an hour or so?"

"He's going to run us down, not use the gun." I loosened the boat hook, telescoping the sections out until the whole twelve-foot length was floating along the surface. I told her that if we could use it to fend off, I might be able to cut his dinghy free. Linda took the butt end, and I held on to it about midway.

Two boat lengths away, *Dancer* was pushing up a white bow wave, probably making just under eight knots. Whenever my head dipped below the surface, I could hear the prop whine.

"Push the pole down slightly," I said. "If he sees it, he might cut it right down the middle."

One length away.

I was treading water fast, my breath rushing. The *Dancer* blotted the *Spindrift* from view.

"Riley—"

"Steady. Stay right there. Just be sure to hold it the way I told you, and face away from the boat once I plant it, and get ready to kick."

"Oh God."

I put the knife in my teeth.

Dark Dancer was upon us.

Keeping the pole horizontal, I placed it on the starboard-bow quarter. The force of the boat shoved the pole through our hands, but we held on well enough so that it pushed us away from the bow, and then we were rolling alongside the rushing black hull. Then the flashlight was just over my head, and I heard Nick curse as I turned and swam with all my strength parallel to the stern. The warm oil-smelling exhaust water hit me in the face, and for a panicky second I felt the pull of the prop undertow. I flipped up over onto my back and caught the running white line in my hands. Burning. My hand was burning, but I squeezed tight anyhow. Suddenly I was being dragged through the water so fast my arm felt as if it would be pulled from its socket. I tried to wrap my wrist in the line, but it was too tight to gain any slack. My clothes filled with water. The drag was terrific; I kept sliding farther back on the line, so when I reached up with the knife, the few strands I managed to cut were not in the same place.

"You bastard!" Nick cried. White light illuminated the inflatable dinghy, and the shotgun spoke. Reflexively, I cringed and loosened my grip. A pattern of white froth appeared far to my left, and I realized he had missed intentionally, presumably firing just to scare me. It worked. The dinghy slammed me in the face. Before I could take a good breath, I slid under it, grasping the line with both hands. My arms burned with the stress. I tried to angle the knife back to cut the line and instantly lost my grip. I tucked into a ball and rolled along the dinghy bottom, cradling my head in my arms.

The lower unit of the dinghy's outboard caught me in the side.

The blow to my damaged ribs made me scream, made me open my mouth to the water and begin to drown. I choked, and struggled for the surface, and swallowed more huge gulps of water. It was as if I suddenly became weighted by ten pounds of lead. My head and heart were pounding, but I just couldn't seem to make it. So this is it, a remote part of me thought.

I sensed something above me, and thought briefly that the dinghy was still there, and then my hair was tugged. Linda was behind me, grasping my chin and kicking, pulling me up to the surface, pulling me up to breathe.

I coughed up water, trying to get a clear lungful of air as the pop of the diesel grew closer.

"He's turned. He's coming back, Riley. For God's sake, we've got to get ready to do it again."

I felt about my body. The knife was gone.

Dark Dancer was right behind me now.

I drew in a long shuddering breath, coughed once more. "Give me the pole," I croaked.

Dancer was bearing down less than a length away.

Shoving the butt end down into the water until the whole buoyant length was submerged, I said, "You've got to fend us off."

She nodded fast, and looked over her shoulder. The flashlight was shining from just over the rail inside the cockpit. He surely was holding it, but from my angle the glare made him invisible. The bow settled right on us—he apparently had a hand on the wheel as well. Linda was hyperventilating, the longer to hold her breath. She put her hands on my waist and started kicking for all she was worth, shoving me just to the starboard of the fast-approaching boat. I kicked as well, but mainly kept myself erect in the water, fighting the buoyancy of the pole and keeping it angled back along my side. One swell away, *Dancer* slid down, then bounded up the side, the bow rising, a huge black shape poised above us.

But Linda had measured it right. *Dancer*'s bow landed less than three feet away, and Linda kicked out, her sneakers making a squeak against the polished hull as she shoved both of us out of the way. As the *Dancer* went rushing past, I fought to swing the pole back into position. The flashlight was far outboard of the boat now, and I could see Nick's silhouette as he leaned, apparently expecting to see our two broken bodies float up from his bow wave.

"Put your head down," I whispered to Linda.

He cut the power, but still the *Dancer* surged on. Long enough anyhow, as I loosed the pole between the thumb and forefinger of both hands and its buoyancy pushed it quickly into the air. I aimed just to the right of the flashlight, and grasped the butt end against my hip. From behind, Linda wrapped her arms around my back and held on to the pole as well.

The pole itself was lightweight, the speed created by its buoyancy negligible, but at that angle, and with the inexorable momentum of *Dark Dancer*, when I felt the pole slide over something soft, I knew we'd hit him, and were doing damage. We were shoved deeper into the water. The pole shuddered as something broke at the other end. Milliseconds later, the pole itself snapped. I held one end, and as we floated to the surface, I saw the other end sticking out over the edge of the boat.

Linda and I swam as fast as we could to the dinghy. She made it just before me and was all for untying the line and leaving in the little inflatable. But I felt certain what I would find. And indeed, when I climbed up the Hinckley's swim ladder minutes later, Nick lay on his back in the cockpit, the pole's tip rammed up under his chin, his neck broken. His open eyes were already losing the surprised look and turning glazed.

"Is he dead?" she asked.

I covered his face with my sweater. "He is. For a long time now."

EPILOGUE

I asked the cabdriver to wait. Sylvia stayed downstairs while Geoff and I went up to his study. We sat in his leather chairs near the window and talked as the breeze sifted through the leaves of the oak tree outside. Geoff listened intently as I told him all of it, from the time he dropped me off at my house until Mitchell walked me out of the hospital, free for the second time of police guards.

Geoff's face seemed to age further as I told him of Ellen's affairs with Nick and Cory. He looked at me intently, but did not interrupt. When I was finished, he said distantly, "So they never connected you with the fisherman. The one you actually killed."

"No. The Newport police decided that Beauregard and Lowe

must've had a falling-out. The way his house was trashed and the fact that Beauregard's prints were all over the place made it seem likely. I didn't dissuade them. For the rest of it, the arsenal in Nick's house, the fact that the .22 round that killed Derby matched the rifle in Nick's truck, and Linda's testimony over-shadowed their other concerns. The police found Cory's address book in Alicia's safe deposit box, with Nick's phone number—the last two numbers transposed. The owner of Gansett Marine in Jamestown identified a photo of Nick and pointed out his qua-hog boat. We told the truth, saying that Nick stole the coke from Cory, and as a result Beauregard and Lowe went on a rampage, killing everyone they thought connected, including Ellen."

"And that was enough?"

"You turn in forty pounds of coke and a half million in cash voluntarily, the police look at you differently."

Geoff stared at me for a long moment, but finally he nodded. "You look like hell. Bruises all over. Your nose is broken, isn't it? I thought so in the newspaper photo. The media really took hold of the story. I keep waiting for someone to connect Ellen with it further."

"I know. And it could happen, I suppose. Someone could iden-tify Cory as the waiter in the ad. But really, he had such a bit part in the ad, and he used a pseudonym when modeling. The focus of the media attention is on the charade Nick managed to pull off, the seduction of cocaine, the availability of guns in the street, that whole bit. Mitchell was able to help direct that angle with a few well-chosen comments." I laughed shortly. "If I still had an agency, I'd hire him to start a public relations department. The man's a genius."

"It's gone?"

"I took a rock-bottom offer for it yesterday, but that's all it's worth now. With Nick dead—and me being the one who killed him, justifiably or not—clients are poised to leave in droves. Worse, I can't seem to bring myself to care. The company that purchased it is looking to expand, so they'll hold on to all my employees, and I salvaged enough so that I've got some time before I need to work again."

Geoff nodded absently.

I waited.

"So you've been able to protect her memory," he said softly.

"No. I've protected her public image, and short-circuited some of the ugly comments you might otherwise hear. I know what she did, and I know what I did. I have no reason to share any of it with the newspapers. If she were with me now, the best I could hope for would be that we could forgive each other. Maybe if she were alive we would still go our separate ways. Maybe not."

"You *have* gone on separately, Riley. That you can't change. But you can forgive her, and decide that she would have forgiven you. She was probably on her way down to Newport to tell you the truth when she found you with that other woman."

"That's true. That's what Nick thought, too." I stood up. "I'd better be going now."

He walked me downstairs and out to the cab. He saw my small suitcase in the backseat. "You're not going home?"

"No. I'm going away, take some time. A year maybe."

He put out his hand. "Good luck, then." He started up the steps, then turned back. "Riley—don't be alone too much longer. Ultimately, it will do you no good, and you deserve better." He didn't wait for an answer. Sylvia opened the door when he reached the top of the stairs. She nodded to me slightly.

I told the driver to head to the airport. "Where are you going?" he asked, trying to make conversation.

"I'll figure that out when I get there."

He gave me a long look in the mirror.

I opened the package Linda had given me just before I left for Geoff and Sylvia's that morning. She had come over the night before, with another of her bottles of wine. We had talked till late in the night, and I had offered her the guest room. She had insisted upon the couch, and I settled into the guest room myself. When she slipped under my covers just before dawn, I found I was hungry for her to a degree I could not have guessed.

Nevertheless, when we awoke to the late-morning sunlight, I told her I still planned to leave. "Is it the age difference?" she asked. She lay against my chest, and I inhaled the scent of her as I traced the line of her small, strong back with both hands.

"No."

"My background? We're too different?"

"We're the same, and you know it."

She grinned. "I do. Same cloth." She kissed me, and then moaned, "Oh, Riley, I've already been waiting so long." She rolled off the edge of the bed onto her feet.

"I miss you already," she said. "I think . . . I *know* I love you already—don't even try to say the same to me, I know you don't have a clue about what you're feeling." She tugged the gaily wrapped present from her duffel bag and gave it to me, saying, "Not until you are on your way. Promise."

Inside was a leather jacket. It had clearly seen some use, she had apparently bought it at a secondhand store, but it was still in beautiful shape. There was no card, but a launch service schedule was tucked inside the right-hand pocket. The midnight Fort Adams launch was circled—the *Dauntless*. Linda had dated the schedule one year from now. Along the top she had printed in a clear strong hand, "Let me be your destination."

I slipped the coat on as we sped through the heart of the city, and began to look forward to my journey.